Chasing the Calm

Namaste with a few Detours

Jacqueline Sand
Copyright © 2025 Jacqueline Sand
All rights reserved

ISBN-13: 979-8-218-67470-0

Cover design by: Art Painter
Library of Congress Control Number: 2018675309
Printed in the United States of America

Important Note From the Author:

Hello beautiful souls,

In the midst of trying to remember who I was before becoming a mom, I started writing. At first, it was just a way to escape the chaos and find a little bit of calm. But then it grew. Friends started reading my drafts of *Chasing the Calm* and telling me it was…**really** good? So here we are.

But here's the thing—*Chasing the Calm* isn't your typical romance. It's got all the steamy tension and love story vibes, but it's also packed with a lot of what got me through the tough stuff: Reiki, meditation, sound healing… all the woo-woo things that grounded me when life felt like a hurricane. It's not just about two people finding each other; it's about finding peace, finding stillness, and maybe even finding yourself.

I know not everyone's into that kind of thing, and that's totally cool. But if you're the kind of person who believes there's more to healing than just pushing through, who lights candles not just for the smell but for the energy, and who thinks there's actual magic in a good sound bath…well, this book was written for you.

I poured so much of my heart (and probably a little too much caffeine) into these pages, and my only hope is that it brings you even a sliver of the peace it brought me while writing it.

Sending you all the love,
Jacqueline

For all the wild-hearted girlies and barefoot dreamers.

CHAPTER 1

ALEX

"Listen, all I'm saying is, the best way to get over her is to fuck your way through LA," my best friend AJ declares, leaning back with his arms crossed like he's just solved world hunger. "You had no trouble doing that *B.C.*"

I blink. "*B.C.?*"

"Before Catia," he explains, like it's the most obvious thing in the world. "You were like a one-man population boom."

I snort, shaking my head. "Things are different now." I came back from Pablo's retreat feeling like I'd been spun through a spiritual washing machine and hung out to dry. The idea of just diving back into the LA dating pool feels…shallow.

AJ huffs out a laugh. "Look, man, I don't get it. Catia's gone. She's off with that Portuguese guy now, right? That soccer dude…Vítor Chávez?" He says the name like it's dripping in cheap cologne and hair gel. "The world practically popped champagne when they announced their engagement—what, two weeks after you guys broke up? Impressive turnaround. I couldn't tell if I was more surprised by the speed or the sheer audacity."

I let out a dry laugh. "Yeah, well, I got to play the role of the brooding billionaire who let her slip away. My PR team's still riding that one."

AJ leans forward, eyes sharp. "What really happened, anyway? She just up and ran into the arms of Mr. Euro Goal?"

"Not exactly," I say, stretching my legs out. "She gave me an ultimatum—marry her or let her go." I shrug. "Two years together, and I couldn't say it. Not once."

"Couldn't say what?" He asks curiously.

I stare him down. "I love you." The words feel foreign, like they don't belong to me. "I couldn't force it. I wasn't about to spit out three words just to meet some deadline. So, I let her go."

AJ whistles low. "And she pole-vaulted straight into Europe's most eligible athlete. Good for her, I guess."

"Right?" I laugh, shaking my head. "I practically handed her the gold medal in rebound Olympics."

AJ smirks. "Look at you, all enlightened and shit, swearing off women like you're joining a monastery."

"I'm just saying, it's time I date the most important person in my life," I say, sipping my water. "Me."

AJ raises a brow, unimpressed. "Sounds deep, *Miss* Pierce."

"Look, I know it sounds cliché, but my spiritual healer thinks my fear of commitment is a coping mechanism from having a shitty childhood." I let out a deep breath.

AJ snickers and rolls his eyes. "Dude, come on."

He doesn't get it. None of my friends do; honestly, I don't expect them to. I'm not trying to prove anything to anyone. I've been running in survival mode since I was a kid. Being vulnerable probably sounds as foreign to AJ as it once did to me.

"Well, Friday is Mark's bachelor party," he says, raising his hands to form exaggerated air quotes. "You want to 'find yourself'? How about you 'find yourself' between the long, tight legs of a sexy blonde? Nothing kickstarts a journey of self-healing quite like a little *sexual* healing." He finishes with a wink.

I smirk, shaking my head. He's not entirely wrong. It's not exactly in my nature to live like a celibate monk. Maybe a little fun wouldn't hurt while I'm on this so-called self-improvement project.

CHAPTER 2

Forty-five minutes until I leave for the airport and my suitcase is still half-empty. Packing has never been my strong suit. I blow a stray lock of hair out of my face and toss in the last of my clothes. I don't own much—just a small collection of quality outfits on rotation. Thankfully, that makes packing a lot easier, but still, I can't shake the sense that I'm forgetting something, even as my suitcase starts to fill. Maybe it's not about what I'm packing but what I'm leaving behind.

"Yazzy, come downstairs! Dad's waiting!" Sami calls, squeezing my arm. "Whatever you forget, I'll bring it when I visit during spring break." I grin at her. Sami isn't just my sister, she's also my best friend. Leaving her behind is no doubt the hardest part of all this. But I know I'm headed exactly where I'm meant to be. Everything I've worked for has led me to this moment.

A major film production company offered me a three-month contract to be the full-time yoga instructor for Liam Woods—Hollywood's latest heartthrob, currently training for his next big role as a wellness guru caught in a love triangle. Apparently, turning a movie star into a zen master takes more than just good lighting and a filter. Teaching celebrities was never part of my master plan, but three months of guided breathing and downward dogs with Hollywood royalty? That kind of paycheck could finally get me closer to my real dream. And if I have to listen to a few stories about private jets and mansion remodels along the way…well, I suppose I can survive.

I drag my suitcase downstairs to find my dad waiting by the door, holding out a Tupperware container like it's a sacred offering. "We're so proud of you, *Azizam*," he says gently.

"Your mom and I. If she were here today, you know she'd be your biggest cheerleader." Before I can even respond, I'm pulled into one of his classic bear hugs—the kind that makes your spine crack but also somehow fixes your soul.

My dad is broad with a generous waistline and an even bigger heart. He's one of the strongest, most positive people I know—and, in my completely unbiased opinion, the greatest Persian chef on the planet. "I made your favorite," he says, handing me the Tupperware. "*Gheymeh* and *barbari* for the plane ride." He studies me for a moment, brow creasing like he's about to declare a national emergency. "You've gotten too thin. Don't forget to eat, okay?"

I blink back the emotion welling in my chest and nod. Leave it to my him to remind me—with food and unconditional love—exactly where I come from and how deeply I'm supported. My parents had the kind of marriage most people only dream about, and it breaks my heart that my father lost his soulmate so young. My sister and I grew up with the unwavering certainty that, no matter what, love was the foundation of our home.

"Thank you, Dad. What would I do without your cooking?" I say, cradling the container like it's a little piece of home I get to take with me.

He chuckles, squeezing my shoulder one last time before I step outside to call my Uber. It's bittersweet, but I hold onto the thought that I'll see Sami in just a few weeks. Until then, I have a suitcase full of dreams and a Tupperware of *gheymeh* to keep me company.

—

It's about mid-afternoon when I step off the plane at LAX. The air feels different here—softer, almost like it's trying to convince me that life is a little bit easier in LA. Even with rain clouds hanging low, I can't help but smile, knowing how much the earth here craves it. Even the sky needs a good release sometimes.

A few years ago, walking through LAX would've made me feel like I'd accidentally wandered into a Vogue convention—airbrushed strangers gliding by like they owned the place. But that version of me is long gone. I've spent years nurturing the quiet parts of myself, building a foundation that no one else's beauty or success can shake. Now, I walk through the crowd sending out silent blessings, wondering about their stories, dreams, and heartaches. I hope, in some small way, they find whatever they're searching for.

I spot my name on a sign, held up by a gentleman in a crisp black suit and a smile that looks like it's been practiced for decades.

"Ms. Se-pehr?" he asks, pronouncing it slowly. "Did I say that right? You have a beautiful name. I'm Alfie," he adds, reaching for my suitcase.

"You got it perfectly," I say, smiling. "Thank you for picking me up, Alfie." He nods and briskly walks to bring around a sleek black SUV. I wait under the awning, watching the rain drizzle in steady streams. It feels cleansing, like the whole city is rinsing off yesterday.

Once we're on the road, I catch Alfie's gaze in the rearview mirror. His calm energy is almost meditative. I lean forward. "So, Alfie, have you worked for Liam long?"

His eyes crinkle with an easy smile. "A good while now. Long enough to have plenty of stories, but only the good ones."

I chuckle, sinking back into the plush leather as the city blurs by. I know the basics—Liam Woods is old Hollywood money. His family practically helped build Los Angeles. His mother, Grace Woods, is a living screen legend. He's basically West Coast royalty. A small knot of nerves forms in my stomach as these thoughts swirl around in my head. I close my eyes for a moment, silently repeating my mantras of confidence. *I am grounded. I am capable. I belong here.*

I glance back at Alfie. "Have you enjoyed working for him?"

He shifts slightly in his seat, his hands steady on the wheel. "The Woods family has been very generous to me and my family. I'm forever grateful for the opportunities they've given me." His words are kind, but there's a twinge of something beneath them, like the aftertaste of an unspoken truth. It doesn't take much to read between the lines. I get the sense that Liam might be a tougher boss than I anticipated. Still, I've handled plenty of challenges before and I'm more than ready for this one.

I offer him a polite smile before turning to look out the window. We're cruising through Beverly Hills. It's the kind of place where even the trees look like they have publicists.

We finally pull up to a set of grand black iron gates. They swing open, revealing a long, scenic driveway flanked by guest houses that are bigger than most hotels. A serene pond shimmers to the left, ducks gliding across the surface like they're contractually obligated to look picturesque. Horses graze lazily in a paddock because, *of course* they do—this place is basically a Pinterest board that inherited a billion dollars.

When the main house comes into view, I lose my breath. Calling it a mansion would be an insult. It's a castle masquerading as a home, dripping with old-world charm and the kind of grandeur that makes you check your shoes for dirt.

The front doors swing open, and I'm greeted by a petite redhead with thick-rimmed glasses and a smile that could power a small village. "Yasmine! You made it!" she chirps. "I'm Elliot. Liam is just *dying* to meet you. Wow, you're even prettier than I imagined!"

I barely have time to respond before she's off, practically jogging through the foyer. I hurry to keep up, my eyes taking in the vaulted ceilings, chandeliers dripping with crystals, and marble floors so polished I can see my soul.

Elliot whisks me into the sprawling kitchen, where I'm introduced to Carlos, the chef, and Gertrude, the head maid.

"Welcome to the team, Yasmine," Gertrude says warmly. "We hope you enjoy your time here."

"Thank you," I reply, genuinely touched by her kindness. Elliot doesn't miss a beat, zipping us through the library, Liam's office, ten extra bedrooms, the pool, and finally, the gym.

She spreads her arms wide like she's unveiling the Taj Mahal. "And this," she grins, "is where the magic happens. Morning yoga at 8 a.m. sharp and evening meditation just after dinner. Liam takes his training *very* seriously."

I nod, half-wondering if Liam is training to become a yogi or just preparing to achieve inner peace while navigating his twenty-seven bathrooms.

Finally, Elliot leads me to my home for the next three months—a charming one-bedroom guest house nestled five minutes from the main estate. I step inside and nearly gasp. It's stunning: a sleek kitchen, cozy bohemian living room, and even a yoga nook with a meditation cushion. It's like my dream moodboard exploded and landed perfectly in this guest house.

"Wow," I breathe. "This is incredible. Thank you."

Elliot beams. "I'm so glad you like it. Get settled in, and I'll call you when Liam's ready."

She waves cheerfully and heads back to the main house, leaving me to soak it all in. I stand there for a moment, absorbing my new reality. This beautiful space, my life for the next three months—it's surreal, and I'm more than ready for it.

—

I've just finished dinner when Elliot's text pings on my phone.

Elliot: Master Liam is ready for your presence ;) Pop over now please!

I roll my eyes, stifling a laugh. I half expect him to be sitting on a velvet throne, sipping champagne while someone fans him with palm leaves.

By the time I get to the mainhouse, Elliot's already waiting at the front door, practically buzzing with enthusiasm. "He's just inside. Follow me!" she chirps, flinging open the massive doors.

I step in, as the faint crackle of a fire seeps through from the library. And there he is—Liam Woods, leaning casually by the fireplace like he's auditioning for the cover of *GQ*. He's tall, polished, and practically dripping with the kind of confidence you only get from a lifetime of people telling you you're perfect. He turns at the sound of my footsteps, his eyes sweeping over me in a way that feels more predatory than polite.

His lips curl into a smirk that I'm pretty sure has been rehearsed in mirrors. "Well, if it isn't the infamous Yasmine Sepehr," he drawls, voice low and deliberately smooth. "I've been meaning to meet you ever since I saw your face in *Aspire Magazine*. Gen Z's latest yoga guru, huh?" His gaze lingers just a little too long before he adds, "If anyone can teach me about deep, *deep* healing, it's you."

I resist the urge to roll my eyes into another dimension. Instead, I keep my smile steady. "I'm happy to be here," I start, but he cuts me off with a flick of his hand like he's shooing away a waiter.

"Elliot showed you to the guest house, right?" he asks, stepping closer. "But honestly, I'd prefer you stay in the main house. Easy access, if you know what I mean." He winks like he just handed out the punchline of the century, and I'm pretty sure he expects applause.

My stomach twists—not from nerves, but from his sheer audacity. I glance at Elliot, who looks completely unfazed, like she's seen this show more times than she can count. I half expect her to whip out popcorn.

I take a slow breath, keeping my voice even. "If that makes things easier for your training, I'm happy to do what's best."

His grin stretches wider, all sharp teeth and smugness. "Perfect. I'll see you tomorrow morning, bright and early. But…I'll let you know if I need you sooner." The way he says it feels less like a promise and more like a warning.

As I step back into the hallway, I can't shake the feeling that training Liam Woods is going to be less about yoga and more about surviving his ego. I mean, I've led guided meditations in the middle of Times Square, so I'm not exactly a stranger to chaos. But Liam Woods? He's giving off big *Namaste…but make it narcissistic* energy.

And I've got three whole months of it. Lucky me.

CHAPTER 3

It's Friday night, and I'm really not in the mood for Mark's bachelor party. *The Velvet Room* is LA's most exclusive gentlemen's club—the kind of place where the entry fee costs more than a beach house. Three hundred grand a year for velvet curtains, women so stunning they could make a priest consider his options, and the kind of privacy that even the FBI would envy. That's the price tag for exclusivity in this town.

It used to be my scene—hedonism dipped in luxury. But lately, I feel like I'm stuck somewhere between the guy I was *B.C.* and figuring out who the hell I'm supposed to be now.

I've never been the white-picket-fence type. A house full of kids? The same dinner routine every Thursday? I'd rather be waterboarded. Or maybe that's just because I've never met anyone who made that life seem appealing.

Catia definitely wasn't that person. She was more of a trophy—a walking status symbol I didn't even realize I was flaunting. Dating a supermodel felt like an achievement, another box checked off on the "Look How Successful I Am" list. But it was never about her. It was about how she made me look.

Which is exactly why she left.

We fought about it all the time—her pushing for marriage, me dodging the question like it might give me a rash. So when she finally walked out, I wasn't heartbroken. My ego, though? Shattered.

That's what Pablo's been working on with me. Learning to separate myself from my ego, understanding that wounded pride isn't real pain. But when you've spent years living in a world where ego is currency, letting it go feels like cutting off a limb.

Pablo calls it "reptilian dominance mode," like I'm some kind of prehistoric lizard fighting extinction. He's not exactly wrong though. But maybe the guy I've been isn't the guy I'm supposed to be anymore.

My phone buzzes, pulling me out of my thoughts, and I glance down. AJ. Probably calling to make sure I'm not about to bail. "Hey, man. What's up?" I answer, already bracing myself.

"You know what's up. We've got reservations at *Catch*. I'm picking you up at nine. And you're not driving, because I'm planning on getting you plastered," he announces, sounding way too excited for my current energy levels.

I pinch the bridge of my nose. "Listen, man…getting plastered is the last thing I want to do. I just got back from a ten-day spiritual retreat. My body is basically a temple right now. A work of art meant to be worshipped."

"Perfect," AJ quips without missing a beat. "We'll get those girls at *The Velvet Room* to worship your body *all* night long. See you at nine." He hangs up before I can argue.

I let out a long sigh and shake my head. My friends mean well, and I can't fault AJ for trying. They think I'm in some kind of post-Catia spiral. The truth is, I'm just changing. For the last two decades, I've been laser-focused on building wealth—an unstoppable machine fueled by ambition. Women were secondary. And Love? It wasn't even on the radar.

Pablo says it all ties back to fear—a fear of losing something I can't replace. And he's not wrong. I learned early on that nothing is promised, and the people you love can disappear without warning. Maybe that's why I've always clung to things I can control—things that can't be taken from me at 30,000 feet up in the air.

—

Nine p.m. rolls around faster than I'd like. I hear the low growl of an engine, and when I step outside, AJ is already pulling into my driveway in his Ferrari, headlights cutting through the evening haze. I greet him with our usual handshake and a solid pat on the back.

"AJ, my man," I say with a grin. "Listen, I'm driving tonight. I want to take my new car out for a spin." In reality, it's less about the car and more about control. A small part of me doesn't trust myself tonight. I don't want to go overboard, and driving forces me to stay grounded.

AJ raises an eyebrow, clearly skeptical, but after a moment, he shrugs. "Alright, dude. But only because I'm just as hyped as you are to take that beast for a ride."

My new Bugatti is one of only five made this year. I've always had a thing for exclusive, limited-edition masterpieces—the kind that aren't just modes of transportation but pieces of art. My garage holds over twenty supercars—it's like a billionaire's midlife crisis threw up in there. But if I'm being honest, these days they're just an excuse for me to drown out the chaos rattling around in my head.

We walk toward the garage, which is massive enough to be its own compound, separate from the house. When we reach the car, its sleek black frame catches the overhead lights, all polished curves and quiet power. "Not bad, right?" I ask, running a hand along the hood.

AJ whistles low, his eyes widening. "Damn, man. Consolation prize for your breakup?" He slides his hand over the side of the car like he's touching something sacred.

I laugh. "I ordered it a year ago. Honestly, though, this is probably my last car purchase for a while. Get in, brother."

We slide into the leather seats, and when I hit the start button, the engine roars to life, the vibration thrumming through the cabin like a pulse. AJ leans back, still grinning. "Why the change of heart? You've always loved your cars."

I rest my hands on the steering wheel. "Material things never gave me real happiness, you know? Sure, they're exciting for a moment. But genuine fulfillment? You don't have to chase that. I'm trying to detach from that part of my life."

AJ listens but doesn't respond. I know it's hard for him and most of my friends to understand this shift. I built my entire world around ambition and luxury, and they've only ever known me as the guy who couldn't get enough.

We pull into *Catch's* valet, where the lineup of sleek sports cars and black SUVs basically screams, "Congratulations on your trust fund!" The buzz of conversation drifts from the entrance, guys in thousand-dollar jackets already working their best fake laughs.

As we step out, I spot Mark heading toward us. "Hey, man!" he shouts, grinning like he just won the lottery. He's already buzzed, eyes shining with that pre-wedding glow. "Glad you made it! Tonight's gonna be epic. We'll make you forget all about everything that went down."

I force a smile. Everyone assumes I'm heartbroken and spiraling, but tonight isn't about me. It's about Mark. I clasp his shoulder and give him a firm pat. "Don't worry about me. Tonight's your night. Let's make it one to remember."

Mark laughs and nods, his eyes gleaming. We've known each other since our Harvard days. He wasn't my closest friend back then, that title belongs to AJ, but I was the one who introduced him to Poppy, his fiancée. So, in a way, I take a little credit for his happiness.

"How's Poppy?" I ask as we make our way to the entrance. "She doing something for her bachelorette?"

Mark groans but can't hide his grin. "A whole week in Cabo. The girls went *all* out. She dropped two hundred grand on the trip. But hey, whatever makes her happy, right?"

Mark isn't exactly hurting for cash. He's one of the heirs to a global media empire, along with his three siblings. Poppy was a whirlwind romance for him. I met her while I was studying abroad at Oxford. Mark came to visit me for a week and was instantly smitten. But their love story didn't really start until two years after graduation when fate seemed to bring them back together. I watch the way Mark talks about her and it's obvious he found the real thing. True love, the kind that sticks. It works for some people. For him and Poppy, it makes sense.

We enter the restaurant and instantly we're ushered into a private room, all dim lighting and polished tables. About fifteen of us are crammed around a hibachi style counter, a mix of close friends and familiar faces. The energy is electric, but the moment people catch sight of me, there's a shift. Sympathetic glances, the inevitable, "How you holding up?"

The downside of living such a high-profile life is that every relationship I've ever had plays out under a public microscope.

Everyone thinks they know the story—secondhand rumors masquerading as truth.

"A toast!" AJ stands, pulling be back from my thoughts. "My man Mark is about to get tied down, but I see some of you single brothers out here, and we're about to blow this town wide open tonight!" Laughter erupts, and we down our shots. The sake burns smooth and strong.

Before I can set my glass down, Mark slides up with another shot in hand, his expression half-serious, half-grinning. "Alex," he says, clinking his glass against mine. "The only wedding gift I need is to see you come back to your old self. We've missed you, man. We need the real Alex back."

I laugh, shaking my head. There's no point trying to explain myself tonight. They don't want introspection or self-discovery over shots of sake. They want me to throw my head back and party like old times. So, I do the only thing that makes sense—I take Mark's shot... and every other one my well-meaning friends shove into my hand. Sometimes, letting the night take over is easier than fighting it.

—

By the time we pull up to *The Velvet Room*, I'm more than a little buzzed. The line outside snakes around the block. Mark strides up to the bouncer with the kind of confidence that only someone with his last name can pull. A few quick words, and the velvet rope lifts like it's been waiting just for him.

We step inside and the shift in energy is immediate—dark lighting and pulsing bass. Our hostess, Marissa, materializes with a smile so bright I'm pretty sure it's sponsored. She's petite, with platinum blonde waves, fishnet leggings, and a leather skirt that screams *'bad decisions encouraged.'* "Follow me, boys," she purrs, voice syrupy sweet. She winks. "We'll take *very* good care of you tonight."

Mark slings his arm around my shoulders and grins at her. "It might be my bachelor party, but the real VIP here is my man Alex." He gestures toward me like he's auctioning me off. "Make sure he gets your *best* girls tonight."

Marissa's gaze flicks to me, scanning me from head to toe with a slow, approving smile. "Alex," she practically purrs, eyes gleaming. "Of course I know who you are. You're even more handsome in person. I have just the girl for you."

I smirk, shaking my head as I clap Mark on the back. "You're too much, man. I'm here for you, not me."

But Mark just laughs, waving off my protests as we follow Marissa up a sleek staircase to the VIP lounge. It's decked out in plush seating, gold accents, and a panoramic view of the dance floor below. A group of women appear like they've been summoned—scantily clad, waving light streamers, carrying buckets of Dom Pérignon and Patrón.

The music thrums as they cheer and dance around us, draping a 'Groom' sash over Mark's shoulders. He raises his arms like a victorious king, and everyone laughs. More shots are poured, toasts are made, and for a moment, the chaos feels contagious.

Mark strides over, grinning as he shoves another tequila shot into my hand. "C'mon, Alex, one more for me!" he shouts over the music. I hesitate for half a second before clinking glasses and downing it. The burn is smooth and familiar, and my head starts to spin, the room tilting just slightly out of focus.

That's when Marissa reappears, practically gliding toward me with a tall blonde in tow. "Alex, darling," she says, her voice sweet and smooth. "I have my best girl for you tonight. This is Skye—you're very lucky because she's in high demand. But I promised I'd take care of you."

Skye steps forward and I take her in—wavy blonde hair falling just above her shoulders, a pink corset top, and a white leather skirt that clings to her like it was painted on. Her face is all glossy perfection—false lashes, sculpted cheekbones, and full lips. I can't tell what's real and what's enhanced, but at this moment, with alcohol clouding my judgement, I'm finding it hard to care.

"Hi, you," Skye purrs as she slides her hands around my neck, her touch featherlight but deliberate. Her eyes lock onto mine with a kind of laser focus that leaves zero room for misinterpretation. "Are you going to let me show you a good time tonight?" I pause, somewhere between amusement and wariness. Her confidence is magnetic, almost overwhelming, but something about her feels...rehearsed. Of course, she's getting paid to be here. That's literally the job.

Mark and AJ's voices cut through the haze like bad influences incarnate. "Let's go, Alex! Get it!" they shout, grinning like kids hopped up on sugar and chaos.

I exhale a laugh, shaking my head. "You guys are ridiculous."

But Skye stays close, her arms looped around my neck, her body moving softly with the music. I feel her chest press into me as she sways, and before I know it, my hands settle at her waist, instinctive and unthinking. The room blurs in neon streaks as we move together, the bass thrumming beneath us. Her hair brushes my cheek as she leans in, her voice low and warm. "Let's go somewhere quieter," she murmurs, breath grazing my ear. "Just you and me. I know we'd have fun."

I hesitate, the buzz in my veins pushing me one way while my conscience tugs me back. I've been down this road before. Nights like this are easy, predictable…and never lead anywhere real.

"Skye…" I trail off, not sure how to finish the thought.

Her eyes soften as she tilts her head. "No strings. No expectations. Just a good time." She shrugs one shoulder, the gesture both disarming and deliberate. Her fingers brush the back of my neck and slide down my back. Maybe it's the alcohol, maybe it's the part of me that doesn't want to overthink everything tonight, but my reluctance starts to dissolve. I close my eyes for a second, clearing my head. When I open them, she's still waiting.

"Okay," I finally say, my voice quieter than intended.

Her smile widens as she slips her hand into mine. "Come on," she whispers. And just like that, I let her lead me up the stairs to *Luxe Haven* above, a place designed for exactly this kind of escape.

—

The moment we step into the hotel room, nostalgia hits—not the comforting kind like sipping hot cocoa with grandma at Christmas. No, this is the kind of nostalgia that drags old ghosts to the surface. The kind that clings to your skin like regret.

I blink hard, willing the spiraling thoughts away. I don't need this right now. But the alcohol buzz is burning off, replaced by a dull ache pressing at my temples. The laughter, the music—all of it evaporates, leaving behind an uncomfortable silence that feels heavier than the room itself.

Skye tugs at my collar, her lips brushing close to my ear. "How about we move this to the sofa?" she murmurs, voice silky. "Can I get you a drink, big boy? Champagne? Whiskey?"

I blow a slow exhale. "You're gorgeous, Skye. But… I don't think I can do this tonight. I'm trying to be a better person and all."

Her smile slips, replaced by confusion. "What's that supposed to mean? Being with me makes you less of a better person?"

I wince. "No. Shit—sorry. You can't hold me responsible for the crap coming out of my mouth after tequila." It sounds weak, even to me. I'm just desperate to get out of here. Fast.

The truth? I'm not even sure I could get hard right now. Not because of the tequila—I'm just starting to realize my heart might have been replaced with a decorative ice sculpture—impressive to look at, utterly useless. And yeah, that revelation leaves a gaping, echoey void right in the center of my chest.

Skye tilts her chin, eyes flicking up at me. Her smile sharpens and I can practically see the gears turning in her head. The room suddenly feels smaller, walls inching closer. My pulse kicks up—I'm caught between two shitty options: drown in this moment just to feel *something* or walk away and face the gaping void in my chest—maybe take it out for a drink, get to know it better since it's clearly planning to stick around.

Right now, I honestly can't tell which one's the bigger

nightmare.

CHAPTER 4

YASMINE

It's been raining all week—the kind of steady downpour that makes everything feel slower and blurred, as if the world's been smudged at the edges. But today, the clouds finally break, and sunlight spills through in those golden, syrupy streaks that make everything look like it's been blessed by a filter. The world feels like it's waking up. I feel a rush of energy, this itch to move, to breathe air that isn't soaked with Liam's cologne and unsolicited life advice. Honestly, if I hear one more monologue about "unlocking my inner warrior," I might just shove a chakra crystal somewhere unpleasant.

I pull on a white sports bra and matching running tights that hug me just right. My frame is slim but strong, and it's taken me years to appreciate that. There was a time I actually booked a consultation for a breast reduction, but then my mom got sick, and life had other plans. Looking back, I'm glad I never went through with it. I've learned to love myself exactly as I am—soft spots, strong parts, all of it. I slip into a bright pink lace G-string beneath my gear. No one else will see it, but that's not the point. It's my little reminder that I'm worth celebrating, even if it's just for me.

As I bounce down the hall, I catch Liam watching me from his office. He's leaning back in his chair, fingers steepled, eyes lingering on me just a second too long. I feel his gaze like static, but I don't shrink under it. "Wow… heading out somewhere?" His voice slides in, smooth as silk and twice as slippery. He pushes back from his chair and strolls over, his eyes dragging slowly down my body before landing back on my face.

I plaster on my most polite, zen-master smile. "Just sneaking in a run. Did you need anything before I head out?" I ask, the kind of professional courtesy you extend to someone who signs your checks and occasionally forgets you're not part of the furniture.

He leans in just enough to blur the lines. "Need? No. But I wouldn't mind some company. I can think of a few ways to make a run more… interesting." His voice dips on that last word, like I'm supposed to swoon or giggle or do whatever women usually do when he turns on the charm.

Instead, I laugh lightly, like he just told me puppies invented the internet. "I bet you could," I say, brushing it off with a flick of my ponytail. I remind myself of the line I need to keep firmly in place. The last thing I need is to flirt with my boss. Keeping things professional with Liam is priority number one. And honestly? He's not my type. It's not that Liam isn't objectively attractive—he's practically a walking advertisement for why moisturizers exist. But Hollywood charisma and designer suits don't impress me. Sure, *some* women might melt under his gaze like it's some kind of superpower. But me? I'm proudly radiation-proof. What matters to me isn't dollar signs—it's someone's heart. Their depth.

I squat down to tighten my laces, shooting him a casual glance as I do. If Liam thinks I'm another name to scribble on the inside of his headboard, he's in for a surprise. I'm not here for ego-stroking or designer-label daydreams. I want *real*. Unfiltered. Heart-cracking, soul-stirring connection.

—

My jog starts off like something out of a lifestyle commercial—wide, manicured streets lined with palm trees swaying as if they've been paid to look that graceful. Even the air smells expensive, like eucalyptus and vague superiority. I half expect a drone to fly by, capturing footage for a "Visit Beverly Hills" promo.

A rainbow arcs lazily in the distance, peeking between the fronds as if it's just casually photobombing my morning. I almost want to wave at it. It's all so picturesque I wouldn't be surprised if a golden retriever jogged past with a latte in its mouth. Back home in Connecticut, a run usually involves dodging potholes the size of kiddie pools and hoping the squirrels don't launch an ambush. Here? The sidewalks are so pristine they probably get detailed twice a week.

I find my rhythm, my feet tapping out a steady beat as I pass another jogger—a blonde with hair so perfect it looks like it was styled for a fitness catalog. Her lashes are long and fluttery, her face powdered as though she's expecting paparazzi at mile two. I offer her a smile, but she returns it with a glare that slides down my body like she's scanning for flaws. I don't take it personally. Some people are running from their fears, others are running to show they're ahead of the rest, but I'm just running to feel alive.

Bob Marley's voice filters through my headphones, and suddenly I'm back in my parent's kitchen, barefoot on cool tile, the scent of cardamom in the air. She'd blast his songs on lazy Sundays, swaying her hips as if she was auditioning for a reggae music video. She used to say his voice was liquid sunshine on a rainy day. Mom always had these little sayings, what she called her "mom-isms," and my favorite was the one about rainbows. She used to tell us that no two people ever see the same rainbow, a personal phenomenon shaped by our perspective. Now, I finally understand. Life isn't a single truth we all share—it's a mosaic of experiences, shaped by who we are, what we've lost, and what we hope to find. And maybe the real beauty isn't in the rainbow itself, but in the quiet reminder that even in the same storm, we're all seeing something different—and that's what makes it *human*.

Just as her words echo in my mind, I catch a glimpse of her favorite flowers, gardenias, lining the front yard of a nearby house. My chest tightens in that familiar way grief tends to sneak up. I slow down, taking a deep breath as the floral scent fills my lungs. It's sweet, another little reminder that she's still with me somehow.

And then it happens.

A tidal wave of cold, muddy water crashes over me, soaking me from head to toe. I stand there, stunned, blinking through wet lashes as the shock sets in. My arms shoot out instinctively, droplets flying from my fingertips in a dramatic sprinkler effect. "Oh, for the love of…" I grit my teeth and mutter, half to the universe and half to myself, begging for strength and inner peace.

Twenty feet ahead, a sleek Bugatti screeches to a stop, as if the driver suddenly remembered what brakes are for. The door swings open, and I brace for some LA hotshot to saunter out, toss me a half-hearted apology as if that would make everything okay. Or even worse, ask ME for an apology for being an annoying insect in the way, though I was rightfully on the sidewalk.

What I get instead is…well, not that.

A very tall, very towering man steps out, and my internal monologue screeches to a halt. The sun is framing him like it's part of his personal entourage. When he reaches up to slide down his sunglasses, it's as if he invented the move himself. His eyes are a molten shade of hazel, like someone poured liquid gold into his irises just to mess with the rest of us mere mortals. I swear, the entire universe is holding its breath right now, including me.

As he gets closer, I notice more details. The white t-shirt shirt that clings just right to his chest, his toned biceps and tanned forearms that could probably bench press a small car, and the low collar revealing enough skin to suggest he's in a constant state of "just woke up like this." His hair, a perfectly tousled shade of light brown, is practically starring in its own shampoo commercial.

He stops a few feet in front of me, close enough that I can smell cedar and something that can only be described as "expensive man." He doesn't say a word.

We're just…staring. Not talking. Just standing there in silence, dripping in mud (me) and cinematic lighting (him), both of us basically locked in an awkward stand-off of ogling. I'm pretty sure my brain has short-circuited. Is he alright? Did he hit his head? Should I wave my hand in front of his face? Is he mesmerized or malfunctioning?

I shift slightly, the silence stretching longer than it should. "So… do Bugattis usually come with surprise showers, or is that a special feature?" I finally say, aiming for humor but landing somewhere near awkward. *Nothing.* Just more of that intense, slow-burn stare. His jawline could cut glass, but apparently, words are a limited resource.

The muddy water dripping down my body is completely irrelevant now. I should be annoyed, but instead, I feel a heat rising up my neck that has nothing to do with embarrassment and everything to do with… whatever *this* is.

"I'm guessing you're the artist behind this masterpiece?" I say, aiming for levity as I give a small, theatrical wave of my arms to present my drenched state like a wet exhibit. My smile is casual, but the moment I glance down, my confidence evaporates.

Oh no.

My brilliant idea to wear an all-white outfit suddenly feels like a rookie mistake. My sports bra, now soaked through, leaves nothing to the imagination. My nipples are practically making an introduction of their own. And that brightly colored G-string? It's putting on a full Broadway performance beneath my now transparent leggings.

"Oh… oh no," I mutter, wide-eyed, as I clap my hands over my mouth in disbelief, heat rising to my cheeks. *Of course,* this would happen. Some moments in life really test your ability to laugh at yourself. This one just took first place.

CHAPTER 5

ALEX

5 Minutes Ago

I unintentionally rev my engine as I swerve out of *Luxe Haven's* driveway. The growl of my car is loud enough to wake the dead, but I don't care. I couldn't get out of there fast enough. Last night was a crash course in humiliation.

Skye pulled out every trick in her arsenal to seduce me, and my body responded like it was on strike. Zero. Zilch. My dick might as well have been in a coma. She tried to laugh it off, but it was the kind of awkward that clings to the air like bad cologne. I made my excuses, practically ran out the door, and now I'm cruising down Sunset Boulevard as though I can outrun the embarrassment.

My phone vibrates again in the cupholder. The screen lights up with a string of unread texts and missed calls. There are at least ten from AJ and the guys, who all want a play-by-play of the night. Not happening.

I grip the steering wheel tighter and shake my head. The last thing I feel like doing is explaining why the night didn't end the way everyone assumed it would. The stories they can slap on like badges of honor during brunch recaps. But there's nothing to tell. Because the truth? It isn't fun or exciting, it's… hollow, and no amount of expensive champagne is enough to fill that empty space.

I crank the stereo to drown out my thoughts, the city waking up around me as I speed toward home. As my mind starts to wander, I barely register the road in front of me.

And then I see her.

She's standing on the sidewalk like some ethereal vision in all white, her long, wavy black hair catching the sunlight like a halo. She's tall and lean but somehow impossibly curvy, the kind of figure that makes reality feel like it's glitching. For a split second, I forget where I am, who I am, hell, what I am.

Is this heaven? Because if it is, and this is what your angels look like God, I swear—no more sins. I get it now. The hype makes total sense.

A familiar pull stirs low in my body, and I blink in surprise. *Well, look at that. Maybe I'm not broken after all.*

Unfortunately, while I'm busy gawking at this goddess like some lovesick fool, my Bugatti barrels straight into a massive puddle. A tidal wave of muddy water explodes across the sidewalk and all over her.

She's completely drenched.

I groan and drag my hands down my face. *Seriously, God? I'm trying here. You don't have to be a jerk about it.*

I slam on the brakes and swerve to the side of the road. My heart is hammering, and I have no idea what my game plan is, but I know I can't just drive away. I'm supposed to be working on being a better person, and something tells me leaving a beautiful, innocent woman covered in sludge isn't part of that plan.

So, I take a deep breath, step out of the car, and brace myself for whatever comes next.

I try to shake off the pounding in my head before stepping out of the car. The sun feels like a personal assault, stabbing straight into my skull. I reach for my sunglasses, ready to remove them out of habit, but I wince the second the brightness hits. Nope, not putting myself through more unnecessary torture. I decide to leave them on, at least until I get a clearer look at the woman standing in front of me.

Holy…

'Sexy' doesn't even come close. She's not just beautiful; she's breathtaking in a way that makes you question if you're awake or dreaming. Her face is soft but striking, with none of that cold, aloof prettiness I'm used to from the women in my orbit. No forced pout or plastic perfection. Just raw, natural beauty.

Thanks to me, she's drenched from head to toe, her all-white outfit clinging to every inch of her toned, curvy body. And it's doing absolutely nothing to hide what's underneath. A hint of soft pink presses against the front of her sports bra, her nipples outlined by the damp fabric. Lower down, I catch a glimpse of hot pink lace that's just barely visible through her leggings.

My throat goes dry.

I know I'm staring, probably like some slack-jawed idiot, but I can't tear my eyes away. She's unlike the models or actresses I've grown numb to over the years. She's in a whole other league entirely.

Suddenly, I realize she's been looking at me, her brows slightly raised, as if she's debating whether I'm just clueless or full-blown insane.

Say something, I tell myself, but apparently, I've lost the ability to form words.

Great. Just great. First, I drench her in muddy water. Now, I'm standing here like a mute psycho. Stellar impression, Alex.

"I'm guessing you're the artist behind this masterpiece?" she says, gesturing to her drenched body with a wry smile and a graceful sweep of her arms. Her voice, soft with a little rasp, slides through me like a slow, electric current. And just like that, my dick decides now is the perfect time to wake up.

Fantastic. Thanks for joining us, buddy.

I scramble for unsexy thoughts. Grandma at Sunday church service. That one time I got stung by a jellyfish and my brother had to piss on my leg. The week I almost died from food poisoning after a carne asada burrito from Chipotle—definitely karmic payback for eating at Chipotle when I live in Southern California.

I give my head a subtle shake, trying to break free of her spell and clear my throat. "Sorry… I didn't see the puddle there."

"It's alright," she says, waving it off. "Can't blame you for an accident. I just wish I'd worn something other than white. Pretty sure I'll be giving the entire neighborhood a free show on my way home." She lets out a light and melodic laugh, and for some reason, it lands right in the center of my chest.

"Do you live around here? I can give you a ride home if you'd like." I immediately regretted saying it as the words slipped through my lips. *Please don't think I'm a stalker. Please don't think I'm a stalker.*

Her head tilts slightly, considering me. "Oh, no, it's okay, but thank you for offering."

"It's really the least I can do…" I try to sound casual, but internally, I'm spiraling. *Great. She totally thinks I'm a creep.* I try to salvage it with something cool and effortless. "But no pressure. I mean, it's up to you. It's cool. Or, you know, if there's anything else I can do to make up for… uh, getting you wet."

Oh, God. Seriously? I want to hurl myself into traffic. Who says that?

Her lips twitch, and for a moment, I think she might actually burst out laughing. Instead, she shakes her head and smiles a real, genuine smile. "You're very kind, but I'm okay. Um… maybe if you have a towel or a T-shirt, I could borrow it? If not, no worries."

Borrow. That means she'll have to give it back. Which means I'd have an excuse to see her again. My heart gives a hopeful kick, but of course, my car is devoid of anything practical. No towels, no extra shirts, just an empty coffee cup and my own questionable decisions.

Screw it. I grab the hem of my shirt, pull it over my head, and hand it to her.

I run a hand behind my neck and glance at her with a slight grin. "This is the best I can do. But take care of it, okay? It's my favorite."

Her eyes widen slightly as she takes it. Her fingers brush mine, and I swear the contact sends a ripple down my spine. She looks up at me, lips curving into another soft smile. "I'll take good care of it," she says, her voice quieter now.

I try to remind myself to breathe, but it's not easy when she's standing there in front of me, wearing the remnants of my dignity and every bit of my attention.

CHAPTER 6

YASMINE

I'm pretty sure my mouth is actually watering as this real-life Michelangelo statue peels off his shirt right in front of me. And *wow*. His body is ridiculous. Like s*hould come with a warning label* ridiculous. Sculpted abs, broad shoulders, and arms that look like they could carry me *and* all my emotional baggage without breaking a sweat. But it's not just his physique. His deep hazel eyes have this genuine sincerity, like he doesn't even realize how insanely attractive he is. And the way he speaks? Chivalrous, humble, and effortlessly kind—an honesty that isn't curated.

Case in point: he's literally giving me the shirt off his back so I don't have to flash the entire neighborhood on my way home.

I take his shirt, trying not to look like I'm mentally building a shrine in his honor. "Thank you. Seriously, this is really sweet."

He smiles, and I swear it's the kind of smile that could probably melt the polar ice caps. But I remind myself to stay grounded. Deep breaths, Yasmine. Just because a man is hot and kind doesn't mean I need to lose my head.

Still, I was tempted when he offered to give me a ride home. But something tells me Liam values his privacy like it's the secret to eternal life, and the last thing I need is him freaking out over some shirtless Greek god dropping me off.

So instead, I hold up the shirt with a grateful smile. "You've officially saved my dignity. And probably the dignity of a few pedestrians."

His laugh is warm and genuine, and for a second, I'm reminded that there are still good people in the world. And maybe I've just met one of the best of them.

"This is the best I can do, but take care of it, will you? It's my favorite," he says in his deep, dark voice. He grins and gives me a wink, making my insides practically disintegrate.

Our fingers brush as he hands me his shirt, and I swear I feel a jolt of electricity through my entire body. Did he feel that too? Or am I just living out a paperback fantasy in real-time?

Is he expecting me to offer to exchange numbers so I can return his shirt? Shouldn't he be the one asking for my number? Although it is 2025—haven't we evolved past those outdated gender roles? Wait… what is happening? I'm a confident, spiritually grounded woman. These spiraling thoughts have no place in my head. I take a deep breath and do what I always do. Listen to my gut. "I'll take good care of it," I say warmly. "How can I return it to you?"

His grin widens, and he reaches into his pocket, pulling out a sleek business card. Of course, he has business cards. He probably hands them out at yacht parties and private polo matches.

"Here. Just contact me when you're ready to return it."

That smirk? I'm toast. Absolutely scorched. I take the card, glancing at his name, and mentally prepare myself to replay this moment in my head for… well, possibly forever. It's a good thing my pants are already wet from the puddle because, at this point, I'm not entirely sure *what* is responsible for how my body is reacting.

The things I'm going to do with this man in my imagination tonight… let's just say I'm going to need some *deep* meditation to cool me down.

CHAPTER 7

ALEX

I give her one last look—a slow, deliberate once-over—and flash a smile that's probably doing a terrible job of masking how much I don't want to leave. But I force myself back into the driver's seat, rev the engine, and pull away before I do something stupid. Like ask for her entire life story.

The hum of the car would usually calm me down. Not right now. My mind keeps snapping back to her. That smile—soft and unguarded, like she doesn't know how to be anything but genuine. And damn, if I ever needed proof I wasn't as broken as I thought, she was it. I'd convinced myself I'd gone numb, that I was incapable of feeling anything more than surface-level attraction. But this girl? She cracked something open, and I'm not sure I want it shut.

When our fingers brushed as I handed her my shirt, I felt something—a pulse down my back, enough to make me grip my steering wheel a little tighter now. It wasn't just excitement. I've felt excitement a million times before. This was something… else.

She's special, I can already tell. Thoughtful, gentle, probably one of those people who rescue injured birds and meditate at sunrise. But then that body…I've never seen anything like it. Curves that defy reason. The kind that makes you forget what you were saying mid-sentence. Her waist was impossibly small, and those tits? Absolute perfection, and I've seen my fair share.

She's a walking contradiction, the kind that messes with your head. Like an angel who dabbles in sin just for fun. And maybe that's why I can't stop thinking about her. It's basic biology, really. My attraction to her is primal, automatic; there's no sense denying it.

But there's a catch. Something about her doesn't feel…casual. That thought alone makes my pulse spike and my defenses rise. I'm not the guy who changes for anyone. I never have been. But as I think back to this woman, I wonder what it would feel like to let her unravel me.

Not that I'm ready to admit that, not even to myself.

I exhale sharply as I pull into my driveway and cut the engine. Something tells me she's the kind of woman I'll never be ready for.

CHAPTER 8

YASMINE

Well, that was… interesting.

It's been a long time since I've felt such an instant, magnetic pull toward someone. But I know better than to let my guard down. My focus needs to stay razor-sharp. I'm here for one thing, and it doesn't involve getting sidetracked by devastating smiles and biceps that look like they were engineered to distract.

As I jog back to Liam's, wearing Alex's—yes, I took note of his name from the business card with its embossed font and the scent of old money—soft shirt, I can't help but get lost in the smell of it. It's fresh and clean, reminiscent of the ocean breeze crashing over the Pacific Coast, with a hint of something warm and familiar…like cinnamon toast on a winter morning. I have to physically shake my head to snap out of the tiny daydream that almost snuck in—one that involved me stealing his shirt permanently and living happily ever after in it.

Great. Now I'm mentally moving in with his clothing. Not weird at all, Yasmine.

It's worse when my imagination takes the wheel and swerves straight into Rom-Com Territory. I'm suddenly curled up next to him on a Friday night, his arm slung around me, popcorn in hand, watching some cheesy horror flick while I pretend I'm not terrified of clowns. I can practically hear him laughing at me when I flinch, his hand slipping into mine, squeezing gently…

Wow. Okay, Yasmine. Reel it in. My mom always said I had a vivid imagination, capable of taking reality and stretching it into places no one else would dare. Right now, it's steering me straight into a dangerous cul-de-sac with no U-turn. The last thing I need is to hand my heart over to someone who probably has a "no breakfast" policy and an assistant to track his conquests.

Not that I'm as fragile as I was back when Mom passed away. I've done the work. Years of therapy, self-reflection, rebuilding my strength one deep breath at a time. But even after all that, there's still a small part of me that remains tender. And tender doesn't do well with someone who probably has a rotating door policy on emotions.

With that thought, I make a decision right here and now. Alex can stay safely tucked into the back of my mind—a daydream, nothing more. I'll let him resurface occasionally, maybe in my bed, in the shower, or…okay, okay, focus!

Hot doesn't even begin to cover it. And that free sidewalk show? The moment he tugged his shirt over his head, time practically slowed down. I'm talking slow-mo music video vibes, with wind gusting dramatically and birds soaring off in the distance. Ridiculous? Yes. Accurate? Also yes.

But I know better. Attraction this strong? It's like standing too close to a bonfire. You can only admire the flames for so long before you start to sizzle.

—

I quietly slip through one of the back doors of Liam's main house, making sure to avoid any chance of running into him. It's not that I have a problem seeing him; it's just that my brain is still spinning from that sidewalk encounter with Alex. Every detail replays in my head like a slo-mo movie scene I can't stop watching. I can still feel the weight of his shirt on my shoulders, the warmth of his touch lingering where our fingers brushed.

I need space. Time to breathe. To pull myself together before I spiral any further into this intoxicating daydream. Meditation. That's what I need—a way to quiet the noise and clear the heat that's fogging up my mind.

I make my way to my room, already craving the stillness waiting for me inside. As soon as I enter, I practically collapse onto my bed. The soft linen sheets crinkle beneath me as I sink into my plush pillows. A faint scent of lavender from my essential oil diffuser drifts through the air, usually enough to calm my nerves—but not today. Alex's shirt still clings to me, warm and slightly oversized, and for some reason, I hesitate to take it off.

I close my eyes, hoping to sort through the whirlwind of what just happened. Instead, my brain hits replay. Frame-by-frame flashes of him fill my mind. His ripped abs, his broad shoulders, those forearms that look like they could build entire cities. His skin was golden and sun-kissed in a way that felt unfairly perfect. But considering the dreary LA weather we've been stuck with for months, I'd bet money on a tanning salon—of course, I think, rolling my eyes—classic LA pretty boy.

I need to clear my head. Fast. Only one person can snap me out of this. I reach for my phone and dial her number. She picks up after the second ring, her familiar voice instantly quieting the chaos in my head.

"Hey, Sis! Sorry, one sec… Over here!" Sami says, her voice muffled by the sound of whistles and cleats scraping against turf. "What's up?"

"I need a distraction," I confess. "Preferably one that doesn't involve me mentally moving into a stranger's bed."

"Who is he?" she presses, her curiosity practically crackling through the phone.

I let out a breath. "Just some LA… I don't know… player. But the hottest one I've ever met."

Sami's laugh is sharp and knowing. "Yazzy, listen, I know this isn't what you want to hear, but maybe hooking up with a boy toy isn't the worst thing in the world. In fact…" Her voice lowers conspiratorially. "It could even do you some good. Clear your head… clear the cobwebs…"

"Sami!" I sit upright, scandalized but grinning. "I do *not* have cobwebs! I am lasered clean, thank you very much."

She cackles like she's scored a point in some unspoken game. "Seriously, though. When was the last time you did something just for you? Since Mom died, all you've done is throw yourself into work, into helping everyone else. You deserve to have some unattached fun."

My stomach twists, and I close my eyes briefly. She's right. I know she's right. But that doesn't make it easier to hear. "Okay," I sigh, "You're officially *not* giving me the advice I called for. So I'm gonna let you go. Good luck with practice."

"Alright," she says, though her tone has a teasing edge. "But think about what I said, okay? You're not marrying the guy. Some mutual fun is a win-win! Positive vibes all around—which, let's be honest, is *totally* your thing."

I shake my head, a reluctant smile tugging at my lips. "Love you, Sami."

"Love you more. Now go manifest some good energy!"

I hang up, her words lingering in the back of my mind. I exhale and I peel off my soaked clothes and toss them straight into the wicker laundry basket. Mud splatters on the floor, but I'm too busy trying not to think about *him* to care.

I glance down at Alex's shirt and bring it to my face to breathe him in. It's probably borderline creepy, but if anyone ever bottled this scent, I'd be their best customer. My eyes drift closed as excitement rushes through me, pooling low in my stomach. It's been years since I've felt this kind of fire—a pull so instinctive it nearly knocks me off balance.

I internally shake my head at myself before heading into the bathroom. The shower hisses to life, steam curling around the glass. I crank the notch up to near-boiling—exactly how I like it. The kind of heat that could burn away indecision and hesitation.

But of course, my mind has other plans. Instead of peaceful, meditative thoughts, I'm replaying every second of my run-in with Alex. My eyes drift shut, and the bathroom dissolves into a haze of fantasy. I can almost feel Alex's presence, his breath hot against my neck, his mouth trailing down, each slow glide of his tongue igniting a path from my collarbone to the swells of my breasts. My nipples harden under the imagined touch, standing at attention despite the steam swirling around me.

A low ache pulses within me, and I cup my breasts, squeezing to ease some of the tension, but it's not enough. My hands wander lower, gliding over my slick, wet skin, following the path I imagine his mouth would take. When my fingers brush between my thighs, I'm already drenched, not from the shower but from something far more primal.

I trace lazy circles over my clit with my thumb, imagining that it's actually his, the firm press of his thumb driving me to the brink of ecstasy. My other hand slides over the seam of my slit, teasing, dipping. I'm tight, almost unbearably so, sometimes even a tampon is a struggle. But right now? I'm so wet that my middle finger slides inside with ease. I begin a slow rhythm, pressing and grinding, my thumb working in tandem, stroking the embers in my core.

Pleasure hums low in my stomach, building in slow, lazy waves. But it's not enough. It's never enough. I've never been able to orgasm from sex alone; only my own touch has ever brought me over the edge. But even now, as my pulse quickens, satisfaction feels just out of reach.

My eyes snap open. I shake my head as though I can banish the vision of Alex from my mind. But it's useless. His phantom touch lingers, seared into my senses.

This is ridiculous. I just met the guy, and I'm practically writing sonnets in my head. I blame it on the lack of romance in my life. When you spend your days contorting celebrities into downward dogs, your imagination tends to wander. But still…something about him felt different. I can't quite pin it down, but I know I'm not wrong. My intuition is annoyingly sharp like that.

I towel off and pad back into my room. I should meditate. Center myself. Think about literally anything else. Instead, I flop back onto my bed, staring up at the ceiling like it's holding the answers to the universe.

Sami's voice pops into my head, all sass and unfiltered truth. But I try to remind myself, I'm here for one thing: to do my job, save up, and move on. No distractions. No messy entanglements. And definitely no shirtless, chiseled, Bugatti-driving distractions. I roll over and bury my face in the pillow, groaning into the plush fabric. I can't even lie to myself. I'm already consumed by him. And if I'm being really honest? I don't mind it one bit.

CHAPTER 9

ALEX

It's been three days. Not that I'm counting or anything. But yeah, three days and not a single word from her.

Who am I kidding? She's definitely too good for me in every way that counts. That face…it was something else entirely. I can't get her eyes out of my head. Soft yet piercing, the kind of green you only see in emeralds and fantasies. And those long, dark lashes, curling in a way that only natural lashes can, fanning out to make her eyes look even more hypnotic. Her nose had that cute, slightly upturned thing going on and a few freckles scattered across the bridge practically begged to be kissed. Or nipped. Maybe both. If I get the chance, I won't be able to stop myself. I'm already prepared to issue a formal apology to her freckles for what I'm planning to do to them.

But none of that is what really did me in. What hooked me was how she carried herself. Graceful. Real. No Hollywood pretense. She wasn't playing a part or angling for attention. She just existed, effortlessly, like she had no clue she was drop-dead gorgeous. And for a brief, stupid moment, I thought fate had thrown me a curveball. Something real. Something rare.

But three days of radio silence? Yeah, fate might've been on a coffee break. I groan, rubbing my temples. Should've just grown a pair and asked for her number. No waiting around, imagining her slipping out of reach while I sit here debating what could've been. Lesson learned. Next time, if there is a next time, I'm not leaving anything up to chance.

I flop onto one of the heavy wooden sun loungers on my patio deck like a deflated balloon. It practically groans under me, probably because it knows I'm about to spiral. It's solid and probably weighs more than my last relationship, and I love it for that. My house is perched in the Hollywood Hills, overlooking the entire west side of Los Angeles all the way to the Pacific Ocean. It's so high up it feels like my private sanctuary, where the world's chaos can't touch me unless I let it.

I stare at the skyline but it doesn't stir anything in me. For some people, home is a place. A street, a memory, a feeling. For me? It's always been… complicated. Ever since I was nine, I've had a one-track mind. If emotions show up uninvited, I squash them like I'm playing Whack-a-Mole. So, I don't put much stock in places or permanence. But sitting here now, staring at the city that never stops moving, I can't help but wonder if the thing I'm avoiding isn't home—it's connection.

I sigh, resting my head back against the lounger. Deep thoughts, gorgeous view, emotionally unavailable billionaire—cue the violins.

My phone chimes, and I pick it up, expecting another pointless group chat where people pretend to care about each other's vacation photos. Instead, it's a text from an unknown number with an area code I don't recognize.

Text: Hi Alex, it's the girl you turned into a human puddle the other day. No hard feelings ;) Would you like your shirt back? - Yasmine

My heart does a ridiculous leap like I'm back in high school reading a secret note in class. It's her. And now I know her name. *Yasmine.* Of course, that's her name. She couldn't be anything simple or ordinary. No, she gets a name that sounds like poetry. Graceful, unique, unforgettable. Just like her. My thumb hovers over the keyboard, ready to fire off a response, but nothing comes to mind. *Me.* Blank. This *never* happens. I'm usually effortless. Smooth. Borderline arrogant if I'm being real. I always know where I stand with women because they make it obvious. But Yasmine? She doesn't just turn heads. She could make the whole damn world pause. She's the kind of woman who belongs in a painting. On a pedestal. Not because she asks for it, but because the universe insists.

And now, here I am, a guy who's built his life around control, suddenly feeling like I'm trying out for a team I didn't even know I wanted to be on. My pulse kicks up as I stare at the screen. The problem isn't what to say. It's that nothing I type feels good enough for her.

I begin: **I'm so happy to hear from you! When are you free to meet?**

I pause, reread it, and immediately cringe. Desperate, much? I delete it and try again:

Me: There you are. Shirt or no shirt, I'd like to see you. I'm free whenever.

I stare at the message. Is it too forward? Too casual? What happened to my game? I'm the guy who roasts my friends for sending texts like this, and here I am, one step away from throwing out a "u up?" Before I can spiral further, I hit send and toss my phone onto the side table like it's radioactive. Nope. I can't sit here staring at the screen, waiting for those damn three dots. I need to move. I leap off the lounger and dive straight into my pool. The water cuts around me as I push through each lap with everything I've got. The cool burn in my muscles is the only thing that keeps me from being entirely consumed by this wild mix of excitement and panic.

Because yeah, I'm thrilled she texted me. But beneath that thrill, there's this uneasy whisper in the back of my mind—What if she's about to become the one thing I'm not ready for?

I surface and take a deep breath, slicking my hair back. My phone buzzes. I swim to the pool's edge, water dripping down my face as I climb out.

Her reply lights the screen.

Yasmine: I'm free tomorrow unless you've already lent out your next favorite shirt.

I laugh—an actual laugh—and it catches me off guard. I drag a towel over my face like it might wipe away whatever the hell is going on inside me. I tap out a quick response.

Me: Guilty as charged. But I've got plenty of shirts to spare.

I hit send and sit back, a grin pulling at my lips. Maybe I'm in trouble—but if this is trouble, I'm not sure I mind.

CHAPTER 10

YASMINE

I'm meeting Alex tonight.

It's supposed to be pretty casual, just dropping off his shirt. so why is my heart doing this ridiculous flutter like I'm sixteen and he just asked me to prom?

I told myself I wasn't looking for anything serious. I've repeated that mantra enough times to convince almost everyone around me, including myself. But maybe I do want something more. And maybe, *God help me*, I want it with someone like Alex. Even though I wouldn't dare admit that out loud. Not to my friends, not to my sister, and definitely not to myself.

I shove the thought down, take a deep breath, and head for the shower.

Alex asked me to meet him at *Toru*, a sushi spot in West Hollywood that practically screams *celebrity hot spot*. It's cute, but if he thinks money and ambiance are going to make me swoon, he's got the wrong girl. I'm not the type to be dazzled by VIP sections and overpriced cocktails. I prefer places where you don't need reservations three weeks in advance just to get your chopsticks.

Still, I can't deny there's something kind of… sweet about it. In a ridiculously extravagant way.

I shower, primp, and prep to the nines. I even brush on some mascara and eyeliner. Makeup isn't really my thing, so when I find myself debating bronzer versus blush, I call it a day. My outfit is simple but cute—a coral, off-the-shoulder dress with a floral print I picked up in India during yoga training. It's loose and airy, falling just above my knees. No cleavage. That's right, I'm not giving anything up that easily. If Alex wants more than small talk over sushi, he will have to work for it.

I catch a glimpse of myself in the mirror, and smirk as I brush out the waves in my hair. A spritz of my favorite essential oil blend—jasmine, gardenia, and a hint of peach, all of my mom's favorite scents—completes the look. It's grounding, exactly what I need. Because as much as I want to play it cool, I can't ignore the butterflies or the hope that maybe tonight will be more than just a shirt drop-off.

My phone buzzes, and I glance down.

Alex: Still on for tonight, or did I scare you off?

I smirk and type back.

Me: Scare me off? Please. Takes more than that to intimidate me. Almost ready to head out.

A few seconds later, my phone lights up again.

Alex: Good to know. I'd hate to think my charm wasn't working ;)

I pause, my finger hovering over the screen, his words sending this unexpected warmth through my chest. I've met enough people in this city to know most keep things surface-level, wearing their ambitions and insecurities like armor. But this? It feels…different.

I type back.

Me: Is this where I'm supposed to swoon, or do you save the good stuff for in-person?

Alex: Oh, I save the best for when it counts. But I'll let you decide if I'm worth swooning over.

I laugh, shaking my head. I'm not one for snap judgments. Everyone's walking their own path, carrying their own stories and challenges. And Alex? I'm open to seeing him as he is, with no projections and no assumptions.

I toss my phone into my bag, grab my keys, and head out the door with a flutter of excitement that feels both ridiculous and oddly perfect.

—

As my Uber glides up Toru's pristine driveway, it's like entering a billionaire's playground. Ferraris and Lamborghinis are parked along the curb as though they own the place, their glossy paint jobs practically winking at me in smug superiority. They look like they've been polished by unicorn tears and manifesting crystals. A cluster of hopeful paparazzi hovers near the front and back entrances, cameras at the ready as if they're hunting for Bigfoot—if Bigfoot wore Louboutins and drank $20 matcha lattes.

A few years ago, all of this—the cars, the photographers, the whole glitzy scene—might have made me feel wildly out of place. But now? Not so much. I've done enough inner work to know that confidence isn't defined by the car you drive or how many people scream your name outside a club. Besides, I once led a meditation session for a billionaire who cried for thirty minutes because his dog wouldn't look him in the eye anymore. So, I know firsthand that money can't buy inner peace—or apparently, dog loyalty.

My Uber stops, and I take a breath, squaring my shoulders. I grab Alex's shirt from the backseat and step out with what I hope is casual elegance, even if I'm internally repeating my mantra, *Confidence is a practice, not a feeling.*

Walking into the restaurant is like stepping into a movie scene where everyone knows their mark. Toru radiates calm in a way that feels almost ironic given the chaotic energy just outside. Soft indie electronic music hums in the background, the kind you listen to when you want to feel artistic but still understand the lyrics. It's serene, luxurious, and just pretentious enough to make you feel like you should be whispering your order in Japanese.

The crowd is as dazzling as the setting—a seamless blend of Hollywood elite, business moguls, and effortlessly chic Angelenos. Everyone seems to shimmer under the warm light, their laughter bubbling like champagne, filling the air with that distinct air of money, success, and professionally whitened teeth. This place might scream luxury, but at its core, it's just another restaurant with people trying their best, just like anywhere else.

A group of impossibly tall Amazonian models glides past me, legs for days, draped in tiny designer miniskirts and sky-high stilettos that look more like weapons than shoes. They're basically a moving editorial spread. Polished, radiant, and loud in that carefree, *we're too pretty to worry about gravity* kind of way.

One of them, a leggy blonde with a Russian accent thick enough to spread on toast, leans toward her friend, whispers something, and glances back at me with a laugh. It's about as subtle as a Chanel bag at a flea market. I catch myself smiling, partly because I'm spiritually evolved enough not to take it personally, and partly because the mental image of me trying to balance in five-inch stilettos is comedy gold. I'm five-foot-nine, but next to them, I feel like I've wandered onto the set of

Supermodel Avengers. And honestly? I'm okay with that. I'd make a killer sidekick.

A booming voice cuts through the buzz. A man in his mid-50s, built like a linebacker in an Armani suit, approaches the model brigade with a grin so wide it probably requires its own zip code. "Catia, Svetlana, Vivianne, Elana! I've been waiting for my favorite women all day!" They squeal and practically drape themselves over him like he's the last lifeboat on a yacht gone down. I half expect someone to hand him a rose and call it a wrap. He beams at the leggy blonde as he ushers them toward the back, likely to one of those exclusive private rooms for the rich and semi-famous.

"Excuse me?"

I snap my head back to find the hostess standing there with a mildly annoyed expression, the kind that says she's two minutes away from filing me under "trespasser." She's dressed in a miniskirt and heels so high I'm half convinced she moonlights as a tightrope walker. Honestly, do all the women here follow the same uniform code, or is this just a parallel universe where fashion sacrifices comfort in the name of exclusivity?

I offer her my best *I'm totally supposed to be here* smile. "Hi, I'm Yasmine. I'm here to meet Alex Pierce."

Her expression does a 180 so fast I almost get whiplash. "Oh! Yes, of course, right this way, madam." She gestures for me to follow her, all polished professionalism now, like I just upgraded from 'random civilian' to 'VIP list.'

I fall in step behind her as she weaves through the bustling dining area. The tables are packed with beautiful people. Like, *unreasonably* beautiful. The kind of faces that seem faintly familiar because you've probably scrolled past them on

Instagram. We stop in front of a sleek, unmarked door tucked discreetly into the wall. The hostess offers me a polished smile and opens it with the smoothness of a magician revealing a trick. I half expect a drumroll to start up.

And suddenly, the room steals my breath away.

It's stunning. Intimate. The walls are wrapped in dark, rich wood, creating a sanctuary that feels like stepping into a luxurious secret. One entire side of the room is glass, offering a view of the entire Los Angeles skyline. The city lights sparkle like diamonds. For a second, I feel like I'm floating between two worlds—one I belong to and one I'm just borrowing for the evening. I take a grounding breath, reminding myself this is just dinner. Just dinner… with a man who sent my pulse into overdrive when he took his shirt off. No pressure, right?

And then I see him. Alex. He's sitting at the far end of the table, leaning back like he owns the moment, and honestly, he probably does. He's wearing a dark suit over an open-collared shirt, an effortless cool that feels borderline unfair. When his eyes meet mine, his face breaks into a smile—not the polite kind, but the kind that sends an uninvited ripple right through me. Like he knows a secret I don't, and he's just waiting for me to catch up.

"Yasmine," he says as he stands. His voice is low and smooth, with just enough roughness to make my pulse spike even more.

I step into the room, my sandals tapping lightly against the polished floor, and I can feel the weight of his gaze, steady and warm, with every step. "Wow," I say, glancing around as I approach. "This place… it's stunning."

His smile deepens as he pulls out a chair for me. "You're stunning." The way he says it, so casual as if it's just a simple fact, catches me off guard. Compliments usually roll off me like water, but not this time.

I sink into the chair next to his, and for a moment, my stomach starts fluttering with butterflies. But then Alex leans in just slightly, his gaze locking onto mine like I'm the only person in the room, and all those thoughts of doubt? They dissolve like champagne bubbles.

CHAPTER 11

ALEX

The warm glow of *Toru's* lanterns casts a golden light across the table, and Yasmine practically glows in it. Her hair is swept to one side, her eyes glittering like they've been hoarding hidden wonders. I'm not usually the nervous type, but sitting across from her now? I'm practically malfunctioning.

"Yasmine…" That's all I manage to get out. Seriously? That's my grand opener? Her name? Real smooth, Pierce. But what the hell am I supposed to say when she looks like *that?* Effortlessly gorgeous, like she just rolled out of bed and decided to casually ruin my life. The kind of beauty that makes you lose track of your own name, let alone hers. I can't screw this up. This could be the rebound of the century. Hell, after tonight, Catia might just be "that ex with the accent…whatever her name was."

Yasmine smiles at me and for a moment I get lost. Those lips…forget it. Full, pink, and permanently pouty, like they were crafted just for me. I have to physically stop myself from staring at her mouth like a starved man eyeing dessert. Focus. One goal tonight: don't be an idiot.

She hands me the shirt I lent her, neatly folded. "Here," she says, a hint of amusement in her eyes. "I washed and pressed it for you."

I glance down at it, pretending to be perplexed, purely because she makes me act like an idiot when I'm around her. "What's this?"

She giggles and I'm hit with this ridiculous urge to make her do it again. It's soft, unguarded, and totally different from the performative laughter I'm used to. She's genuine, like she actually lives in her own skin, not someone else's idea of perfect. "Your shirt. You know, since I had to borrow it after you tried to drown me."

"Oh, that." I grin, leaning back. "Completely unintentional, I swear. But maybe fate's got a flair for the dramatic."

Her gaze flickers to mine, softening. "You think that's what it was? Fate?"

I shrug, feigning nonchalance. "Maybe. Or maybe I just need to work on my driving skills."

Her eyes light up. "I've always wondered if things like that are random. Or if maybe there's something bigger at work."

I arch an eyebrow. "You mean…like God?"

She laughs, but it's not dismissive—more like she's amused by the simplicity of the question. "Maybe. Or whatever name you want to give it. Do you believe in that kind of thing?"

I hesitate. It's not that I haven't thought about it. I just haven't been asked. Most of the women I date don't exactly ponder the meaning of life over sushi. Their deep thoughts are more along the lines of, *Does this filter make me look too tan?*

"I don't know," I say with my honesty. "I've thought about it, but I'm not sure I buy into the idea that everything's part of some master plan. Bad things happen to good people all the time. Doesn't make sense if someone's up there pulling the strings."

Yasmine nods, listening like she's genuinely interested. "Maybe it's not about sense. Maybe it's just about feeling connected. To each other, to the world…to something bigger than ourselves." I study her for a beat, struck by how unfiltered she is. She's not trying to sell me on anything and it's disarming in the best way.

"You sound like my healer in Mexico," I chuckle, shaking my head. "The guy practically had me hugging trees. I swear I bonded with a cactus."

Yasmine laughs, and it's the kind that reaches her eyes. "Hey, maybe the cactus needed a hug."

"Maybe I did," I say before I can stop myself. Her smile lingers, soft and knowing. For a moment, the room feels smaller, like it's just the two of us and the rest of the world is on mute.

"So…do *you* believe in something bigger?" I ask, genuinely curious now.

She shrugs, thoughtful. "I don't know everything, but I do believe in connection. In energy. You can feel it when it's real."

Her words settle between us. "You've got a different way of looking at things," I say.

Her eyes crinkle with a smile. "I'll take that as a compliment."

"It was," I say, meaning it.

And that's when I hear it: a voice sharp enough to cut glass. "Alex?" I look up, and there she is—Catia, standing in the doorway like she's waiting for a red carpet to roll out beneath her feet. Her eyes narrow on me, and she smirks like I've just been caught red-handed doing something scandalous.

"What a surprise," she purrs, striding forward with the confidence of a runway model who owns the damn runway. "I didn't expect to see you here."

I force a smile that probably looks more like a grimace. "Catia...always a pleasure." Her eyes flick to Yasmine, sizing her up in about two seconds flat. Yasmine, to her credit, doesn't even flinch. She just gives Catia a serene smile, like she's above whatever game Catia's trying to play. And I swear, I could kiss her for it.

Catia leans in with a pout. "I've been calling you, Alex. I thought we could talk…you know, for closure." Closure? I resist the urge to laugh. Closure for what? Her world tour of infidelity?

Before I can respond, our waitress swoops in like a divine intervention. "Mr. Pierce," she says, practically sparkling with good timing. "Would you like to start with your favorite sake?" She hands the menus to Yasmine and me, completely ignoring the storm cloud that is Catia.

I turn to Yasmine, who's now fully immersed in the sushi options. Calm. Unbothered. Impeccable. If this were a class contest, she'd already won by a landslide.

Catia lets out this dramatic huff, like the universe just dared to inconvenience her. She lingers a moment longer, probably waiting for me to crack, to flinch, to do something. But I don't take the bait. Not today, Satan.

CHAPTER 12

Catia exudes a power that would make weaker souls tremble. I can't deny she's beautiful, but there's something fragile in the way she moves, like she's gripping too tightly onto something that's slipping away. And that something is probably Alex. I don't know their history, but it's written all over her expression—whatever happened, it didn't end the way she wanted.

Alex studies his menu with the kind of focus normally reserved for bomb defusal, jaw tight and fingers tapping lightly against the table. It's like he's trying to will her out of existence. I glance up at him, voice soft, "If you'd rather reschedule, I won't mind. It seems like she might need to speak with you."

His eyes flicker to mine, a bit surprised, then harden as he shifts his gaze back to Catia. "Catia," he says firmly, "If you want to talk, call Eduardo to set up an appointment. But I'm pretty sure I'm booked up for the next half century. Now if you'll excuse me, I need to get back to my date."

My heart does this ridiculous flutter at the word "date," and I take a sip of my water to hide the smile creeping onto my face.

Catia's laugh is sharp and condescending, like she's auditioning for the role of Evil Queen. Her gaze sweeps over me with all the grace of a TSA pat-down. "Your *date*? Her?" She raises a perfectly sculpted eyebrow and smirks. "Looks more like your latest charity project."

Oof. There it is. But I don't flinch. Alex's shoulders tense, but before he can speak, Catia leans in, practically dripping venom. "Not your usual type, Alex," she purrs, her eyes flicking back to me with disdain. "But I suppose even billionaires need a change of scenery now and then." She gives a shrill laugh, like she's said something brilliant. "Though I must say, she looks more suited for a farmers market than a fashion runway."

I take a slow breath, finding my center. I refuse to let her pettiness find a home in my spirit. Catia turns to me, smile stretched tight and brittle. "What's your angle? You must know he's not exactly the type to settle down. Or maybe that's not part of your master plan?" Alex shoots out of his chair, the scrape of metal against wood slicing through the air. His eyes are flinty, voice low. "That's *enough*, Catia."

She tilts her head, catlike and unapologetic. "I'm just being honest. She deserves to know how disposable your 'dates' usually are."

I hold her gaze, unblinking, and smile. A real one. "I'm sorry you're hurting, Catia," I say gently. Her smirk flickers, just for a second. "But I'm not going to absorb your pain." I tilt my head, voice softening even further. "I hope you find peace."

Her eyes narrow, like I just spoke to her in a foreign language. She expected a fight, not empathy. Her lips part as if she wants to say something, but instead, she tosses her hair over her shoulder and turns on her heel, her stilettos echoing away like distant gunfire. At the doorway, she pauses, glancing back with a venomous smile. "Good luck, darling," she coos. "You're going to need it."

The door clicks shut behind her, leaving a vacuum of silence in her wake. Alex exhales, running a hand through his hair as he sinks back into his chair. He glances at me, eyes softening with a mix of surprise and appreciation. "Are you okay?" he asks, his voice quieter now, like he's genuinely concerned.

I grin, reaching for my water. "Are you?"

He lets out a laugh, shaking his head. "You're… something else."

"Thanks," I say, lifting my glass. "But I think I liked it better when you called me your 'date.' That had a nice ring to it." He grins wider, the tension melting away. Whatever storm Catia tried to bring with her? It's suddenly gone now. And here, in this moment, it's like the room is ours again.

Alex shakes his head, chuckling. "I'm sorry you had to deal with that. Here I am, trying to impress you with fancy sushi and—"

"And you did," I interrupt, raising an eyebrow. "Besides, I'm not exactly the 'fancy dinner' type. I'd probably be just as happy at a food truck."

Alex's eyes light up. "Food trucks? You just jumped ten notches up the scale. I know a place in Venice that makes the best breakfast tacos you'll ever have."

I laugh. "I'll believe it when I taste it. LA is notorious for thinking it invented tacos." His smile is easy and warm, and I feel a crackle of electricity run up my spine. My eyes flick to his strong hands resting on the table. I picture them gripping…some *very* NSFW things. Heat rushes to my cheeks, and I quickly reach for my water.

Alex notices, and his grin turns wicked. "Careful, you'll need a refill if you keep blushing like that."

I roll my eyes, but I'm smiling too. "Confident, aren't we?"

He leans forward, voice dropping to a near whisper. "I call it optimistic."

The waitress reappears with a warm bottle of sake. She pours two cups, and Alex slides one my way, lifting his own. "To new beginnings," he says, voice steady and warm.

I smile, lifting my glass to meet his. "I'll drink to that."

We clink glasses, and as I lift mine to my lips, my eyes stay locked on his. I take a slow sip, the warm sake sliding down my throat. His smile deepens, and there's a glint of something wicked in his eyes. A simmering heat pools low in my stomach, and I know I'm in trouble. Alright universe. Let's see where this night takes us.

CHAPTER 13

Yasmine runs her tongue over her lips as I pour our sixth shot of hot sake. I catch myself grinning like an uncontrollable idiot but don't bother reining it in. "I have to admit," I say, sliding her glass across the table, "it's refreshing to meet a yoga instructor who isn't on Instagram every five minutes doing headstands on the beach in a bikini, hashtagging it #NamastayBlessed."

She laughs, "There's no red carpet for teaching someone how to breathe through a panic attack. And seeing someone let go of their pain? That's better than any spotlight."

I stare at her, completely hooked. She's smart, honest, and, God help me, ridiculously sexy when she talks about something she's passionate about. I chuckle and shake my head, leaning back to breathe. "Yasmine, I've been here many times, but tonight is the most special."

She raises an eyebrow, lips curving into a knowing smile. "Is that so?"

I nod, lifting my sake cup in a mock toast. "Must be the company." She blushes and it's so adorable my chest feels warm. "You know," I say, meeting her gaze, "I don't think I've ever met anyone who could make me second-guess myself."

She raises an eyebrow, intrigued. "Second guess yourself?"

I lean in a little closer, the space between us growing smaller. "You'd be surprised. I've made billion-dollar decisions with less hesitation than figuring out what I should say to you next."

"What makes talking to me so different?" Her eyes twinkle with warmth.

I take a breath. "I'm used to people wearing masks, even when they don't know they're doing it. But you…you're just you. And that's rare."

She lets the silence settle around us, soft and unassuming, like a blanket. "I think people wear masks because they're afraid," she says finally. "Afraid of not being enough, or worse, being too much." Her voice is calm. "But the truth is we're all just trying to figure it out."

I run a hand through my hair, exhaling an amused laugh. Her words thread through me and I find myself saying things I don't expect. "Sometimes I wonder if I'm chasing distractions," I admit quietly. "Success, money, women…all of it. Because when you're constantly chasing something, you don't have to sit still and feel what you're afraid to feel."

Her gaze softens, and she reaches across the table, placing her hand over mine. The touch is light but sends a wave of calm through me. "Sometimes we chase things because we think they'll fill the empty spaces inside us. But distractions are tricky. They can feel like movement, like progress, but keep us circling the same place." A small smile plays on her lips. "But here's the thing. Those uncomfortable moments? That's where the real stuff happens."

I raise an eyebrow. "Even if it's messy?"

She nods. "Especially if it's messy. That's usually when the best things make themselves known."

For a moment, something loosens inside of me. "You make it sound almost doable."

She shrugs, her grin widening. "Well, the way I see it? You've survived everything life's thrown at you so far. Sitting still for a moment? I think you've got this."

She says it without an ounce of drama—just quiet honesty. I shift slightly and turn my hand over, brushing my fingers against hers before threading them together. Her skin is soft, her touch steady. "Can I tell you something?" I ask, leaning in slightly.

Her hair falls over one shoulder as she mirrors my movement. "Of course."

"I think this is the first time in forever that I'm not afraid of sitting still."

Her smile widens, "Then maybe this is where things start to change."

She squeezes my hand, a small but deliberate gesture. I lean in just a fraction more, wondering if I'm imagining the tension humming like a live wire. She stays perfectly still, like she's daring me to close the distance. Her eyes flick to my mouth for the briefest second and I'm done pretending I have any self-control left. My thumb brushes against her cheekbone as I pull her close. Her breath mingles with mine, our lips barely an inch apart. And then I press my mouth to hers, slow and tentative, like I need to memorize how she tastes. She responds almost instantly, like she's trying to hold back but can't.

Our kiss deepens without either of us planning it, shifting to something darker, more desperate. She's sweet, warm, and completely addictive, and it makes me greedy. I pull her closer until there's no space left between us, my hand moving to her lower back, pressing her against me as if I can't bear the idea of distance. She gasps against my mouth and it's the sexiest sound

I've ever heard. I swallow it, tilting my head to kiss her deeper. Her hands slide up and around my neck, fingers threading into my hair, tugging just enough to make me groan against her lips. I feel her tremble, but she doesn't pull away. Instead, she presses in closer, matching me with the same hunger I'm drowning in. Our mouths move together like we're trying to learn every secret hidden in the other's kiss.

When we finally break apart for air, her cheeks are flushed and her lips slightly swollen. I brush a strand of hair away from her face, my thumb lingering at the corner of her mouth as I stare at her, completely wrecked. "Wow," I murmur, my voice hoarse.

Her eyes are bright, a little dazed but amused. "Is that your expert opinion?"

I grin, brushing my nose lightly against hers. "More like a personal confession." She lets out a soft laugh and for a second, the world outside this moment falls away. Just her, just me, and whatever this is between us. It doesn't feel fragile. It feels like the start of something inevitable.

"Shall we take this back to my place?" My voice is low, almost a growl, barely masking the hunger beneath it.

Yasmine's eyes flick up to meet mine, and she nods breathlessly. "Uh-huh."

We rise from our seats, but neither of us lets go. Our lips find each other again, hungry and unrestrained, the heat between us spreading like wildfire. Her soft moans ignite something feral in me.

As we reach the exit door, the night air ignite goosebumps along her exposed skin. I trail my fingers down the nape of her back, unable to stop touching her. Yasmine, in the glow of candlelight, is stunning, elegant and serene. But Yasmine, slightly tipsy and utterly unguarded? *Pure temptation.* Her raven dark hair is loose, soft waves brushing down her shoulders, and her makeup is smudged just enough to give her that perfectly ruined look.

My driver, Raul, glides to the curb with impeccable timing, like a chariot summoned by fate. I'm going to have to give the guy a raise.

Yasmine tilts her head up at me, a mischievous glint in her eyes. "You have a driver? He's fast."

I grin, brushing a strand of hair from her face. "He knows when something's urgent." Her laugh turns into a sigh as I pull her closer, my lips brushing the shell of her ear."

Raul steps out swiftly and rounds the car, opening the back passenger door for us. His eyes flick to Yasmine, and his usual professional demeanor softens into a smile as he holds out a hand. "Nice to meet you, I'm Raul."

Yasmine lifts her gaze to his, returning the smile. "Pleasure to meet you, Raul. I'm Yasmine," she says warmly, extending her hand.

Before their fingers even touch, I slide an arm around her waist and pull her flush against me, the possessiveness in the gesture undeniable. "Raul," I warn, my voice low and rough, "eyes front."

Yasmine lets out a soft, melodic laugh that makes the tension dissolve into something warmer. "He's just being polite," she whispers, brushing her lips lightly against my ear as though she knows exactly what she's doing to me. I don't respond with words. Instead, I guide her into the back seat with a firm but gentle pull, my pulse thrumming. The second the door closes and the privacy screen is up, I pull her onto my lap so she's straddling me.

Her hands press against my chest, eyes locked with mine, and I know—this is just the beginning.

CHAPTER 14

YASMINE

I'm grinding on Alex's lap like I've completely forgotten who I am. All I know is how good this feels. The friction is maddening, every rock of my hips against his hard, unyielding thighs sending sparks through my bloodstream. His hands grip my waist with a kind of possessive desperation, fingers digging in like he's afraid I'll disappear if he lets go.

His cock is thick and straining against his pants, hot and unrelenting, and I can feel every delicious inch of it pressing against my soaked panties. A low groan slips from his mouth, rough and guttural, and it sends a pulse straight to my core. I'm wet, embarrassingly so, and the way his eyes darken, jaw clenched tight, tells me he knows it too.

"Fuck, Yasmine…" His voice is low, reverent almost. His hand slides beneath my dress, fingertips brushing the edge of my panties, and I swear I see stars. He teases the fabric aside, one finger slipping through my slick heat, and I whimper into his mouth, pulling him closer, crashing my lips against his like it's the only way to stay tethered to the earth.

His tongue tangles with mine, our kiss messy and desperate, punctuated by the wet, sinful sounds of his fingers gliding over me. The heat in my stomach tenses, coiling with each deliberate stroke. His thumb circles my clit, lazy and confident, like he's got all the time in the world to unravel me. And tonight, he does. I'm shaking, barely holding it together when he slides a finger inside me, just enough to make me arch, back bowing against him. My body clenches instinctively, and he groans low in his throat, a sound that makes me want to drag him under and never let him surface.

"So fucking tight…" he growls against my lips, his voice thick with need. "I can't wait to feel you all around me."

A shudder rips through me, and I kiss him harder, my hands fisting in his hair as he slides his finger deeper, curling just right. His thumb never stops its maddening circles, each one perfectly timed with the erratic pounding of my heart. I grind down harder, chasing the friction, desperate for more.

His other hand grips my waist, holding me steady as I lose myself in the rhythm he's set. The slick, filthy sounds of his fingers working me over are shameless, echoing in the confined space of the car. I'm spiraling, my body wound tight, and when he slides in another finger, I gasp, my body tensing from how long it's been. He stills, eyes flicking to mine, dark and searching. I nod, breathless and biting my lip. His gaze softens, just for a beat, and he leans in, capturing my mouth in a kiss that's somehow gentle amidst all this chaos. When his fingers push back in, filling me inch by inch, my world tilts off its axis.

It's not just hot; it's devastating. I'm wrecked and we haven't even made it to his place. "Yasmine," he breathes against my mouth. He curls his fingers just right, and I swear I see God. "You're so fucking perfect."

My head falls back, mouth open, and his lips find my throat, trailing open-mouthed kisses along my skin. "If your fingers feel this good…" I gasp, words barely escaping my lips. "I can't imagine…" His thumb presses down, and I lose my train of thought, too consumed by the burn building inside me. I'm so close, right there, and he knows it. He strokes faster, rougher, each movement pushing me higher until I'm coming apart, shattering in his arms. My orgasm crashes through me, a tsunami I can't contain. I cry out, my body clenching around his fingers, wave after wave of bliss shaking me to the core.

He watches me unravel, his eyes heavy-lidded and possessive, and it's the sexiest thing I've ever seen. I'm still shivering, still clinging to him, when his car finally glides to a stop. Raul, the world's most considerate driver, doesn't so much as blink when Alex opens the door.

"Come here," Alex murmurs, scooping me into his arms like I weigh nothing. His hands are still damp with my release, glistening under the moonlight—a wicked reminder of what just happened. My legs are shaky, and he smirks, clearly pleased with himself.

He kicks open the door to his house but I'm barely processing it because he's kissing me again, deeper this time, like he's claiming me. I'm wrapped around him, hands fisted in his shirt, mouth open and hungry. We just about make it inside when he pushes me against the wall, his mouth crashing back to mine. There's nothing gentle now; it's raw, unrestrained, like we've given up pretending this isn't happening.

I can't think, can't breathe. All I know is his hands are everywhere—my waist, my hips, sliding up my dress to pull it over my head. It hits the floor and I don't even have time to be self-conscious because he's looking at me like I'm a goddamn miracle. "Yasmine," he breathes, hands roaming over my bare skin. His eyes are dark, almost black with desire. "You're so fucking perfect."

My cheeks flush and his mouth finds mine again as his hands explore my body, like he's memorizing every curve, every shiver. I'm arching against him, desperate and needy, and when his mouth trails lower, I realize I'm done for.

"Tell me you want this," he whispers, his breath hot against my skin. His hands grip my thighs, spreading me wider.

I don't just want this. I *need* it. I meet his gaze, unflinching. "I want everything." And I mean it. Every single thing he's willing to give.

CHAPTER 15

ALEX

I don't waste another second. I spread her with my hands and dive in like a man starved. My tongue strokes over her, tasting her slick heat, and the sound she makes—half gasp, half moan—is the hottest thing I've ever heard. This isn't some fleeting fantasy. This is Yasmine, naked and writhing from my touch, right here in my entryway like a living dream.

I glance up, catching sight of her killer breasts. So full, flushed, and perfect. They bounce with every shuddering breath, and I can't resist them. My hands slide up her waist, brushing over the soft curve of her ribs until they cup her, reverent and greedy all at once. I squeeze, and she lets out a broken whimper that unravels me. I rise to my feet and capture one of her nipples in my mouth, sucking gently before flicking my tongue over the sensitive peak. Her body arches into me, her hands clutching my shoulders, her nails biting into my skin like she can't get close enough.

"Alex…" My name falls from her lips, pleading, and I swear I'm addicted. I trail my tongue back down her body, tasting every inch of her. Sweet, creamy, and intoxicatingly *her*. When I reach her center again, I spread her thighs wide and press my tongue deepe, savoring her like she's my last meal on earth. She tastes better than anything I could've imagined. Like strawberries on a summer evening, deliciously maddening. I finally understand what that song is about, and at this moment, I don't know if I could ever go without it.

Her fingers tangle in my hair as her hips grind against my mouth, chasing every flick and stroke. I feel her trembling and hear the way her breaths come faster, and it fuels me. This isn't about proving something to myself; it's about her. It's about how her body responds to me and how she's unraveling in my hands. It's raw, electric, and something I didn't even know I was missing until now. And I'm not sure I'll ever be the same again.

"Oh God… Alex… *fuck!*" Her voice shatters the air, raw and breathless. I swirl my tongue in tighter circles before sucking her throbbing clit into my mouth. She arches into me, a trembling mess of soft whimpers and whispered curses. Her pretty little pussy is like silk against my tongue. It should feel like a sin, tasting her like this, consuming her in such an unholy, intimate way. But there's nothing vile about it. She tastes like heaven, and right now, she's my only salvation.

Her fingers tremble as they cup my face, grounding herself while I continue to worship every inch of her. "Please," she whispers, barely able to form the words. "I need you."

I lift my gaze to meet hers, her eyes glossy and wild, cheeks flushed. She's never looked more ethereal. "You have me, angel," I rasp, the words spilling out before I can even think. And the thing is, I meant it. More than just this moment. The weight of it hits me hard, like the impact of a wave I didn't see coming. I've never said those words to anyone before, and yet here I am, whispering them to a woman I've only just met. But the idea of tomorrow without her? It twists something deep inside me. She's more than just a fleeting desire. She's something *more*. Yasmine is not like anyone else, and the connection we've made feels like she's rewritten something inside me. Her breath catches as I press a lingering kiss to her inner thigh. "Let me show you," I murmur, my voice low and rough.

With every touch, every moan that falls from her lips, I know one thing for sure: we've moved far beyond one-night stand territory. The thought tugs at something deep inside me. Surely, this isn't just physical for her? Because it sure as hell isn't for me.

Her pulse thrums beneath my lips, and I know I have my answer. And right now, I'm willing to risk everything to see what we can become.

CHAPTER 16

YASMINE

I run my hands down Alex's chest, tracing the defined ridges of his muscles. His abs are nothing short of a sculpted masterpiece. A faint sheen of perspiration clings to his skin and he looks like a vision pulled straight from my wildest fantasy. My fingers tremble as they drift lower, following the deep V carved into his hips, a path that leads me right to the edge of his waistband. I unbutton his pants and ease the zipper down, the sound slicing through the air. I slide them down in one smooth motion and he stands in front of me, completely bare.

My movement falters as I take him in. His cock is the biggest thing I've ever seen, pulsing with heat. I wrap both hands around him, gently testing his length with my grip. He lets out a flustered groan that sends shockwaves straight through me. Suddenly I feel a sense of power, knowing I'm the one pulling these sounds from him, unraveling him with nothing more than a touch.

"Yasmine…" he whispers against my lips. I lean further into him and he grabs my ass with both hands, lifting me as though I weigh nothing. Instinctively, my legs wrap around his waist, and I can feel the heat of him—hard, throbbing, and unapologetically alive, pressed against my stomach.

His mouth is hot against mine again, our kisses urgent and consuming as he carries me up the stairs. I'm barely aware of how we make it to his bedroom, too lost in the feeling of him. When we reach his bed, he lays me down with surprising tenderness as he climbs over me, caging me beneath him. Our mouths finally part and he groans again, his voice breaking. "Tell me what you want, angel."

I arch into him, desperate, needy. "You. I need your big, hard cock inside me… *now*."

His eyes flash. "Look at you," he whispers, his tone low and sinful. "Begging so sweetly… my perfect, good girl." Through the ragged symphony of our unsteady breaths, I catch the faint, unmistakable sound of foil tearing. My pulse quickens as he slides on a condom, his movements dripping with urgency. He leans forward, his mouth brushing against my ear, "Ready for me, angel?"

My whole body answers before my voice can. Through shuttered eyelids, he grabs his hard cock and lines it to my entrance. I hitch my breath as he slides himself up and down my slit to wetten his tip with my juices before he slowly pushes into me. I bite down on my lip to stifle my whimpers.

"It's ok, angel, I'm right here with you. Do you trust me?" There's something in the sincerity of his voice, and in that moment, I know he would never hurt me. I nod, digging my nails into his shoulders as I hold on tight. He pushes in a little more and the pressure feels so intense, but in an incredibly pleasurable way. Thankfully, I'm wetter than I've ever been in my life. He peppers my face with kisses as he pulls out a little before pushing back in further. He's maybe only a quarter of the way in, but I already feel so filled to the brim. I'm stretched to the max around his enormous rock-hard cock, wrapped so tightly around him that I swear we can feel each other's pulses inside me.

He groans so beautifully and tightens his jaw like he's holding onto every ounce of his restraint. He gently slides out again, and this time it's smoother and easier. He thrusts slowly like this for a while, just with the tip, and I'm so sensitive that I can feel every ridge of the head of his cock sliding in and out of me.

"Alex…" The moment his name slips from my lips, it's like a spark ignites between us, a heat that spreads through every inch of my body. The pleasure is so consuming, so raw, that I arch beneath him, offering more of myself. I *need* more. I've never needed anyone like this. A shudder runs through his body as he presses his forehead to mine. His eyes are squeezed shut, his jaw tight like he's holding something back. Words, emotions, I don't know, but the tenderness in the way he moves makes my heart ache. No one has ever touched me like this, like I'm something sacred. This isn't sex. This is an unspoken gravity, pulling us in deep, weaving something invisible between us. And I know he feels it, too.

His rhythm shifts, still controlled and deliberate but with more urgency now. He fills me inch by inch, and my body responds instinctively, tightening around him as a deep, overwhelming pleasure blooms within. My breath catches, and suddenly, I'm falling again, spiraling into something unstoppable. "Oh, God," I cry as the wave crashes over me.

My nails rake down his back and I know I'm marking him, branding him with my pleasure. This is a revelation, a seismic shift in my reality, having gone from never being able to orgasm with another person to unraveling multiple times in one night. Alex groans and his control unravels. He buries his face in the curve of my neck, his lips brushing my skin as he gasps, "Yasmine, you feel so…*fuck*… I don't think I can hold on." The rawness in his voice makes me ache for him even more. I press my mouth to his neck, kissing and tasting his sweat-slicked skin. He lets out a strangled moan, his body seizing as he surrenders completely.

"Fuck… FUCK." The words tear from him, broken and desperate, as he throbs inside me, spilling into me in hot, endless pulses. His release is so powerful that it seems to break something open inside us. Even in the throes of his pleasure, he never loses that gentleness. He never pushes beyond what he knows I can take. And that restraint makes my chest tighten with something more potent than lust.

His body collapses on mine and I've never felt more safe and cherished. He trails feather-light kisses along the curve of my neck, each one like a silent vow whispered against my skin. A shiver runs down my spine and I turn my head just enough for my lips to brush the tip of his nose. The intimacy of the gesture makes my heart ache in the sweetest way. He leans in slowly, giving me time to pull away if I want to, but I don't. His lips brush against mine, slow but sure, a kiss that feels like a promise.

The world outside fades into nothingness and I drift away in his arms, cradled by the steady rhythm of his breathing, into the best sleep of my life.

—

Sunlight streams through massive floor-to-ceiling windows, pulling me from sleep. For a moment, I lie there, suspended between sleep and reality, unsure of where I am. Then it all comes rushing back.

Alex.

I sit up slowly, the bedsheets slipping down to my waist as I take in the sleek opulence surrounding me. Everything about the space is pristine, curated, and impossibly perfect, just like him. But the other side of the bed is empty. My stomach twists as I glance at the untouched duvet. It's as if he never even slept here.

A flicker of something unfamiliar stirs in my chest—not quite disappointment or surprise. I knew what I was getting myself into by stepping into bed with a billionaire playboy. I'm not naive. But for a fleeting second last night, something felt different. Real. Or maybe I just wanted it to be.

As soon as I swing my legs over the side of the bed, I realize that I'm very much naked and I can't exactly wander his house like this. I head to his closet, hesitating for a second before stepping in. The space is absurdly large. Rows of tailored suits hang in perfect order.

I rummage through a section of folded T-shirts until I find something soft and worn. It's gray with *"Stanford"* printed in faded crimson letters—an old college shirt. The fabric is thin and loose, almost comically oversized, but I tug it over my head anyway. It drapes down mid-thigh and the sleeves nearly swallow my arms. I look at myself in the mirror and can't help but laugh. I look ridiculous and oddly endearing, like I'm playing dress-up in his life.

I walk back to his room and realize that my clothes are scattered everywhere throughout his house, like breadcrumbs leading me back through the night. My dress hangs off the edge of a sleek black chair; my bra is looped around the staircase railing, and, oh God, my panties are crumpled somewhere near the kitchen island. I laugh softly under my breath as I gather each piece, the memories of how they ended up there heating my cheeks.

"Good morning."

I turn, clutching my clothes to my chest, and see Alex standing in the doorway. His hair is a little messy, and his jaw is darkened with the beginnings of a 5 o'clock shadow. He's holding a paper bag in one hand and a coffee cup in the other. His gaze sweeps over me, lingering on the shirt, and something flickers in his expression—surprise, amusement, and something hotter, deeper. "Is that my shirt?" he asks, his voice rough and low.

I flush, tugging at the hem nervously. "I, uh… I didn't have anything to wear, and I didn't want to…"

"It's fine," he cuts me off, stepping closer. "More than fine." His eyes darken as he takes me in, the way the oversized fabric clings to me in some places and drapes in others. "You know, to be honest, I never liked it when women wore my clothes," he murmurs, almost to himself. "But on you? That's the hottest thing I've ever seen."

My cheeks heat as he sets the bag and coffee on the counter, closing the space between us. "I can't take my eyes off you," he murmurs, brushing a stray strand of hair from my face. I can feel my pulse quicken under his touch. *Get a hold of yourself, Yasmine; just a second ago, you were ready to sneak out and never see this guy ever again.*

"What's in the bag?" I manage, in a weak attempt to say words.

Alex's lips curve into a boyish grin as he gestures to the bag. "*Wayki Tacos*. Best in L.A. You said you'd never tried them, and I couldn't let that stand."

I can't help but smile, the tension in my chest easing just a little. "You remembered?"

"Of course, I remembered," he says, leaning casually against the counter. "You looked at me last night like I'd just told you Santa was real when I mentioned them. Figured I couldn't leave you hanging."

"Are they really worth the hype?" I ask.

He raises an eyebrow, already reaching into the bag. "Only one way for you to find out." He pulls out a neatly wrapped breakfast taco and hands it to me, the warm, toasty aroma filling the air. "This one's the classic. The *'Wayki Original.'* Trust me, it's life-changing."

I unwrap it carefully, the warm, freshly-made breakfast taco nestled in its foil wrapper. "No pressure, right?" I say, shooting him a playful look.

"None at all," he replies, his grin widening. "But if you don't love it, I'm rethinking everything."

I take a cautious bite, the warm tortilla giving way to perfectly scrambled eggs, smoky bacon, and a hint of melted cheddar. The flavors hit immediately—rich, savory, with just the right kick of spice. My eyes widen in delight, and I can't help the little moan of approval that escapes.

"Oh my God," I say around a mouthful, covering my lips with my hand. "This is… insane."

Alex laughs, clearly pleased. "Told you. They're addictive. You're officially ruined for all other tacos."

I take another bite, savoring the combination of textures and flavors. "Why didn't you lead with this last night? You could've won me over in ten seconds."

He smirks, leaning in a little closer. "I think I did just fine without the tacos." My cheeks flush and I glance away, pretending to be very interested in unwrapping the rest of my taco.

"Hey," he says softly, his tone shifting. "I'm glad you stayed."

The words are simple, but the way he says them makes something stir in my chest. "Me too," I admit, my voice barely above a whisper.

He holds my gaze for a moment longer before grabbing his own taco. "Okay," he says, his tone lightening again. "Next time, I'm getting you *The Wayki Bliss*. Total game changer."

"Next time?" I tease, raising an eyebrow.

Alex grins, his confidence returning in full force. "Oh, there's definitely going to be a next time."

I smile at him, "I think these tacos might be my new favorite thing.

He looks at me with the most seductive come-fuck-me face and says, "I think you wearing my old college shirt might be my new favorite thing." And the way he's looking at me like I'm the only person in the world makes me think he means it.

CHAPTER 17

ALEX

We curl up in my living room as I watch her relish her second taco. Usually, I'd be gone by now. That's my routine. But this morning was different. *Yasmine* is different. So, instead of slipping out the door, I found myself braving an early morning line at *Wayki Tacos*, determined to show her that LA does have the best tacos in the world.

A smear of sour cream clings to the corner of her lips, and I'm already moving toward her before I even realize it. "Hold still," I say, my voice lower than I mean it to be. I swipe my thumb across her mouth, the softness of her skin igniting something primal in me. But then, *Jesus*, her tongue flicks out, grazing my finger as she licks it off.

A spark shoots through me, straight to my core, and the tension between us snaps. I grab her by the waist, pulling her against me with a force that's just shy of desperate. Her lips part in surprise, but I'm already there, brushing my mouth against hers, tasting something entirely unique to her. Her moans are like gasoline to fire. Her arms wrap around my neck, pulling me closer. I trail kisses down her neck and she leans back to give me more access. My hands roam higher under the oversized shirt that's been driving me crazy since the moment I saw her in it. I tug it off, and she lets it fall without hesitation, revealing creamy, golden skin and curves that make my mouth go dry.

My hands cup her breasts, their perfect weight filling my palms as her back arches into my touch. Her eyes flutter closed and I can't help but lean down to kiss her again, harder this time. Her taste is intoxicating and every sound she makes feels like a revelation. At this moment, nothing else matters. Not my rules, not my past, not the voice in my head telling me this shouldn't feel so good. All that matters is her.

I lower myself down to her ankles and her legs part instinctively. Her eyes meet mine, wide and full of trust, and it hits me like a punch to the gut. She's so beautiful, it's almost painful. I've never been this obsessed with anyone—never felt this need, this hunger, this pull. Yasmine isn't just someone I want for a night. I'm absolutely transfixed by her, and I need more of her. I dive into her as if she's all mine. Her body tenses when I reach her center and I look up to meet her eyes. "Relax," I murmur, my voice rougher than I intended. "Let me take care of you."

She nods, her hands gripping the edge of my sofa as I lower myself before her. I kiss her there first, soft and teasing, and she lets out a broken moan that makes me ache. Her taste is intoxicatingly addictive, like everything about her. I start slow, my tongue gliding with deliberate precision, wanting to learn every single thing that drives her wild. Her hips buck against me, and I pin them down gently, holding her in place as I take her deeper into this.

"Alex," she breathes, her voice a mix of surprise and desperation. I'm losing myself in her. Every moan and whispered plea pushes me closer to the edge of control. Her body tightens and when I flick my tongue just right, she cries out, her body trembling as she falls apart. Watching her come undone, knowing I'm the one who did this to her, ignites something primal in me.

I don't stop; I *can't* stop. She's like a drug. She's like a vision I'll never forget.

CHAPTER 18

YASMINE

Alex surprised me this morning, and I'm not going to lie; it knocked the breath out of me. I half expected him to slip out quietly, avoiding the awkwardness of a morning goodbye. But there he was, standing in front of me with that disarming smile that made me feel like I was the only person in the world.

My heart does a ridiculous little flip, and even though I tell myself to stay grounded, I can't help but feel this fluttering warmth spread through me. I know I shouldn't be this excited. Maybe my judgment is clouded by post-orgasm bliss, but right now, in this moment, I choose to live in the now.

Alex rises slowly from between my legs, his eyes smoldering with an intensity that makes my brain short-circuit. Coherent thoughts? *Gone.* My vocabulary? *Deleted.* I'm pretty sure I forgot my middle name. He presses a devastatingly slow, deliberate kiss to my lips. The taste of myself on him sends another flash of heat through me and I realize I might actually combust.

"You're incredible," he bites out, like he's barely holding it together. I swallow hard, trying to keep it cool, but I swear the room tilts. His gaze isn't just dark with lust; it's something else, something deeper, and…is that softness? It throws me completely off balance. I was prepared for toe-curling pleasure, but this? Emotional eye contact after orgasms? *Danger zone.*

I manage a wobbly grin. "You're just saying that because I didn't pass out."

He lets out a low chuckle. "I'm saying that because you're the best damn thing that's ever happened to my living room." I laugh, but the way his eyes hold mine makes my heart skip. As much as I want to be cautious, I find myself pulling him closer anyway, because if this is how I'm going out? What a way to go.

I look up at him, my fingers brushing against his jaw. "Alex," I whisper, and though I don't finish the thought, I think he hears it anyway.

"I know, angel. I'm right there with you," he murmurs as he nuzzles his face into the side of my neck. I can feel his incredibly hard erection pushing up against my stomach through his sweatpants.

"More…I need more of you," I struggle with his waistband with shaking hands. I don't know what's overcome me. Everything feels so heated and intense. His mouth urgently finds mine, and we're kissing like mad. Alex kicks off his sweats in one swift movement without taking his mouth off mine. I'm still trembling in his arms, my body humming with the aftershocks of pleasure.

In one effortless motion, he lifts me off the sofa, carrying me upstairs to his bed in his strong, muscular arms like I weigh nothing. His lips crash against mine again, fierce and demanding, and I kiss him back with everything I have, every ounce of fear, hope, and desire coursing through me. He lays me down gently like I'm something precious, and when he pulls back to look at me, his gaze is searing. "You're so fucking beautiful," he murmurs, almost reverently.

A shiver runs through me at his words. We've only known each other for one night—technically just a handful of hours—but no one has ever looked at me the way he does, like I'm the only thing in the world that matters. It's surreal and unnerving in the best way. His gaze feels like gravity, pulling me in with a force.

And for someone I just met, it's wild how much it feels like I've known him forever.

He pulls off his T-shirt, his eyes never leaving mine. My heart races as I take him in, his body laced with a magnetic confidence. "Tell me if it's too much," he says softly, his lips brushing against my ear. "I'll stop if you need me to."

I shake my head, my fingers threading through his hair. "I don't want you to stop. I want this. I want *you*."

He groans and kisses me again, his hands claiming, worshipping. He quickly grabs a condom from his nightstand and rolls it on at record speed. Then he's back on top of me, and when he finally enters me, the sensation is overwhelming. A perfect mix of pleasure and fullness that makes me gasp.

"So fucking tight…are you okay?" he asks, his voice tight with restraint.

"Yes," I manage, my nails digging into his shoulders. "Don't stop."

He moves like he's savoring every second. My body arches beneath him, my breaths coming in shallow gasps as he sets a rhythm that has me spiraling higher with every thrust. "Yasmine," he groans, his voice raw and unguarded. "You feel fucking incredible." The way he says my name is like a desperate mantra. I've never felt this connected to anyone before.

As the intensity builds, he picks up the pace, his movements harder, deeper, more urgent. My moans entangle with his, and the sounds of our bodies moving together fill the room. I can feel myself teetering on the edge again, the pleasure almost too much to bear. "Alex," I cry out, my hands clutching at him like he's the only thing keeping me grounded.

"You're going to ruin me, aren't you?" he groans as he brushes his lips against mine. The euphoria hits me like a tidal wave, my entire body trembling as I cry out his name over and over again. He follows moments later, his own release shuddering through him as he collapses on top of me, his breaths hot and heavy against my skin.

For a long moment, neither of us move. We're tangled together, our bodies slick with sweat, our hearts pounding in unison. Alex lifts his head, his gaze locking onto mine. "I don't think I can ever get enough of you," he says softly, brushing a strand of hair from my face.

My heart swells at his words and I realize with startling clarity that I feel the same way. I don't want this to end.

CHAPTER 19

The weekend passed in a blur of tangled sheets, soft laughter, and stolen kisses. My entire world, compressed into the walls of my house, wrapped up in Yasmine. I've never felt this captivated, like I'm standing in the eye of a storm.

But now, as she stands in my foyer, slipping on her sandals, a knot forms in my chest. It's irrational. I mean, we've only known each other for a handful of days. Technically, just the weekend. And yet, the thought of her leaving feels heavier than it should.

"I'm still not sure why you won't let me drop you off," I say, leaning casually against the doorframe, hoping my nonchalance hides the fact that I don't want to watch her walk out that door.

She glances up, her eyes soft but cautious. "That's okay," she says, tucking a loose strand of hair behind her ear. "I already called an Uber."

I push off the frame and take a step closer. "I could've called one for you," I murmur.

Her smile is sweet but resolute. "I know. But I don't want to trouble you."

Trouble me? She is the only part of my life right now that doesn't feel like trouble. There's something more behind her words, though. I don't press her. Maybe she doesn't want me to know where she lives. Maybe it's too soon? I get it. Hell, maybe she's smarter than me in keeping boundaries. *Boundaries*. The word feels ridiculous after the way we've spent the past 48 hours.

"Okay," I say finally, even though it doesn't sit right. "But I'm walking you out."

She nods, biting her lip, probably unaware of how much that small action tempts me to cancel her damn ride and lock the door behind us. The Uber pulls up at the edge of my driveway. She turns to me and the weight between us is so thick I could cut through it. "I had a good time this weekend," she says softly.

"Good?" I smirk, stepping closer. "I was aiming for unforgettable." She rolls her eyes as she steps toward me, rising on her toes to press a final kiss to my lips. I hesitate, the words caught in my throat. I'm not used to saying things that make me seem vulnerable, but it feels like I don't have a choice with her. "Yasmine," I start. Her brows knit together in that way that makes my heart do something absurd. "This doesn't feel like a one-time thing to me." I manage to admit outloud.

Her lips part, surprise flickering across her face. For a second, I panic, wondering if I'd misread everything. But then her expression softens. "Me neither," she admits. Relief washes over me as I reach out and press my lips to hers. A kiss that promises *see you soon* instead of *goodbye*. Our lips linger, soft and unhurried, and for that brief, fragile moment, everything else fades away. The world is just us.

Finally, we pull apart and she offers me one last look before slipping into the backseat. I watch as the car disappears down the hill, already too aware of how empty the house feels without her in it.

Damn it. She's becoming a problem. A beautiful, dangerous problem. And I don't want to fix it.

CHAPTER 20

My heart is floating somewhere above the clouds after the weekend I just had. What was supposed to be a one-night thing with Alex somehow turned into something I can't even put into words yet. All I know is that I'm happy. A smile plays on my lips as I grab my bag from the passenger seat and head toward the side entrance of Liam's house, hoping to slip quietly into my room. I could really use a hot shower and a long nap. I tiptoe past the hall toward the stairs but I don't even make it three steps before I hear his voice.

"Yasmine."

I freeze mid-step. *Great.* I slowly pivot, already bracing myself. There he is—six foot one and scowling, standing in the doorway with arms crossed like some kind of brooding Marvel villain. "You're *just* now getting back?" His gaze narrows. "You've been gone all weekend."

I take a slow, grounding breath. *Stay Zen, Yasmine.* "Yeah," I say casually. "I ended up spending the weekend at a friend's house." I say, keeping my tone light as if I don't notice the storm brewing behind his eyes.

His perfectly sculpted jaw is set tight, and his eyes flick down to my dress, which is the same one I wore out on Friday night. I watch as his realization sinks in. "In the same clothes as Friday night?"

I glance down at myself like I just noticed. "Huh. Would you look at that? Guess I didn't stop home to change into my royal ball gown."

Liam doesn't laugh—tough crowd. "With who?" He steps forward, looking like he's trying out for *Interrogator of the Year.*

I shrug. "Just a friend. It's still the weekend, Liam." My voice stays breezy, gently hinting that I'm technically still off the clock.

His jaw tenses, and for a second, I swear I see a tiny crack in his perfectly curated Hollywood mask. He shifts his weight, arms crossed casually. "So…busy week ahead?"

I keep my tone light. "The usual. Sessions with you, my own practice. Nothing out of the ordinary."

He nods slowly, his gaze dipping just for a second like he's gathering the nerve for something. Finally, he clears his throat. "There's this charity gala on Thursday night. *Children of Tomorrow.* It's kind of a big deal, and I was thinking…" He pauses, meeting my eyes. "It might be nice to have someone like you there. For balance."

I blink, caught off guard. "You mean as your date?"

He gives a tiny, almost bashful shrug. "Why not? It's for a good cause."

I smile politely, shaking my head. "Liam, I'm flattered. But that's not exactly part of my job description."

His lips press into a line before he leans in, his voice quieter now. "Yasmine, it's not for me, it's for the kids."

I stare at him, fighting the urge to laugh at the sheer earnestness in his tone. Is he seriously pulling the *'think about the children'* card?

"Look," he continues, straightening up again, "these events can be a lot. Having someone like you there, someone who isn't caught up in all the glitz, it'd really help."

I exhale, feeling the weight of his expectation. "Okay," I say slowly, "but only because it's for the kids."

Liam's face softens, but not in a way that feels warm, more like a cat who just cornered a mouse. "Perfect," he says, his voice oozing with satisfaction. "I'll have my stylist handle everything. Wardrobe, accessories, the works." His tone makes it clear this isn't generosity. It's control, wrapped up in a shiny package. His way of making sure I show up looking exactly how he wants.

I force a polite smile, though my stomach turns slightly. "Of course." He means well, I think. I can handle one night of forced glamour and polite small talk. Besides, if nothing else, it's an opportunity to practice patience. As I excuse myself, I remind myself to stay calm and centered. *I am a tree in the storm, rooted and unwavering.* Let Liam be Liam. I've faced bigger challenges than a man with a fragile ego and a penchant for control.

Once in my room, I close the door behind me and as if on cue, my phone buzzes. *Alex.* My heart makes a ridiculous little leap at his name, and I can't help but smile as I open his text.

Alex: I thought about waiting for the 3-day rule, but screw it. I can't stop thinking about you.

A smile breaks across my face, unbidden and unstoppable.

Me: Since we're breaking the rules…I haven't stopped

thinking about you either. It's safe to say you've officially bent my chakras out of alignment ;)

Alex: On the contrary, I was beginning to wonder if all yoga instructors have the ability to bend reality because I'm still recovering from the way you wrapped me around your finger…and other places.

My face heats up instantly and a laugh escapes my lips before I can stop it—this man. I sit cross-legged on my bed, trying to play it cool, but before I can think of a response, I see three little dots pop up, and then his next message comes through.

Alex: Are you free Thursday night?

My smile drops. I haven't told him about Liam due to the iron-clad NDA I signed, but I also don't want to lie to him.

Me: I'd love to see you, but I can't. I have a work obligation. How about this weekend?

I hesitate before hitting send, wondering if "work obligation" is the right way to put it. But what else can I say?

The reply comes almost immediately.

Alex: My family's in town for the weekend, and while I'm sure you'd love to see my dad try to lasso the Wi-Fi router like it's a wild horse, I wouldn't subject you to that. How about next Tuesday?

My smile returns to my lips as I type back. Alex briefly mentioned his family's Midwestern roots, and while I'd love to meet them one day, he's right—now is a bit too early.

Me: Sure, Tuesday sounds great :)

I sit there for a moment, staring at the screen, another soft smile tugging at my lips. Alex feels like the first uncomplicated thing in weeks. A rare, grounding breath of fresh air in a whirlwind I didn't choose. His text is easy, warm, and exactly what I didn't realize I needed.

The gown hangs on my closet door like something out of a dream. Midnight blue and undeniably stunning. It's strapless with a sculpted bodice that hugs every curve—daring but not over the line, with just enough leg revealed by the high slit to make a statement. Liam's stylist had all but insisted on it, and while I wouldn't have chosen it myself, I can't deny its beauty. If nothing else, I'm glad for the excuse to wear something this breathtaking. I pull it on carefully, the cool silk gliding over my skin, and when I look in the mirror, I almost gasp. The makeup artist Liam hired really worked her magic. She gave me soft, smoky eyes, perfectly arched brows, and a hint of blush on my cheeks. My lips are a deep rose and my hair is swept to one side in loose waves that cascade over my shoulder.For a moment, I barely recognize myself.

A soft knock at the door pulls me from my thoughts. "Yasmine? Ready?" Liam's voice is muffled but familiar, a mix of charm and impatience. I take a deep breath and step into my silver stilettos. They add a few inches to my height, elongating my legs and giving me even more of a confidence boost. I grab the matching clutch that Liam's stylist left me as I make my way to the door. When I open it, Liam stands there in a black tuxedo so precisely tailored it's practically smug. His blond hair is slicked back with too much shine, and his thick, musky cologne hits me like a wave.

His eyes drag over my body, slow and deliberate, before his lips curl into a smirk. "Yasmine," he drawls, his gaze lingering on the slit of my dress, "you wear that like you're trying to cause trouble. Not that I'm complaining."

A prickling discomfort settles over me but I manage a smile. "Shall we?" I gesture toward the grand staircase. "Don't want to keep the kids waiting."

He chuckles, stepping closer, cutting through the air between us. His hand brushes my arm in what's supposed to seem casual but it just makes me uncomfortable. "Ready when you are," he murmurs, his eyes locking onto mine with a little too much intent. "But try not to steal the spotlight from me, yeah? Wouldn't be fair." His tone is playful, but there's an edge of ego beneath it that makes my stomach twist.

I feel his eyes on me as I descend the staircase and it makes my skin crawl, but I remind myself this is just one night. One night of playing Liam's perfect companion. After this, I can go back to being the yoga instructor, the woman who's here to help him nail a role, not stroke his ego.

And next week? Next week is for Alex.

CHAPTER 21

The ballroom is an opulent display of wealth and excess, every corner dripping with extravagance. The hum of conversation is constant, punctuated by bursts of polite laughter and the soft chime of silverware against china.

My family is a little slice of Montana amidst the glittering crowd, standing tall for the *Children of Tomorrow* charity gala. After my mother's death, we made it our mission to carry her torch. Her legacy of kindness and service is woven into every fundraiser and cause we support. She was a force in the world of philanthropy, and this gala was one of her favorites.

I sit at our table, slowly swirling the amber liquid in my glass. The crowd—billionaires, celebrities, and power players—blurs into a sea of familiar faces and rehearsed smiles.

My father, Clint, sits at the head; his weathered hands, which once wrangled wild horses, now rest loosely around a glass of sparkling water. Cole, my eldest brother, sits beside him, seeming disinterested as he scrolls through emails on his phone. Despite being a tech giant in the wild, he's always ready to switch from CEO to dad mode at any second. Meanwhile, my older brother Lucas nurses his bourbon, his gaze drifting across the room like he's watching paint dry, searching for anything that might hold his attention for more than five seconds. Zane, the youngest Pierce of the family, is sprawled on his chair, his tie loose, just one drink away from starting a brawl, or a dance party. He's the wildcard, always has been, but there's a grin on his face that keeps my dad's steady gaze from turning to disapproval.

Usually, I'd be out there, working the room with practiced charm, brokering deals, securing partnerships. But tonight? Tonight, none of it matters. All I can think about is Yasmine. Her laugh, the way she smiles and moves, the way she makes everything else feel so far away. *This is a disaster.* The thought of her has been on the back of my mind all week, distracting me like an itch I can't scratch. I'm completely hooked, and I wonder if she's thinking about me too. I'm sitting here, lost in my phone, rereading my last text conversation with her for the tenth time. We've been messaging each other all week, talking about everything and nothing.

"What's got you grinning like a damn fool?" Lucas's voice cuts through, smooth but teasing. "Or should I say who?"

I glance up, caught, and pocket my phone, but Zane's already zeroed in, eyes glinting with mischief. "Oh, don't you dare stash the evidence now. Spill it, lover boy."

Cole leans back in his chair, raising one brow. "Let me guess, it's business." He gestures with his glass. "If it's not, well, then hell must've frozen over."

"Business doesn't make you look that stupidly happy," Lucas says, swirling his drink. "Unless you've figured out how to make A.I. fall in love with you."

Zane laughs. "Knowing Alex, he's probably wooing her with 'fascinating data points.'" He mimics swiping at a screen. "'Look at this projection, babe; it screams romance.'"

I reach over and shove Zane's shoulder, and his chair scrapes backward. He dodges with a loud laugh.

"Boys," Dad mutters, shaking his head, though there's a soft smile playing at the corners of his mouth.

Lucas leans in, tone quieter now. "Seriously, though. You seem happier, somehow."

They're all watching me now. I sigh and lean back in my chair. "There's someone," I admit, the words unfamiliar but strangely right.

Zane's fist slams the table in triumph. "Called it!"

Cole smirks and takes another sip of whiskey. "I'll believe it when I meet her."

Dad lifts his glass with a nod that feels more like a silent blessing than a toast. For a brief moment, the usual chaos melts. They don't know Yasmine yet, but when they do, I know they'll get it.

Before I can tuck my phone away, a commotion near the entrance snaps my attention to the other side of the room. The buzz of conversation falters, replaced by a rising wave of excited murmurs and the rapid click of cameras. I turn in my seat, craning my neck to see what's causing the fuss. Paparazzi, stationed just outside the ballroom, have swarmed the entrance, their cameras flashing like fireworks. The crowd parts to reveal whoever's just arrived.

And then I see her. Yasmine.

For a second, I forget how to breathe. She's glowing, radiant and…ethereal. But she's not alone. Hollywood's golden boy, Liam Woods, stands beside her, grinning like he's just won the lottery. His hand rests on the small of her back as he guides her into the room, leaning in close to whisper something in her ear.

She laughs, tilting her head just enough to catch the light, but all I can focus on is Liam's hand on her.

My stomach twists. *So this is the work obligation.* Bitterness rises in my throat like bile. I sit frozen as they walk across the room, pausing to greet people who flock to them like moths to a flame. Liam basks in the attention, his every gesture calculated and smooth, while Yasmine stands at his side, gracious and poised. The whole thing feels like a performance, and I'm the fool who bought a ticket.

She didn't owe me anything, I remind myself. We've only just met and barely had time to figure out what we are. Still, the sight of her on Liam's arm makes something in me ache. I can't do this. I push back from the table, the legs of my chair scraping against the floor. A few people glance my way, including my brothers, but I don't care. I grab my drink, downing the last of it before setting the glass down a little too hard. Without a word, I make my way toward the exit, my jaw tight and my hands clenched into fists at my sides.

CHAPTER 22

The soft sound of chirping birds in the distance sets the perfect tone for my session with Liam, not that I'm particularly looking forward to his presence this morning.

Surprisingly, I did enjoy the gala last night. And no, it wasn't because of Liam. He was his usual charming, self-absorbed self, parading me around and introducing me to everyone as his "date." I cringed internally every time but kept my mouth shut. I wasn't about to stage a PR crisis moment in the middle of a charity event. The final announcement that the gala raised over twelve million dollars last night made it all worth it. That money will change lives—funding college tuition, mentorship programs, and tutoring sessions for underserved communities. That's the real headline, not the celebrity drama.

Just as I reach for my yoga mat, my phone rings. Sami's name flashes on the screen. I smile, already bracing myself, and sure enough, she doesn't even wait for me to say hello. "Yasmine! Why are you on the front page of *Hollywood Gossip*?!"

I blink, confused. "What are you talking about?" There's a pause, and then my phone buzzes with a text. I open it and immediately see what she means. It's a photo from last night of Liam and me at the entrance to the gala. He's flashing his toothpaste commercial smile at the camera, his hand resting just a little too low on my back. I'm looking up at him, mid-laugh, and from this angle, I look…affectionate. Fond, even.

I shake my head and let out a small sigh. "Sami, it's *Hollywood Gossip*. The clue is in the name. It's gossip, not reality."

"But Yasmine, it looks—"

"It's not," I cut her off gently. "Trust me."

She's still muttering about how ridiculous it is, but I manage to steer the conversation toward lighter things for a moment before we say goodbye. As soon as the call ends, I grab my mat and head downstairs. As I make my way to Liam's yoga room, I can't shake the article's image from my mind, or the fact that Liam is probably loving every second of this.

Just as I finish setting up, the door opens, and in he strolls, radiating smug confidence like it's a designer cologne. His grin is wide as if he's picturing himself in a slow-motion entrance scene, complete with dramatic lighting. His gaze sweeps over me like I'm another priceless piece of decor and it makes the hair on the back of my neck prickle. Calm, officially disrupted. If inner peace had an escape route, it would've bolted right out the window by now.

"Morning, Yasmine," he drawls, his voice low and silky as he steps closer. He looks me up and down, his smile deepening. "Didn't think you could outdo yourself after last night, but here you are, proving me wrong."

I force myself to take a slow, steady breath. Inhale for four, exhale for four, like I'm teaching a toddler how to calm down, except the toddler is me. This yoga room is starting to feel like a box, the walls scooching in.

"Good morning, Liam," I reply, keeping my tone neutral as I straighten up. "We'll start with some breathwork today, then ease into a full flow."

He watches me a beat too long, his smile still firmly in place like he's auditioning for *Hollywood's Smuggest Bachelor*. "Sounds perfect," he says, stepping onto his mat with a lazy stretch that looks more performative than practical. "Though I must admit, I've been looking forward to our one-on-one time all morning."

Of course, you have.. I internally roll my eyes so hard they hit the back of my head. I try to channel every ounce of patience I have. If he's expecting flirty banter, he's about to be severely disappointed. "We'll start with a grounding exercise," I say. "Close your eyes, lengthen your spine, and bring awareness to your breath."

Liam closes his eyes for a moment, but after a beat, he peeks one eye open and grins. "You know," he says, his voice thick with faux casualness, "this whole spiritual-guru-in-a-love-triangle plot is starting to feel eerily familiar."

I tilt my head, maintaining my calm but genuinely confused. "Familiar how?"

He opens both eyes and leans forward slightly, resting his forearms on his knees. His grin widens. "Well, my character is trying to navigate his feelings for two women while the world watches. Sound familiar?" He winks.

"I'm not sure I follow," I say, keeping my voice even.

He shifts his posture, deliberately taking his time. "I'm just saying…It seems the press got the wrong idea about us, especially after that glowing front-page feature this morning. But don't worry, I'm sure your little date from last weekend will understand. If he's mature enough, that is."

The air in the room shifts, my calm replaced with something heavy and unsettling. I blink, piecing it together as his words sink in. Realization hits me like a tidal wave. The picture and the story are too convenient. Too perfectly timed. And Liam's tone is dripping with self-satisfaction. "Did you orchestrate this whole thing, Liam?" My words are calm but direct, my gaze steady on his face.

He doesn't even try to deny it. Instead, he shrugs with exaggerated innocence. "Me? I mean, can I help it if the cameras caught our best angles?" He rests his palms on the mat behind him. "Let's just say I have friends who like to make sure the world sees things from the right perspective."

My stomach tightens. The truth of his intentions hangs between us, sour and undeniable. He *wanted* to make it look like there was something between us, to plant seeds of doubt in someone else's mind. "I see," I say softly, pressing my palms together in front of my heart.

"Hey," he says, his grin not faltering. "These things happen in Hollywood all the time."

I meet his gaze evenly. "Yes, they do. But I'm not here to play a role in your PR game, Liam."

He raises his hands like he's surrendering, but his smile doesn't waver. "You're too serious, Yasmine. Relax. Breathe."

"I am breathing," I reply calmly. "And we're here to focus on your practice, not headlines."

His smirk fades slightly as he realizes his attempts to rattle me have fallen flat.

"Shall we move into warrior pose?" I suggest with a serene smile, rising to my feet.

He hesitates for a beat, then gets up with a reluctant nod. As I guide him through the pose, I remind myself of the truth that Liam can't touch. I know who I am. His world may be smoke and mirrors, but mine isn't. I have no control over his games, but I can choose not to play them.

—

The air in Beverly Hills is crisp and breezy, scented with freshly mowed lawns and way-too-expensive roses. My feet pound the pavement in a steady rhythm as I weave through tree-lined streets. The massive mansions and perfectly pruned hedges blur into the background as I focus on my breathing. Inhale peace, exhale…whatever the hell this knot in my chest is.

I came out for this run to clear my mind, but apparently, my mind missed the memo. No matter how many miles I put between me and Liam's estate, one thought keeps circling back like a stubborn boomerang. Alex. He hasn't texted me all weekend. He said he was with family, which I get, but it's Monday afternoon. Wasn't he supposed to resurface by now? A simple "Hey, I'm alive" wouldn't kill him.

I slow to a jog as I approach the towering iron gates of Liam's estate, its sprawling gardens mocking me with their relentless perfection. I stop, hands on my hips, catching my breath. Inhale calm, exhale doubt. That's the mantra, right? Peace doesn't always waltz in gracefully. Sometimes, you have to drag it in by its hair.

I head inside, feeling…well, not lighter, exactly, but maybe a touch less twisted. Frustration still simmers under the surface, but I decide it's fine. Maybe frustration is just part of the ride.

Back in my room, I grab my phone, thumb hovering over the screen. I open my chat with Alex and type out something casual, or at least as casual as I can manage.

Me: Hey, just checking in. Are we still on for tomorrow? Hope your weekend didn't involve too many awkward family dinners.

I hit send and stare at the screen for a second, like it's going to spit out answers if I glare at it hard enough. When it doesn't, I toss it onto my bed with a huff and head for the shower. The hot water is pure magic, washing away my sweat and tension. I close my eyes, forcing myself to focus on the here and now instead of mentally dissecting every non-existent text from Alex. I finish rinsing off, wrap myself in a towel, and pad back into my room.

The screen lights up. Nothing.

A familiar pang shoots through me. I close my eyes and try to shove it back down. I know better than to tie my peace to someone else's texting habits. He's probably busy. Or his phone fell into a volcano. Both are equally plausible.

I pull on fresh clothes, yank open the curtains, and let sunlight flood the room. If there's one thing I've learned, it's that I can't control other people—or their inexplicable disappearing acts. But I can control how much headspace I give their silence. I grab my journal, flipping it open with purpose.

Maybe Alex is caught up in something. Maybe he's just bad at this. Or maybe I'm overthinking like it's a national pastime.

Either way, I'm done waiting around for a ping from his end. I've got things to do, goals to chase, and at least three affirmations to repeat until I actually believe them.

I am calm. I am centered. I am not going to obsess over a guy who can't text back.

One more deep breath, and I set my pen down. Whatever happens next, it's not going to derail my peace.

CHAPTER 23

ALEX

The weekend crawled by at a pace that would make glaciers look efficient. My brothers didn't miss a beat hounding me about my abrupt exit last Thursday. Thankfully, the sheer force of my simmering anger must have been enough to signal them to back off. Either that, or they finally got tired of poking the bear.

Now it's early Monday evening, and I've spent the entire day barricaded behind computer screens, drowning in reports and numbers that demand my attention but fail to keep it. I'm staring at graphs like they hold the meaning of life, but all they do is blur into meaningless lines. Turns out, spreadsheets aren't great at distracting you from things you don't want to think about, like *her*.

The low hum of my computer fills the silence of my office, interrupted only by the occasional clink of melting ice in my glass. The sleek design and framed art that cost more than most people's mortgage usually make this space feel like a temple of focus. But today? It just feels like a very expensive cage. No matter how I position myself, the walls seem to close in. Typically, this is my sanctuary, where data and strategy sharpen my mind like a blade. But right now, all the numbers on my screen might as well be a word search because Yasmine is the only thing I can think about. And as much as I hate to admit it, the silence has never been louder.

I glance at my phone, sitting face down on my desk, and I know there's a message waiting. She texted earlier but I didn't even open it. I don't want to hear from her. I don't want to think about her. Yet I can't stop. Her laugh echoes in my mind.

The way she looked at the gala, like she didn't have a care in the world, like she wasn't keeping secrets from me. And Liam—his hand on her back, how he leaned in like she belonged to him.

I drain the rest of my whiskey and set the glass down harder than I mean to, the sound cutting through the room like a whip. Catia's voice creeps in, uninvited. *She's a gold digger, Alex. These girls are all the same. They see your money and your name and latch on like leeches. Don't let her fool you.* At the time, I'd brushed it off. Catia's bitter—always has been, and of course, she'll never approve of anyone I date after her. But now I wonder if she was right. I thought Yasmine was different. She wasn't like the rest of the girls at these events, flashing fake smiles and calculating their next move. But seeing her with Liam? It's like a slap in the face.

I rub my temples, my mind drifting back to memories I try not to visit. *My mother, her laugh, the warmth of her hug.* And then the accident. The emptiness it left behind. I've spent my life building walls, keeping people at arm's length because it's easier that way. Safer. With Yasmine, I let my guard down, even for a moment, and now I'm paying for it.

The soft clatter of the door opening pulls me out of my haze. My assistant, Eduardo, strides in, clipboard in hand, dressed in his usual tailored perfection. The man could make a coffee run look like a Milan fashion show. "Evening check-in before I head out," he announces. But then he stops, narrows his eyes, and raises one impeccably shaped brow. "Oh no. I know that face. You're either about to acquire another company or have personal drama. Spill."

I exhale and rub my temples again. "Just run me through my schedule for tomorrow, Eduardo."

He taps the clipboard like it's a gavel. "Fine. But I reserve the right to judge later." He flips a page and glances down. "Morning strategy meeting, investor calls—yawn. Afternoon and Wednesday morning completely blocked off for 'Yasmine.' Romantic mystery time or whatever it is you do on dates. So…still keeping that sacred or should I open it up?"

I lean back, the weight of it all settling deeper. "Open it up," I say, my tone flat. "Cancel Yasmine."

Eduardo's pen freezes mid-air. He looks at me over the top of his frame. "Really? Cancel 'Yasmine'?" He pauses, softening his voice. "I mean…you blocked time for a woman. That's practically a marriage proposal for you."

"I'm sure," I say, sharper than I intend. I sigh and add, "Just clear it."

Eduardo watches me for a moment, then scribbles something down. "Okay. Done. But for what it's worth, some things are worth the emotional risk. I've risked plenty of heartbreak in the name of brunch alone."

I snort despite myself. He gives me a small, satisfied smile before disappearing through the door. The silence feels heavier now as Eduardo's words sink in. It's almost laughable—him giving *me* advice on risk. My entire career is built on mastering risk, knowing when to play the odds and when to walk away. And the dumbest gamble I could make right now? Betting on a drop-dead gorgeous *liar.*

CHAPTER 24

YASMINE

2 weeks later.

Sami and I linger at *Café Blessings*, our chosen lunch spot after tackling Runyon Canyon. The scent of citrus blossoms and fresh bread drifts through the air, blending with the murmur of nearby conversations and the occasional clink of silverware. We've been here a while, savoring the kind of unhurried sunny afternoon that feels special, especially since it's her first time visiting LA.

Most of the hike was spent unraveling everything from the past few weeks. Alex's maddening radio silence, the sting of it, and my absolute confusion over how I'm supposed to feel. Sami's take was blunt, of course, but honest. *He was a fling, nothing more, don't let an LA 'fuckboy' derail me from my goals.* She has a way of delivering truths like they're casual observations. And she isn't wrong.

Our Buddha Bowls and iced teas are long gone, and I can't help but smile as Sami launches into an exaggerated retelling of some high school drama, complete with wild hand gestures. One guy from a nearby table actually flinches when she mimics throwing a dodgeball. It feels good to laugh again, even if there's still a faint ache in my chest. But it's quieter now, like background noise I've learned to live with.

"Okay, fine," Sami says, leaning back in her chair with a satisfied sigh. "LA's not as overrated as I thought. But next time, we're getting fries. None of this healthy post-hike, namaste-your-gut bullshit."

I laugh. "Deal. You survived kale; you've earned fries."

She raises her glass. "To balance."

"Cheers to that." I grin as I hand the server my card to pay.
But then something—or someone—catches my eye by the
entrance.

Alex.

He walks in like he owns the place. Handsome as ever, wearing
a navy button-down, fitting like it was tailored by the gods, and
exuding a confidence that makes the rest of us look like we're
trying too hard. My breath stumbles, and before I can reel it
back in, I spot the woman clinging to his arm. She's tall,
blonde, and the kind of stunning that makes you wonder if she
wakes up every morning bathed in soft lighting. She looks like
she belongs in a perfume ad, casually draped across the deck of
a yacht with a flute of champagne in one hand and no actual
cares in the other. She slides into the seat across from him, and
the way they lean in, heads almost touching, feels way too
intimate for a casual brunch chat.

My chest tightens, and for a second, the room feels like it's
been put on a spin cycle. I blink and grip my glass a little
tighter, forcing myself to remember: *You're fine. You're calm.
You're the picture of grace.* Except that grace is currently losing a
battle with the urge to stage-dive into their conversation and
yell, *Really? Perfume-ad perfect?*

"Sami, don't look, but oh my God, Alex is here," I whisper, my
voice tight. Of course, she immediately looks. Her eyes follow
my gaze, locking onto him in seconds. Her eyebrows shoot up
before narrowing in sharp assessment.

"*That's* him?" she asks, her tone dripping with curiosity and judgment. I nod, barely remembering to breathe. She glances back at me, concern softening her features. "Okay, yeah…he's insanely hot. Like, offensively hot." She pauses, crossing her arms. "But no guy, especially not some quick fling, is worth it."

I let out a shaky laugh despite myself. "You're right."

Sami links her arm through mine and tugs me toward the exit. "Let's go. You're way too amazing to waste even five minutes watching some guy with hot billionaire vibes play romantic musical chairs."

The corners of my mouth lift as I let her lead me outside. I glance back once as the door swings shut behind us. The hurt is still there, but Sami's right. No man, no matter how magnetic, is worth my peace.

We step into the LA sunshine, and Sami launches into another story, her voice pulling me back into the present. The steady rhythm of our steps on the pavement and the warmth of her laughter remind me *I'm stronger than this*. And I'm not about to let Alex, or anyone else, make me forget it.

CHAPTER 25

ALEX

She was here. I saw her. The ethereal, breathtaking, completely unattainable woman who turned heads without even realizing it. Everyone was watching her. And she was oblivious to it all. Because Yasmine isn't like the rest of LA, she doesn't thrive on attention. She doesn't bask in the spotlight.

Unlike the woman sitting across from me right now. Nina's father happens to own a global media empire, one Lucas and I have been circling like vultures for years. She also happens to have an insufferable crush on me. I have never been interested in her. Not before and definitely not now. Not when my mind is consumed by someone else entirely. Someone with dark, mesmerizing hair and a laugh that still haunts me in the quiet moments I won't acknowledge.

But Yasmine is off limits. She has to be. Because I refuse, *refuse*, to be vulnerable again. Vulnerability is a loaded gun, and I already pulled the trigger once. And now? Now, I'm bleeding out. And the worst part is it hurts even more than my breakup with Catia, which is absurd. Laughable, even. I spent years with Catia. Yasmine? I spent a handful of days with her. Days. And yet she managed to infiltrate my walls and plant herself so deep inside my psyche that I can't even go a single hour without thinking about her. The real kicker is that I *know* I wasn't wrong about her. I make a living reading people. I can spot a liar, a fake, a fraud from miles away. And Yasmine? She wasn't one of them. She was good. Genuine. Which is why it makes absolutely zero sense that she betrayed me like that.

"And can you believe Mathilde wore last season's Balmain like no one would notice? We *all* noticed." A shrill laugh yanks me from my downward spiral, and I blink back into the present. Nina is cackling like she just told the joke of the century. Meanwhile, I'm sitting here giving the performance of my life, nodding along, feigning interest. Somebody hand me an Oscar.

God, I miss talking to Yasmine. With her, the conversation was easy, deep, and meaningful. Nothing like this constant stream of vapid nonsense Nina keeps spitting out. I stare at my drink, wondering how much I'd have to down to make this lunch more bearable. Maybe the whole thing. Maybe the entire bottle. But alcohol isn't going to fix the reality in front of me. Yasmine and I were never meant to be. I have to accept that.

But damn it, she's still going to haunt me. She already carved her name into my bones, and no amount of time, distance, or meaningless lunches with women like Nina will change that.

And for that? I don't know if I should hate her or thank her.

CHAPTER 26

Two and a half years later.

The salty ocean breeze tickles my skin as I step barefoot onto the yoga deck's smooth, sunsoaked wood. Nearby waves crash in a steady rhythm, blending with soft laughter as my students gather, their mats unfurling with satisfying pops.

This place—my place—feels like I've plucked it straight out of my wildest daydream and dropped it right here in Tulum. *The Hana Elise Yoga Center* sits gracefully on a gentle rise, overlooking endless stretches of water as far as the eye can see. I named it after my mom, the woman who first taught me the magic of movement and stillness. The main deck is an open-air sanctuary under a thatched palapa roof. The beach below is just a few steps away. Sometimes I hold meditation sessions right there on the sand, the tide's gentle push and pull setting the rhythm for our breaths. Even the ocean's in sync out here.

Today, my center hums with life. A group of teacher trainees scatter under the pergola. Nearby, a few students lounge in a shaded corner, sipping fresh coconut water. I walk through the space, greeting everyone with a smile, my heart practically bursting with gratitude.

It's surreal sometimes, how far I've come. This isn't just a place for yoga—it's a sanctuary for healing, for growth, for connection. It's everything I dreamed of, and then some. Every misstep led me to this, and I wouldn't trade it for anything.

I lean against the wooden railing as I watch the waves crash and retreat, crash and retreat. Two and a half years I've poured everything into this place. Heart, soul, sanity…and maybe a few tears. Okay, a lot of tears.

And it's enough. I'm not just content—I'm proud. I built this. I did it. But still…My fingers trace idle patterns on the railing, grounding me. It's not that I've sworn off relationships. It's just…I haven't felt that spark in a long time. That soul-thrumming, body-tingling, mind-spinning feeling that makes you do reckless things like leave toothbrushes at each other's places or consider joint Netflix accounts.

Maybe it's timing. Maybe it's fear. Or maybe I've just cocooned myself so deeply into this life I've built that the idea of someone untying those threads feels too risky. But if I'm being honest, there's a part of me that just misses being held. Not because I'm broken or incomplete—I'm fine, really. But sometimes, you just want someone strong and solid to wrap you up, say nothing, and make the world feel a little less sharp around the edges.

I tilt my face toward the sun, letting its warmth sink into my skin. That part of my life might be waiting for me somewhere out there—or maybe I've already walked past it. Either way, I'm good. Alone, but not lonely. Fulfilled, but still open. Ready to see what's next whenever the universe decides to show up with it.

And if it doesn't? I've got palm trees and the ocean on speed dial. Not exactly a bad backup plan.

—

The soft shuffle of footsteps pulls me out of my mat-straightening trance. I glance up, expecting a student, but it's Pablo standing at the edge of the deck, his serene presence unmistakable. My face breaks into a grin.

I first met Pablo at a retreat when I moved to Tulum, still wobbly with self-doubt but fiercely determined. He saw something in me back then—potential, maybe, or sheer stubbornness—and he helped me shape this dream into reality. His guidance and calm certainty nudged me from "hopeful dreamer" to founder.

Behind him, Alyssa, my operations manager, strolls in, balancing a stack of fresh towels. She's running the next class, but she knows I love to fuss over setup. Call it a quirk, or control issues. Whatever. "Look at you, actually working," she teases, setting the towels down with a flourish.

I laugh, tossing her a playful glare. "It's my ritual. Can't break tradition."

Pablo chuckles, his voice like warm honey. "I'd expect nothing less."

"Pablo," I say, crossing the space to hug him. His arms wrap around me in that grounding, all-is-right-in-the-world kind of way.

"Yasmine," he says, pulling back, eyes crinkling with genuine affection. "It's been too long."

"Come in," I lead him to the shaded lounge where the sea breeze does its magic. "How's Carmen and the kids? I haven't seen them in forever."

Pablo's face lights up with pride. "They're wonderful. Carmen's working on a new community project, and the kids…well, Mia just turned twelve. Can you believe that?"

"Twelve?" I laugh. "I swear she was nine like…yesterday."

He nods, bemused. "Time's relentless. We'll have to do dinner soon. Carmen would love to catch up."

"I'd love that," I say, genuinely meaning it. Talking to Pablo always feels like a deep exhale.

He settles onto one of the low cushions, crossing his legs like it's second nature. "Your work here…" he gestures around us, "it's remarkable. You've created something truly special, Yasmine."

"Thank you." Warmth spreads through me. Coming from Pablo, it means more than I can say.

His eyes turn thoughtful, a smile tugging at the corners. "I have a proposition for you," he starts. "I'm hosting a retreat next month. Very intimate. Very exclusive. I need a yoga healer I trust—someone with the right energy. Someone who can hold space for real transformation."

I blink, absorbing his words. "You want me to co-host?"

Pablo nods, his smile widening. "Yes. Your presence, your approach…it's exactly what this group will need."

"What kind of retreat is it?" I ask, curiosity flaring.

He leans forward, voice dropping like we're about to swap state secrets. "A spiritual immersion for a very private group. I can't reveal their identities, but I can tell you they're seekers. They want healing, with clarity and purpose. And they need absolute confidentiality."

I hesitate, not because I doubt Pablo, but because the mystery is…well, a little dramatic. "Why all the secrecy?" I ask, eyebrow raised.

"These are people who live under constant scrutiny," he explains. "This is their chance to be vulnerable, to find peace without the weight of public judgment. It has to be private. For their sake."

I nod, absorbing the weight of his words. If anyone could create that kind of sanctuary, it's Pablo. And if he thinks I'm the right person to help, who am I to argue? "I'd be honored," I say, meeting his gaze with conviction.

His smile deepens, eyes gleaming with approval. "Thank you, Yasmine. Together, I know we can create something extraordinary."

As we dive into logistics, excitement bubbles up inside me. This isn't just a gig—it's a calling. A chance to expand, to grow, to share what I love on a deeper level. I don't know who's going to show up, but I do know one thing: this is going to be unforgettable.

CHAPTER 27

ALEX

The early morning sun slices through the glass walls of my home gym, casting sharp lines across polished equipment as I grind through the last rep of shoulder presses. Muscles burning, sweat trickling, and I welcome every bit of it. Pain is predictable. It makes sense. Unlike…well, other things.

Soft footsteps echo from the hallway, delicate and entirely too familiar. I glance toward the doorway and there she is. All legs and tousled blonde waves…wait, is she wearing my old Stanford T-shirt? The one I hadn't seen in months. Did she go rifling through my closet? Jesus.

I suppress a sigh, setting the weights down with a thud. Women parading around in my clothes isn't cute—it's territorial. Like a cat rubbing its scent on everything. Except… My mind drifts back to Yasmine, barefoot and completely unbothered in my shirt, like it had just fallen from the sky and she happened to catch it. She wore it like it belonged to her, like I did.

I shake off the thought, reaching for my water bottle. Sasha leans against the doorframe, stretching in that slow, deliberate way women do when they want you to watch. "Got anything for breakfast?" she purrs, all doe eyes and stretched limbs.

I take a long pull of water, letting the coolness clear my head. "I've got a busy morning. Thanks for last night, but…breakfast isn't part of the arrangement." I flash her a polite smile, the kind you'd give a flight attendant after she hands you a packet of pretzels. Transaction complete.

Her smile flickers—just for a second. Almost like she's shocked. Maybe she thought the Stanford shirt bought her more time. But she recovers, shrugging it off with a grin that's just a little too forced. "Got it."

I crank up the music before she can say anything else, the bass vibrating through my chest. I grab the next set of weights, focusing on the familiar burn, letting it drown out everything else. Especially the fact that, for one brief, stupid moment, I thought about Yasmine instead.

—

I pull into the private lot beneath my office, cut the engine, and step out into the steady pulse of downtown LA. It's early, but the city's already alive with energy, like it's had three espressos and a cold shower before sunrise.

The elevator ride is quick, and when the doors slide open to the top floor, the familiar sharpness of my space greets me. Sleek. Minimal. Controlled. Just the way I like it. No chaos. No surprises.

Eduardo is already waiting by my desk, tablet in hand. He raises a brow. "You're late."

I loosen my collar, dropping my bag by the chair. "Busy morning."

He doesn't flinch, just nods and swipes his screen. "Your nine a.m. is in the conference room."

I grunt in acknowledgment, rolling my shoulders to shake off the tension. Years of grinding, building, conquering. I've outpaced every goal, bought my way into every exclusive circle, and yet…it's like eating gourmet food and still feeling hungry.

Work is my oxygen, but lately, it's starting to feel more like suffocation. Relationships? A complete joke. I've had the world's most beautiful women in my bed—models, actresses, influencers—each one hotter than the last. But none of them…stick. Not because they can't, but because I don't let them.

And I hate that the sight of Sasha in my old Stanford T-shirt this morning made me think of her. *Yasmine.* It's been years, and she's still haunting me like a damn ghost that refuses to be exorcised. None of them compare. Not in bed, not in conversation, not even close. It pisses me off that I still do this. That I still think of her at all. But betrayal leaves scars. And hers? It's carved deep.

My phone buzzes in my hand, and Pablo's name flashes across the screen. For a second, I feel that familiar calm he always seems to bring with him, even through a phone call. I haven't been back to Tulum in years, but Pablo and I have stayed connected. Some people are like anchors; you can drift, but you never really lose them.

"Pablo," I answer, leaning against the glass wall of my office.

"Alex, my friend," his voice is warm and steady, like always. The guy could probably order a pizza and still make it sound like a spiritual experience. "How are you?"

I smirk. "Busy. Always busy."

"Too busy for healing?" He says it like he already knows the answer. And he does.

I rub the back of my neck, staring out at the city. "I'm doing fine, Pablo. No need to worry."

"You've said that before," he replies easily. "But you're still running. I can hear it in your voice." I don't argue. He's not wrong. Pablo's always had this unnerving ability to read me better than I read myself.

"I'm hosting a retreat," he continues. "A very small, private gathering. A chance to disconnect, reflect, and realign. I think it would be good for you, Alex. You've come far, but there's more work to be done. On yourself."

I exhale, pinching the bridge of my nose. A retreat sounds about as appealing as a root canal, but Pablo wouldn't suggest it if he didn't think I needed it. "Where is it?" I ask, more out of habit than interest.

"Tulum," he says, voice steady. "At my center. Perfect for the kind of transformation I know you're seeking."

I let the silence stretch. Maybe he's right. I've been running on fumes, and deep down, I know something has to shift. "Alright," I say finally. "I'll come."

I can practically hear Pablo smiling through the phone. "Good. I'll send you the details. Trust the process, Alex. I believe this will be worth it."

When the call ends, I stare out at the cityscape. Maybe a change of scenery is exactly what I need…or maybe it's the last thing I need. Either way, it's happening.

CHAPTER 28

The morning sun filters through the palms, casting playful shadows across the open pavilion at Pablo's retreat center. The scent of salt and hibiscus hangs thick in the air, and the steady crash of waves provides the kind of ambiance a meditation app would kill for. As I tick off the last items on my checklist, I take a deep breath, feeling both grounded and buzzing with energy "Four attendees," Pablo says, glancing at the handwritten itinerary in his hand. "Each one will have regular private yoga healing sessions with you."

I nod, jotting it down. Four? It's going to be a challenge, but I'm up for it. Still, there's something in his tone that makes me pause. "Anything I should know about these attendees?" I ask, raising an eyebrow.

Pablo gives me that serene smile that always makes me feel like he knows the secrets of the universe. "Let's just say they'll each bring their own unique energy."

I smirk. That could mean anything with Pablo—from reclusive tech billionaires needing a soul reboot to wanderlust influencers meditating in tree poses while snapping selfies. Either way, I'm ready. He steps closer, his expression softening. "These people need this, Yasmine. They're searching for something deeper. I told them you're not just a teacher—you're a guide."

I blink, touched by the weight of his words. "That means a lot, Pablo." I step back to admire the pavilion, hands on my hips like I just conquered an HGTV challenge. It's simple but intentional, just the way I envisioned it. The mats are laid out in a neat crescent facing the ocean, perfectly positioned to catch the first morning rays. *This is where they'll heal,* I think, a slow smile spreading across my face. It's not just a yoga class. It's a sanctuary, a space to pause and unravel the knots that life has tied up. I've been there. I know what it's like to stumble into therapy as a last resort and come out the other side with a new perspective. Sure, some people think yoga is just an excuse for overpriced leggings and eighteen-dollar green juices. And look, I'm not above a good smoothie. But for me, it's always been more. It's how I learned to breathe when life felt suffocating. How I found balance when everything was tilted. Yoga isn't about squeezing yourself into some spiritual stereotype. It's about finding stillness when everything's spinning. If that peace happens to come while folded into child's pose with the ocean stretching out before you, well, that's just a bonus.

"This feels right," I say softly, turning to Pablo. "I can't wait to meet them. To hear their stories, understand their struggles, and help them find clarity through the practice."

"You will do an amazing job," Pablo says, his eyes warm with pride. "You have a gift, Yasmine. You see people as they are. That's rare."

I smile, gratitude swelling in my chest. "Thank you for trusting me, Pablo. I promise to give them my best."

We finish up the last-minute details, and I can already feel the pulse of the retreat—full of promise. I know, as much as I'm here to guide, I'll also learn. Their stories will touch mine, and maybe I'll find some healing of my own, too.

CHAPTER 29

ALEX

My jet slices through the clouds with the kind of effortless grace that only obscene amounts of money can buy. Inside, the engine hums like it's meditating, barely disturbing the curated silence. I should feel at peace in this capsule of luxury, but my brain's doing laps like it didn't get the memo. I turn to the window, eyes tracing the endless stretch of turquoise below. It's the kind of view that makes people quit their jobs to "find themselves." I lean back, tapping my fingers against the leather armrest while my other hand clutches my phone. My VP Greg and Eduardo's voices filter through the speaker as we wrap up my handover.

"I'll be mostly offline for the next two weeks," I say. "No phone, no internet."

Greg laughs nervously. "You sure you can survive that?"

I smirk. "No, but my spiritual guru seems to think so."

Eduardo, ever the optimist, jumps in. "We've got it covered. You need the break. And besides, this might actually be good for you."

I don't answer. He's probably right, but admitting it feels like conceding defeat. I glance at the flight monitor charting our path from LA to Tulum. My life runs on boardrooms and bottom lines, not meditation and kale shots. But Pablo insisted this retreat would jumpstart my so-called healing journey.

The stewardess appears as if my hesitation had its own concierge service, her smile polished to corporate perfection. "Mr. Pierce," she says, her voice dripping with just the right amount of suggestion. "I hope you're having a comfortable flight."

"It's fine," I reply, keeping it short.

Her smile doesn't waver. "Tulum's beautiful this time of year. If you need someone who knows the area…" She lets the subtext hang in the air.

I lean back, smirking. "I'll keep that in mind."

When she finally disappears, I'm already a thousand miles away in my head.

The plane lands smoothly, and the door swings open, letting in a gust of humid air. I grab my leather duffle, sling it over my shoulder, and step into the sun. A blacked-out Escalade gleams on the tarmac, its driver already holding the door open like I'm royalty. I give him a nod before climbing in, savoring the blast of AC.

I'm supposed to be focusing on this retreat, on whatever clarity Pablo thinks I'm going to find, but my mind keeps wandering back to the one person I can never seem to forget. *Mom.* Coming here is Pablo's idea of '*self-work*,' —I'd call it self-inflicted torture, but semantics.

The SUV turns onto a winding road and Pablo's retreat center comes into view—a sprawl of modern architecture tucked into the jungle like it sprouted there naturally. I step out, heat clinging to my skin. Tropical birds are chirping. Of course, they are.

A woman in flowing white glides over, smiling like she's been waiting her whole life just to say hello. "Mr. Pierce, welcome," she says, clasping her hands. "I'm Riley."

"Thank you," I nod. Another attendant shows up, practically materializing out of the foliage. Hospitality on steroids. He reaches for my bag with the grace of someone who's been trained not to startle rich people.

Riley hands me a cool, lavender-scented towel. "For grounding," she explains, like wiping my face with essential oils is going to realign my entire personality.

I play along, dabbing my face. It smells good, at least.

"And here's your welcome drink," she continues, passing me a tiny glass of green liquid. "Organic elixir, designed to rejuvenate."

I take a sip. Lime, cucumber, and something that tastes suspiciously like lawn clippings. I hand the glass back, nodding. "Refreshing," I lie.

Riley launches into a tour, and I trail behind, trying to look interested. Communal spaces with floor-to-ceiling windows, dining areas with wooden tables that probably cost more than a car, and a kitchen where wheatgrass is apparently the star of the show. "We believe food is medicine," she chirps.

Ah because nothing says medicine like quinoa pretending to be pizza.

She leads me past massage rooms, reiki spaces, and something called a 'vibration therapy chamber.' We finally reach the yoga pavilion—a breezy, open-air structure with mats arranged in a U-shape facing the ocean. The floral scent in the air is familiar, but I can't place it. "This is where you'll have your private yoga and breathwork sessions," Riley says, her voice smooth.

"Lucky me," I respond.

We walk back to the main path, and she details my schedule: yoga, group sharing, sound baths, and something called a 'secret journey.' I have no idea what that means, but I'm sure it involves chanting or spirit animals. If I end up howling at the moon, I'm asking for my money back.

Riley finally leads me to my room. Inside, sunlight filters through, reflecting off a massive crystal perched on a table by the window. "This is clear quartz," she explains. "For clarity and healing."

"Good to know," I say, brushing my fingers over it. It's cool and smooth, and I feel...something. Not healed, but less jagged. I'll take it.

Riley gestures to the spread of tropical fruits and coconut water waiting on a low table. "These are replenished daily. If you need anything, just ask."

"Appreciate it," I reply.

She steps back, her smile unshakeable. "We'll send someone to get you for the welcome gathering at five."

I nod, and she leaves, the door clicking shut behind her. For a moment, I just stand there, letting the silence settle. I've been here all of five minutes, and already, the edges are softening. I'm not sure if that's good or terrifying.

But I guess I'm about to find out.

CHAPTER 30

The energy at Pablo's retreat center practically vibrates as I step into the open-air meeting space for the evening's meet-and-greet. The room is alive with laughter, framed by the jungle, where the sunset spills through the trees in streaks of green, crimson, and sunlit yellow—like Mother Nature decided to flex. I take a deep breath, letting the warmth of the moment settle in my chest.

Pablo's here, naturally—anchoring the space with his signature calm. He greets me with a hug that practically radiates serenity, and I spot the rest of the team nearby. Gabriela, our sound healer, whose voice is probably being bottled and sold as sleep therapy somewhere. Emilio, the reiki master who can say more with a single nod than most people can in an entire speech. And Camila, the Ayurvedic masseuse whose nurturing energy makes you half-expect her to pull a weighted blanket out of thin air. They're basically the Guardians of Inner Peace, and standing with them reminds me why I love this work so much. I mentally note not to make any jokes about forming a wellness superhero team. At least, not yet.

Slowly, the guests start to arrive, each one greeted by Pablo with deliberate care. His words always carry that understated reverence, like he's introducing a soul instead of a person. "This is Yasmine, my co-host for the retreat," he says warmly. "She won't just guide you through the practice; she'll help you come home to yourself." No pressure.

The first guest I meet is Alaina. Petite, glowing, and familiar. It takes me a second before I realize I've heard her voice a hundred times on the radio. In person, she seems smaller, more real, like she finally took off her stage costume. There's a shadow in her eyes, but when she smiles—tentative, hopeful—it's clear she's here to heal. Pablo quietly shares that she's been struggling since surviving a terror attack at one of her concerts. My heart squeezes, instantly struck by her bravery.

Next is Ethan, who looks exactly like his business magazine covers: polished, powerful, probably a little allergic to genuine emotion. He's that breed of tech billionaire who would buy an island just to bulldoze it. His handshake is calculated, his smile practiced, and his eyes sharp—like he's calculating the ROI of every conversation. Pablo whispers that he's fresh off a messy divorce. I can't help but wonder what "messy" looks like in his world. Probably less screaming matches and more frozen assets.

Then there's Sofia, a social media influencer whose selfies have probably been retouched by angels. She glides through the room with the kind of confidence that only comes from millions of followers validating your every brunch choice. But when she meets my eyes, there's a flicker of doubt. Pablo mentions she's been struggling with her identity, and I catch the hesitation in her smile, like she's deciding if she's here to heal or gather fresh content for her feed.

The mixer is in full swing, herbal tea flowing like champagne, and I'm mid-laugh with Gabriela and Sofia, feeling that rare click of alignment, like the universe is on my side.

Then the door opens, and the universe takes it all back.

A tall, broad figure steps inside, and the whole room seems to hiccup, as if gravity momentarily forgot what it was doing.

Alex.

He looks different—like my memory of him, but sharper, more rugged. His hair's a little longer, jawline somehow even more defined, as if life's been chiseling away at him for sport. His eyes sweep the room until they land on me. He freezes, and I feel my stomach do an Olympic-level flip. Seriously? Right now?

I set my tea down carefully, like that tiny act of control might stop the storm brewing inside me. Spoiler: it doesn't. I'm rooted to the spot, heart pounding as memories I thought I'd buried decide to hold a reunion tour. His touch, his laugh, his voice—they crash over me, determined to wreck my whole calm, spiritual vibe. *Breathe*, Yasmine. You literally teach classes on how to handle this.

He stares, I stare back. The air between us thickens, heavy with unspoken things. Awkward? Definitely. But also intimate, like the room has folded in on itself, leaving just the two of us in some cosmic staring contest.

Then, blissfully oblivious to the tension thick enough to cut with a chakra wand, Pablo steps forward to greet Alex like they're old friends. I can't focus on what they're saying—I'm too busy trying to ground myself, but my inner peace seems to have taken a sabbatical. Alex finally breaks eye contact, but the moment lingers, his presence now a gravitational pull I can't ignore.

Whatever happens next, one thing is painfully clear: this retreat just got a whole lot more interesting. Namaste to that.

CHAPTER 31

ALEX

Yasmine. She's here.

For a second, my brain flatlines. Not just here—she's standing in the middle of the room, practically glowing, like she landed straight from some celestial plane into this retreat. Her jet-black hair tumbles over her shoulders, catching the sunlight as if it's personally invested in making her look divine. She moves with a confidence I don't remember, like she figured out the world bends for her now. And maybe it does.

I stop mid-step. My heart is slamming so loud I half-expect someone to call security. She's magnetic. There's this energy around her that draws every eye in the room without her even trying. And me? I feel like I'm sixteen again, gawking at the prettiest girl in school while clutching my books and hoping not to faceplant.

A surge of emotions slams into me—frustration, because of course she's here, because the universe clearly enjoys screwing with me. Resentment too, because no amount of success ever really stitched up the wound she left. And maybe something close to vulnerability, though I'd rather call it pride, because standing there, effortlessly captivating, she's everything I swore I didn't need.

But mostly? I'm mesmerized.

Even the air around her seems brighter. I didn't think I believed in energy or auras, but hers is impossible to ignore. Golden, steady, alive. And for one stupid, reckless second, I forget why I swore I'd never let myself feel this way again.

She sees me, too. When our eyes lock, the entire room evaporates. It's just us, standing in the fog of unfinished history. My chest tightens, and I force my legs to keep moving, even though they feel like they've been replaced with concrete. Her expression is unreadable, but mine? It's probably a disaster.

Pablo greets me, snapping me out of the trance. I shake his hand, mumble something about the place looking great, but my brain is still back there, stuck on her. I glance at her again, just once, and catch her doing the same.

Perfect. Two weeks of this.

I square my shoulders, masking how thrown I am. Sure, she looks like some kind of goddess reborn, but I'm not about to let her see how much she still gets under my skin.

Pablo's voice reels me back in, his hand resting on my shoulder as he introduces me to the small group. I nod at each of them, polite but distracted. My gaze keeps flicking back to her, standing there, radiant and calm, hands clasped in front of her like she has all the time in the world.

"And finally," Pablo says, practically beaming, "I must introduce you to someone truly special—Yasmine. She'll be leading the yoga healing sessions throughout this retreat. She's remarkable, Alex, and I'm certain she'll help you in ways you don't even anticipate."

His words hang in the air, wrapping around me like a challenge. Special. Remarkable. And yeah, even with everything that's happened, it's impossible to deny she is. She always was. I clear my throat, the words getting stuck before I finally manage, "It's… been a while."

Yasmine's lips tug into a polite smile, but her eyes stay guarded. There's something flickering there. Recognition, sure, but also a wall so solid it might as well be made of steel. "Yeah… it has," she replies, her tone soft but distant, like she's carefully measuring each word. The silence stretches, taut and heavy. The things we're not saying ripple in the air like static. I wonder if she feels it too, or if I'm just the idiot bracing for impact.

Pablo glances between us, eyebrows raised like he's stumbled onto the world's most awkward secret. "I didn't realize you two knew each other," he says, his tone light but probing. "I trust this won't be a conflict of interest?"

Neither of us responds. Me, because I don't trust my voice not to crack, and Yasmine, because she's too composed to let anything slip.

Pablo waits a beat, then continues with that unnervingly calm authority of his. "Alex, your private sessions with Yasmine begin tomorrow morning. She'll guide you through a yoga practice tailored specifically to your healing journey. I strongly recommend you open up to her and to yourself. Share what you've been holding back, especially about your mother. I believe this could be transformative for you."

The mention of my mom sends a spike of something jagged through my chest. My eyes flick to Yasmine, instinctive. Her expression softens—not pity, just…presence. She's listening without pushing, the same way she did all those years ago. Open but never intrusive. And for a split second, I remember why I ever let her in. She was the only person who made me feel seen without asking me to lay out all the broken pieces. And that realization is like a sucker punch to the ribs.

"You can trust her," Pablo says, his voice low and deliberate. "Completely. Share what you're comfortable with; she'll hold space for it."

Yasmine meets my eyes for a moment longer than I expect. There's something there. Empathy? Understanding? Or maybe I'm just imagining it. Either way, it leaves me unsteady. I shift, rubbing the back of my neck. "Thanks, Pablo," I mutter, voice rougher than I intended. "I'll… try."

I shove my hands into my pockets, already dreading—and maybe anticipating—whatever the hell tomorrow's session is going to bring.

First thing in the morning. Just the two of us.

Pablo shifts his attention to another guest, leaving Yasmine and me marinating in silence thicker than the humid Tulum air. She doesn't bolt like I expect her to. Instead, she steps a little closer, voice soft but firm.

"I'm glad you're here, Alex," she says, her tone professional yet genuine. No sarcasm, no edge, just sincerity. "I think this retreat will be good for you."

Her words settle, and I forget how to respond for a second. There's something in her eyes—steady, unflinching, like she's holding back a thousand things she could say. An unspoken truth hangs there, and it claws at my ribs. Yasmine doesn't seem like the type to lie, play games, or date someone like Liam. The girl I remember was thoughtful, grounded, different. Did I get it wrong? Was there more to the story than I let myself believe?

Before I can unravel that thought, she tilts her head slightly and offers a soft smile. "Good night, Alex. I'll see you in the morning." And just like that, she steps back into the crowd, leaving her presence lingering like the faint trace of her scent.

I watch her go, graceful and unbothered, her laugh spilling easily as she greets others. My fists clench in my pockets, doubt creeping in. Maybe there *is* more to this than I thought. But for now, I keep it to myself, my mind already circling what tomorrow might bring.

CHAPTER 32

YASMINE

The yoga pavilion is perfect this morning—serene and a haven of calm. My thoughts? Not so much.

Seeing Alex last night stirred up more than I expected. Memories I'd shelved—his smile, his warmth, the way he'd look at me like I was the only person in the world—came rushing back like they'd just been waiting for the right cue. But with them came the bitterness, the sting of his vanishing act, and those nights I spent wondering what I did wrong.

I kneel beside the mat and try to center myself. This isn't about the past. It's about healing—for him and for me. Still, I know I can't ignore the tension. Better to clear the air now than let it fester like bad juju during savasana.

The door creaks open, and I look up just in time to catch my breath.

Alex steps in, and I swear the universe flicks the lights up a notch. He's in a fitted white t-shirt that clings to his frame in ways I'm pretty sure violate at least three wellness guidelines, and gray athletic shorts that prove he hasn't skipped leg day. His gaze flicks over the room before landing on me, and for a second, his composure slips. Just a second. But I catch it.

"Good morning," I say, voice smooth, steady. I refuse to let his stupidly good looks throw me off.

"Morning," he replies, his voice rougher than I expected.

I gesture to the mat. "Make yourself comfortable. We'll start with some breathing exercises."

He sits but doesn't relax. His body's still, but his eyes don't stop moving—like he's scanning for exits. I meet his gaze head-on. No sense pretending we're strangers or that the past isn't looming over us like some ghost of bad communication. The air between us is thick with unspoken tension, but I'm grounded. I've worked too hard to let old wounds throw me off balance. I cross my legs, rest my hands on my knees, and lean forward just enough to signal I'm not afraid of this conversation.

"Alex," I begin, calm but firm. "Before we start, I think we should talk. No point ignoring the elephant in the room. I believe it's important to clear the air—for both of us." He blinks, the silence stretching just long enough to get uncomfortable. But I don't back down. If he's going to respond, I want it to be real, not the corporate version of his feelings. I take a slow breath. "I want you to know I don't hold any grudges about what happened between us," I say, my tone soft but clear. My lips curve into a faint smile. "Or, more accurately, what didn't happen."

Alex shifts slightly, his eyes flickering to mine before dropping. His shoulders tighten just a bit.

"You ghosted me," I continue, even and honest. "Yeah, it hurt at the time. I won't pretend it didn't. But I've worked through it. I've let it go."

He stares at me like I've just told him the sky is orange. I hold his gaze, making sure my words land. "This space we're in now, what we're doing here, it's about healing, not our past. You don't have to worry about me holding anything against you. I'm here to guide you with the same care I'd give anyone else."

His jaw clenches. Something shifts in his expression—hurt, maybe? But then his eyes harden. "Hold anything against *me*?"

he says, his voice laced with disbelief. "For what exactly, Yasmine? If anything, I should be the one forgiving you.

Wait…what?

He shakes his head, eyes fixed on me, unflinching. "You lied to me. I wanted to invite you to that charity gala, you know. I was going to ask you to come with me as my date. But you said you had a work obligation. Then I saw you there with Liam Woods." He exhales sharply, running a hand through his hair, the vulnerability slipping through despite his anger. "You don't have to lie, Yasmine. I saw you with him. You looked…close. Like you were together."

I blink, letting the silence stretch just a moment before I speak. "Alex," I say, voice soft. "That's not what it was."

His expression hardens, though there's a flicker of doubt now. "Then what was it?"

I keep my tone even. "It *was* a work obligation. Liam was my boss then, and he asked me to go as a favor. I didn't tell you the details because couldn't. I'd signed an NDA. He was prepping for a movie role, and I was his yoga trainer. That's it."

His eyes narrow, searching my face like he's scanning for a lie. "You weren't with him?"

"No," I say firmly. "I wasn't with him, and I didn't lie to you. I was just doing my job."

His shoulders relax a fraction, the tension bleeding out as my words sink in. "So… you weren't dating him?" His voice is softer now, hesitant like he's bracing for impact.

"No," I say again, a faint smile tugging at my lips. "He was never my type." I hold his gaze, letting the words hang there just long enough. *You're my type.* I don't say it, but the silence does.

Alex takes a long breath, his gaze dropping again before flicking back to mine. His expression is softer, a hint of relief threading through. "I guess I jumped to conclusions," he admits, voice low. "Seeing you there that night…it messed with my head."

I lean forward. "If I'd known how much that night hurt you, I would've told you everything. I'm sorry you carried that for so long."

He studies me for a beat, then his lips twitch into a reluctant smile. "I owe you an apology too," he says, rubbing the back of his neck. "I handled it like an idiot. I should've asked you instead of jumping to conclusions and ghosting you. I'm sorry, Yasmine." His sincerity feels raw, real. And for a second, the tension lifts, replaced by something lighter.

Then, with a smirk, he adds, "You know, we'd probably be married with two-point-five kids by now if not for that misunderstanding."

I blink, then laugh. "Oh, really?"

"See?" he says, gesturing around the room. "Lesson one from this retreat: communicate. Maybe Pablo actually knows what he's talking about."

I shake my head, smiling despite myself. "Well, it's a good start."

He leans back, his demeanor lighter, the unspoken relief still lingering. Whatever happens next, at least we cleared the air.

"Let's begin," I say, voice steady as I guide him. "It's time to breathe."

He closes his eyes, shoulders relaxing as he exhales. Watching him settle, I redirect my focus. My role is clear—to guide him toward healing, not stir up our past.

Whatever questions we have, whatever could-have-beens floating between us, they'll have to wait.

CHAPTER 33

I'm trying to focus—I swear I am—but my brain's been hijacked by sixteen-year-old, hormone-fueled me, and that kid? He's got the attention span of a TikTok scroll and absolutely zero chill.

Yasmine's standing in front of me wearing this simple, flowy yoga outfit—a loose white tank and earthy green linen pants that somehow fit her perfectly. Nothing flashy, nothing designed to grab attention, but apparently, my body didn't get the memo. It reacts like she's strutting around in lingerie. Seriously, what is wrong with me? She's effortlessly sexy, that kind of beauty that doesn't even try, and apparently, that's my kryptonite.

I'm used to women draped in designer everything, precision makeup, and enough high-maintenance energy to power a small city. But Yasmine? She's the opposite. Natural, grounded, real. It's…unsettling. Usually, my brain would short-circuit trying to process how good she looks, but something about her energy—calm, centered, completely unbothered—forces my thoughts to slow down. For the first time in forever, I'm actually…here.

And then there's the kicker. She didn't lie. The thing I'd been clutching onto like a life raft—her betrayal—turns out to be fiction. That tiny detail shifts everything, at least for me. I have no idea where she stands. Maybe she's moved on. Maybe she has a boyfriend. I glance at her hand—bare. Thank God. I don't know how I'd handle finding out she's married. But wait, why am I even going there? Why am I zoning out like an idiot to someone who isn't even looking at me right now?

This retreat is working—just not in the way I expected.

"Close your eyes, Alex," she says gently. "Inhale deeply through your nose and exhale slowly through your mouth."

I hesitate for a second, but I do it. At first, the breathing feels mechanical, like I'm faking meditation. But her voice is so soothing, and I start to notice the rise and fall of my chest, the way the air feels cool going in and warm going out.

"Good," she murmurs. "Today, you're going to introduce me to someone. As you breathe, I want you to picture yourself as a child. Around seven or eight years old. What does that version of you feel like?"

I freeze. My breath catches before I force it back into rhythm. I don't want to go there. I've locked that kid up in a box labeled *Do Not Open.*

"Let whatever comes up surface," Yasmine says, her tone firm but kind. "Don't judge it. Just notice."

A knot forms in my chest, tightening with every breath. Images flash in my mind—me, sitting on the edge of my bed, staring at the floor. My mom's laughter, soft and distant, like a song I only half remember. And then…nothing. Silence.

"What do you see?" she asks, voice pulling me back.

I swallow hard, my throat tight. But something about how she asks makes me answer. "I see…myself," I admit quietly. "Alone. Sitting in my room."

"Good," she says, like it's the most natural thing in the world. "And how does he feel? That version of you?"

The words tumble out before I can stop them. "Scared. Lonely. Like…like everything good could disappear at any second." My voice wavers, and I hate how raw it sounds, but she doesn't flinch.

She lets the silence stretch, giving me space to sit with it. "Keep breathing," she says softly. "That fear, that loneliness—it's still with you, right?"

I nod, even though my eyes are still shut, and I don't want to admit it. "Yeah," I manage. "It's always there. No matter what I do or how much I try to bury it."

Her voice is gentle but solid, grounding me. "That's because that little boy is still waiting to feel safe. To feel seen."

The knot in my chest tightens, then loosens, like something inside is shifting. I inhale deeply, the air filling a space I didn't even realize was empty.

"This is where we start," she says, voice steady. "By acknowledging him. By giving him the attention he didn't get back then. Healing isn't about fixing what's broken. It's about learning to hold those broken pieces with love."

I don't respond, but I let myself sit with that scared little boy, and for the first time, it doesn't feel unbearable.

Yasmine's voice remains steady. "Now that we've connected with your breath and that little boy inside you," she says gently, "let's set our intention for this session to acknowledge your inner child."

My mind buzzes, but I focus on her words. Set an intention. I close my eyes, and that image of me as a kid flickers back—small, scared, alone.

She shifts slightly, and I hear the soft rustle of fabric as she demonstrates the first pose. "We're going to start with a gentle forward fold. Sit tall, knees apart. Let your hands rest on your feet. As you fold forward, think of it as an embrace for that little boy inside you."

I mimic her movements, leaning forward slowly. My hands clasp my feet, and the stretch is deep but…comforting. Her voice continues to guide me. "Think of that child, Alex. He's sitting in front of you. He's been waiting for you, hoping you'd show up. Wrap him in love. Let him know you're here now."

The image sharpens in my mind. Though I'm holding the pose, it feels like my arms are wrapping around him, protecting him. My throat tightens, but I stay quiet, breathing through the swirl of emotions.

"That little boy," Yasmine continues, "has been with you through everything. He stood by you when you felt lost. He carried you through your darkest moments. Love him, Alex. More than anything. Because he's your best friend, and he always has been."

The knot in my chest returns, but this time, it's not suffocating. It's heavy, but it's something I can hold. I inhale deeply, my breath trembling slightly as I let it out.

Yasmine must notice because her voice softens even more. "How does that feel?"

I sit up slowly, hands still resting on my feet. "Honestly?" My voice is lower than usual. "I feel…guilty. Like I should've done this sooner."

Her eyes are warm, unwavering. "Guilt is natural," she says gently. "But it's also something we can work with."

I exhale slowly. For the first time in years, I'm not running from the past. I'm sitting with it, breathing through it. And somehow, it feels okay.

CHAPTER 34

YASMINE

Alex's revelation drops into the room like a punch to the gut, knocking the air right out of it. I feel it reverberate in my chest. My mind stumbles over the image of him as a little boy—so young, so small—losing his mother in a split second of fate that didn't care he was just a kid. That kind of loss isn't just grief. It's a fracture that splinters through your life, sending tiny fault lines into everything you touch.

And yet, here he is. Strong, powerful, carrying himself like nothing has ever touched him. You'd never guess tragedy was woven into the seams of his life, stitched beneath all that confidence. People look at him and see perfection—sharp suits, sharp mind, sharp tongue. But now I know there's something raw and broken just beneath the surface, still bleeding in places he doesn't let anyone see.

That's the haunting thing about life. People walk around with whole worlds of hurt tucked behind their eyes, unspoken stories they never share. We hide our heartbreak in plain sight, cover it with smiles and small talk, pretending the ground beneath us isn't cracked.

Alex's story is one of survival. He's still standing, still moving forward, and it makes me want to hold space for him—not just with healing poses and deep breaths, but with something *real.* The kind of space that lets you finally set down the weight you've been carrying alone. A space that makes you feel seen. Understood. Less alone.

He breaks the silence first, his voice softer than I've ever heard it. "You told me once…that your mom passed away. That it's what led you to yoga." His tone is gentle but searching, like he's offering me a doorway into something raw.

I take a breath, surprised he remembers. The weight of it settles in my chest. I almost never talk about it. Like keeping it buried somehow keeps it from hurting. But right now, it feels right. Necessary, even. "Yeah. My mom," I say, my voice steady. "She had terminal liver cirrhosis. The doctors said it wasn't alcohol-related. She wasn't much of a drinker. It just…happened." The words hang between us. "Two months after we found out, she was gone."

Alex sits up slightly, his attention sharpening. He doesn't say anything, but his deep hazel eyes stay locked on mine.

"I was older than you were when you lost your mom," I continue, "it still changed everything though. It was the kind of loss that flips your whole world upside down. You start questioning everything—your purpose, your beliefs, who you are."

Alex listens, the tension lines on his face softening just a bit. I watch him unravel, if only slightly, like maybe my words are giving him a place to connect.

"My mom had a lot of pain in her life," I say, my voice dropping. "She carried guilt, anger, sadness…and I truly believe it contributed to her liver failure. Traditional Chinese medicine teaches that the liver is tied to these feelings. That idea stuck with me. It made me realize how our emotions can fester if you don't deal with them."

He nods, absorbing it, and I press on. "That's why I do what I do. I know what it feels like to hurt, to lose, to look for something—anything—that makes you feel whole again. Yoga became that for me, and I wanted to share it. Not just for the poses, but for the healing."

He doesn't speak right away, but his gaze lingers, heavy with something I can't quite name. Gratitude, maybe. Understanding. Finally, he nods, voice low and sincere. "Thank you for sharing that. I…I get it. More than I thought I would."

And in that moment, I know more than ever that healing isn't just something I guide others through. It's something we share—a mutual exchange of vulnerability and strength.

—

As the day winds down, I finally retreat to my room, feeling like I just survived an emotional marathon. Holding a private session as a healer isn't exactly light work. Everyone brings their own brand of baggage, and even though I know how to guard my energy, I still feel the weight of their traumas clinging to me like glitter—impossible to shake off.

I light a citrus-and-sage candle in the bathroom, the flame flickering like it's working overtime to clear the air. I step into the shower, and the hot water streams over me, washing away the tension knotted in my shoulders. I grab a handful of sea salt scrub, rubbing it across my skin in slow, deliberate strokes. As I scrub, I set an intention to release everything that isn't mine to carry. Each grain feels like it's scrubbing away layers of other people's heartbreak.

When I step out, my spirit feels lighter, my thoughts less tangled. I wrap myself in a towel, letting the cool breeze from the window ground me. My mind clears, my energy feels renewed, and I can almost convince myself I'm a well-adjusted adult. Almost. But then, as I sit on the edge of my bed, my thoughts drift back to Alex—not just our session earlier, but what he said. The image of him at that gala all those years ago, watching me with Liam, flashes in my mind. He thought I was dating someone behind his back. *Liam.* The guy who once ordered "organic sparkling water" on set and threw a fit when it wasn't fizzy enough. I almost laugh at the absurdity.

But regret creeps in, soft but persistent. What if I'd just told him the truth back then? Would we really be married with two-point-five kids by now? Maybe living in some overpriced house in the suburbs, hosting dinner parties with fancy charcuterie boards and rescuing hyperactive dogs? If I'd explained why I was there with Liam, cleared the air before Alex's imagination ran wild, would we have had a shot? Would I have stayed in LA, tried to make it work instead of burning it all down and starting fresh in Tulum?

I take a deep breath, centering myself before I can drown in what-ifs. Things work out the way they're meant to. That's what I've always believed. I wouldn't be here now, building this life I love, if it hadn't all gone down exactly as it did. And Alex wouldn't be here either, unpacking his own traumas and apparently his entire emotional attic.

But then, a thought flutters in, light and uninvited. If I really believe everything happens as it's meant to, then Alex being here now, at this exact retreat, right when I'm cohosting? I can't help but wonder if maybe—just maybe—the universe is setting up a plot twist I haven't seen coming.

CHAPTER 35

I step into the communal dining room where the staff glides around like wellness ninjas, setting up for dinner. The long live-edge wooden table is buzzing with chatter and laughter, like the emotional landslide Yasmine guided me through never happened. But somehow, I feel lighter too. It's weird—like unloading a truckload of baggage I didn't even know I was carrying.

A small smile tugs at my lips as I grab a seat. I remember when I used to think of Yasmine as some kind of angel sent from above, and after today, I'm pretty sure I was right. How else do you explain someone who can guide you through emotional hell without breaking you in half? It's like she's running a spiritual triage unit, and I'm the most complicated case she's got.

My gaze sweeps the table and when I spot her, my breath stumbles. She's near the head of the table, talking to Ethan and Sophia, her long dark hair falling in waves like it just air-dried into perfection. Of course, it did. Her hair probably wakes up flawless. I'm mesmerized by the way her lashes flutter when she talks, and those damn dimples I tried to forget about are back with a vengeance.

Is anyone else noticing this? Or is it just me? Because seriously, *damn.*

And her dress. Pale pink, loose, soft in all the right ways. I can't help but wonder what's underneath, and that thought's not exactly spiritual. Get it together, Alex. She's here to help you heal, not relive past mistakes. Still, when her gaze shifts to mine and she smiles, it's like she sucker-punched me with nostalgia. I nod back, attempting to play it cool, even though I feel like a toddler with a crush on his babysitter. God help me, this woman is going to be my undoing.

The chef rolls out plates for this carefully crafted Ayurvedic dinner, and everyone settles in. I silently curse my luck when Yasmine plops down between Sophia and Ethan.

Why is Ethan practically sitting in her lap? He's leaning in, laughing way too hard at whatever she's saying, and I can feel my jaw tighten like it's got something to prove. He needs to back off. What's worse is the sudden streak of jealousy clawing at my chest. Yasmine and I are…what? Nothing. We're nothing. So why do I want to punt Ethan out of his chair?

I reluctantly take the open seat next to Alaina, but my focus is shot. My gaze keeps wandering across the table, magnetically pulled back to Yasmine. It's not subtle either. I'm practically broadcasting my obsession in 4K. But then her eyes meet mine again, and for a second, the whole room blurs. It's quick, just a flicker, but it's enough. There's a softness in her gaze, and suddenly, I'm not so sure I imagined it. The connection we had—it's still there, lingering, waiting. I can work with that.

"Alex?" Alaina's voice slices through my thoughts, and I blink, realizing she's been talking to me. Her perfectly arched brow lifts in that judgmental way that says she knows I wasn't listening. "Did you hear me? I was saying I recently switched to this *life-changing* snail mucin serum. I'm thinking of adding it to my brand partnerships!"

I nod, forcing a smile. "Yeah, sounds good." She giggles like it's the funniest thing anyone's ever said, and I barely resist the urge to roll my eyes. I pretend to listen, but my mind keeps drifting back to Yasmine. She's not just beautiful—she's magnetic. And she's sitting across the table from me, out of reach but impossible to ignore.

Alaina keeps talking, but I'm checked out. My brain's running highlight reels of Yasmine—her smile, the way she crinkles her nose, the way her eyes light up when she's genuinely happy. She's captivating, she's infuriating, and she's here. Right here.

Dinner can't end fast enough. I'm out of my chair the second I finish, practically sprinting to my room before I do something stupid. A part of me itches to seek her out, but the louder, more rational voice reminds me that would be a *terrible* idea. I can't let my emotions complicate things—not here, not now. Once inside, I lean against the door, exhaling hard. My mind's a mess, tangled with thoughts of her. Even when I try to shove her out, she lingers like an echo I can't shake.

I rake my hands through my hair, frustrated with myself, but deep down, I know the truth. She's ingrained. And no amount of mindful breathing is going to change that.

—

Pablo's sitting cross-legged on this oversized cushion, his loose linen shirt making him look like he just floated down from a mountaintop to bless us mere mortals with his wisdom. He smiles warmly as I settle onto a cushion across from him. "It's been a while, hermano," he says, his voice soft and welcoming. "How have you been?"

"Busy," I reply, leaning back and trying to absorb whatever Zen magic is swirling around this place. "But I'm glad you invited me, Pablo. I needed this."

Pablo nods, his hands resting gently on his knees. "Tell me, what's been on your heart?"

I hesitate, my gaze drifting to the low table between us, where a candle flickers beside a pile of crystals. Of course, there are crystals.

"Honestly?" I pause, searching for the right words. "Work has been…consuming. It always is. But that's not new." I exhale, fingers tapping against my knee. "If this were my twenties, I'd probably be drowning it all out with overpriced vodka and bad decisions. But now?" I shake my head. "That escape doesn't work anymore."

Pablo's eyes soften. "Would you say that changed after…"

I cut him off before he can crack that door open. "No, this isn't about Catia." I'm not about to spiral down that rabbit hole. "Seeing you after the breakup made me realize it. I never loved her—not in the way she wanted." I shrug. "That breakup was a wake-up call, just not in the way people think."

Pablo nods, not pushing, just letting the silence stretch. "At the risk of going off-topic, I recall you mentioned knowing Yasmine from years ago. May I ask what your relationship was? Share only what you're comfortable with."

I run a hand through my hair. "We met in the most ridiculous, serendipitous way. Like the universe conspired to make it happen. I was hooked instantly. Who wouldn't be?" I smirk. "Things moved fast—maybe too fast. We fell hard. But before it had the chance to be anything real, I did what I do best and wrecked it."

Pablo just nods, unbothered by my self-sabotage.

"We went on one date," I continue. "But it wasn't just a date. It turned into an entire weekend. We talked about everything—no walls, no bullshit. I felt more connected to her in two days than I've ever felt with anyone else."

I pause, leaning back and staring up at the ceiling. "I felt empty long before Catia. Hell, we hadn't even slept together for three months by the time it ended. Imagine that—me, unable to get it up for the world's 'Top Supermodel of the Year.'" I scoff, shaking my head. "But Yasmine…the first time I saw her, it was like my brain just short-circuited. She's the most stunning woman I've ever laid eyes on, and it was like my body made a decision right then and there. My dick basically booked a one-way ticket to Yasmine, and there's been no coming back since."

Pablo's eyes glint knowingly, though his voice stays calm. "Do you feel comfortable continuing this journey with her as your yoga healer?"

"Yes," I say, not even a beat of hesitation.

He smiles. "Then trust the process, Alex. Trust yourself. And trust that the universe has a way of bringing people back into our lives for a reason."

His words hang in the air, landing heavier than I want to admit. He's right, of course, and the worst part? I think he knows it.

—

Later that evening, I head down to the beach, hoping a walk will clear my head. The sun dips low, casting the horizon in a wash of amber and violet. The beach feels almost enchanted, draped in silence except for the whispers of the waves.

The ocean's calm is the complete opposite of the chaos swirling in my head. This retreat has dredged up emotions I've had locked away like they were on a permanent time-out—especially when it comes to my mom. I don't think I ever really processed losing her. Can anyone really process that? Or do we just shove it into some dark corner of our minds and hope it stays there? But now I'm realizing that holding onto that pain is what kept me from moving forward. I'm basically hoarding grief like it's a collection.

I look out toward the water and spot someone standing at the edge, her silhouette wrapped in the soft glow of the fading light. Her green dress flutters in the breeze, blending into the landscape like she belongs there. Effortlessly magnetic. Of course, it's Yasmine. I swear, even the wind seems to be on her side. Her hair practically moves like it's in a shampoo commercial.

I approach quietly, not wanting to break whatever spell she's casting. "It's peaceful, isn't it?" I say softly.

She turns, her eyes meeting mine, and for a second, everything else fades away. Her expression softens, and she smiles—one of those secret smiles that feels like it's just for me. "It is," she says quietly. "I like meditating by the ocean sometimes. There's a kind of peace here that never leaves, even when we do."

I glance at the waves shimmering in the last light of the day. "Do you ever think about how small we are?" I ask, my voice dropping to a whisper.

Her smile widens, like she's genuinely excited to respond. "All the time," she replies. "And that's the beauty of it. Even in our smallness, we matter. We're connected to something bigger."

The waves keep rolling in, rhythmic and unbothered. The glow from the setting sun casts over her face, and I find myself staring, probably for too long. Her beauty isn't just surface-level; it's the kind that seeps into a room and changes the energy. Like she's carrying her own atmosphere.

I look down at the sand shifting beneath my feet. "Coming here has made me think about my mom a lot," I admit, the words tasting strange on my tongue. "I haven't talked about her to anyone in a long time."

Her eyes soften, and she turns fully toward me. She doesn't press, doesn't pry—just waits. Her presence feels like an invitation. I swallow hard, my gaze fixed on the horizon. "When she died, everything fell apart. It felt like chaos took over. My dad tried to be there for us, but he was drowning in his own grief." I trail off, the memories clawing their way up my throat.

Yasmine nods slowly, her expression gentle but unyielding. "That's a heavy burden for any child to carry," she says, her voice soft but firm.

I let out a breath, my voice raw. "I guess I never stopped carrying it. Even now, I can't let myself get close to people. Not really. It's easier to keep things surface-level, not to risk…losing them."

She's quiet for a moment before she speaks. "Grief can feel like…a weight you can't put down. But it's not something you have to fight. It's something you embrace."

I look at her, not quite understanding.

"It's not your enemy," she says softly, her eyes meeting mine with quiet intensity. "Grief is a part of you. It's proof that there was love, that there was a connection. It hurts because it mattered. And grief deserves its place in our human experience, just as much as love and happiness do."

Her words hang in the air.

"When you stop resisting it," she continues, "you start to see its beauty. It's not just pain. It's a reminder of what was good, of the memories that shaped you. And when you see it that way, it becomes lighter. You don't lose the love; you just learn to carry it differently."

I don't know what to say. Her words peel back layers I've kept buried, and I feel…bare. Exposed. "I never thought about it like that," I manage, my voice barely audible.

Yasmine gives me a tender smile, like she's just handed me the missing piece to a puzzle I didn't know I was solving. Her hand rests gently on my arm, and the spark that ignites shoots straight through me. Does she feel it too?

"It's okay to feel it, Alex," she says, her voice layered with something I can't quite name. I catch the double meaning, even if she doesn't.

"Let it all in. Grief, love, healing…It's all part of being human. And there's beauty in that, even when it hurts."

I nod, the tightness in my chest unraveling just a bit. For the first time in years, I feel something close to peace. Not quite there yet, but I can see it on the horizon.

—

It's the third day of the retreat, and I'm about to step into my first-ever Reiki session. I'm still not entirely convinced it's not just glorified hand-waving.

Emilio greets me with so much sereness that I half-expect doves to fly out from behind him. "Welcome, Alex," he says softly. "I understand this is your first experience with Reiki, but don't worry, I'll guide you every step of the way."

He gestures for me to lie down on the table, and I oblige, mentally preparing for him to whip out a dreamcatcher or start chanting in Sanskrit. Instead, he just smiles. "Reiki is a form of energy healing. It's not invasive, and it's not tied to any particular belief system. The idea is to clear and balance the energy in your body—to help you feel more aligned in mind, body, and spirit."

I glance up at him, eyebrow raised. "And how exactly do you do that?"

His smile widens. "Through touch—or sometimes just intention. I'll place my hands lightly over specific points on your body, and we let the energy flow. It's your body doing the work. I'm just the conduit."

I blink. "So, you're like…an energy electrician?"

Emilio laughs, the sound surprisingly genuine. "Something like that."

I exhale, more out of habit than calmness. "All right, hit me with your best shot."

Emilio nods and instructs me to close my eyes and focus on my breathing. I do, feeling weirdly self-conscious. His hands hover above my head, and I can't help but crack one eye open. He's not even touching me, but somehow, I swear I feel…something. I close my eyes again, forcing myself to focus. It's not uncomfortable—just odd. Part of me wants to roll my eyes and chalk it up to placebo, but there's another part that's a little too stunned to argue.

At some point, time fades away. It's just me and the energy radiating from Emilio. It feels like I'm floating, my body weightless on the table. Then, without warning, something shifts. I'm leaving myself, rising above, and suddenly, I'm somewhere else entirely.

I'm standing in a meadow, the air crisp and filled with the scent of wildflowers. Ahead of me is a figure I know instantly, even though I haven't seen her in over two decades. *Mom.* She looks just as she did in the last photo I have of her, her warm brown eyes full of love and her smile so radiant it could light up the darkest night.

"*Mom,*" I manage to say, my voice catching.

She steps closer, and though I know this isn't real, can't be real, it feels more vivid than any memory. She touches my face, her hands soft and warm. "Alex," she says, her voice filled with pride. "You've grown into such an incredible man."

I want to protest, to tell her she doesn't understand, that she doesn't know the mistakes I've made, but she silences me with a look. That same look, the one that used to calm me when I was little, the one that told me everything would be okay even when the world was falling apart.

"You carry so much grief, my sweet boy," she murmurs, her eyes full of love that I ache to touch. "But you don't have to. You never did. Don't you see? You were my joy, Alex. You gave me more love than I ever could have asked for. And that love was everything. It's the whole reason we're here. It's what makes life beautiful. It's what makes it matter."

Tears well up in my eyes as she continues. "Don't let fear hold you back. Love is worth the risk, even if it hurts sometimes. You deserve to feel the kind of happiness your father and I had. And you can."

Her words hit me harder than I expect, and I can't help but think of Yasmine—her wisdom, kindness, and beauty. It's as if my mom is echoing what Yasmine said about grief and love being intertwined.

"Don't be afraid anymore, my sweet boy," my mom says softly. "Live, Alex. *Really* live." Her hand reaches for mine, but she starts to fade just before our fingers meet. My chest tightens, and my throat burns. I try to hold on, freeze this moment, and memorize the warmth in her eyes before she disappears. But she's already gone.

And I'm left behind, drowning in an echo that lingers in the hollow space where she used to be. The meadow fades and I feel myself being gently pulled back into my body.

Emilio's calm and steady voice guides me back to the present. "How are you feeling?" he asks once I open my eyes.

I sit up slowly, disoriented and overwhelmed. "I… I had a vision," I say carefully. "I saw my mother."

Emilio nods knowingly, his expression calm but encouraging. "Would you like to share what you saw in your vision?"

I give him the shortest version I can manage, unsure of how much I want to share because my throat is tight. "She told me she's proud of me and that I need to stop holding on to the past. That I need to stop being afraid of love."

He smiles, as if he's already heard the words I've left unspoken. "That's an important realization, Alex," he says, his tone warm and grounding. "I have some homework for you." Emilio gently places his palm against my chest, right over my heart. "During our session, I sensed a blockage here, in your Heart chakra."

He pauses, his gaze steady. "The ocean has an incredible way of holding space for us, of helping us release what no longer serves us. Tomorrow morning, before the day begins, take a swim. Let the water embrace you, cleanse you. It's one of the most powerful and healing forces on earth."

I thank him and carry his words with me as I make my way back to my room. My thoughts swirl over my vision, my mom; and somehow, it all keeps circling back to Yasmine.

CHAPTER 36

YASMINE

A warm breeze drifts through the palm trees as I guide Ethan to the outdoor dining area. This should be a moment of calm reflection after a deep, meaningful session, but something about Ethan throws the balance off. He seemed "moved," though I suspect it's more of a calculated reaction than genuine emotion. He never fully lets go, like he's gathering data instead of seeking personal growth.

"That was incredible," he says, raking a hand through his meticulously styled hair. His tone is complimentary but I detect a sharp edge lurking beneath it like he's mentally ticking boxes for whatever corporate study he's conducting. "Honestly, I didn't expect it to be so… powerful. I always thought yoga was just some social media thing."

He offers a practiced grin but his gaze flickers around the resort with a telltale spark of ambition. It's as though he's already compiling notes for a future pitch, analyzing every detail for market value rather than spiritual enlightenment. Part of me wants to believe he could be sincere, but I can't ignore the gleam of ulterior motives shadowing his every word.

I laugh lightly. "A lot of people think that. But yoga has been around for thousands of years. It's not about trends, it's about connection—to yourself, your breath, and something bigger than you."

Ethan nods, but it seems he's not hearing my words; he's processing them in a different way, like he's looking at an equation that needs solving.

"That's exactly what makes this so interesting," he says, stepping just a little closer, his voice dropping into more deliberate. "You have something real here, Yasmine. And that's rare."

He smiles, his perfect white teeth flashing. "If you structure this right, your retreats can earn ten times what they are now. Easily."

I blink, taken aback. "Oh, I'm really happy with how things are going. I get to do what I love and people find their way to me when they need to."

"Sure," Ethan says, "but imagine how many more people you could help if you expanded. Franchised. Built out a network of retreats all over the world. You could be the face of modern wellness." He gestures, as if the future is already unfolding before him. "Think about it. Luxury retreats with your name on them, high-profile clientele, an entire movement centered around you. You'd be huge."

I hesitate, not because I don't believe in the power of what I do, but because I never felt motivated by money. "That's… a lot to consider," I say carefully.

He grins, sensing an opening. "I can help with that part. You shouldn't have to worry about logistics, investments, or numbers; that's where I come in. You focus on the spiritual stuff and I'll ensure it reaches its full potential."

His enthusiasm is persuasive and I believe he means it, but something in my gut tells me this isn't just about business.

"Well," I say, keeping my voice warm, "I've never really thought about turning this into something… bigger."

"That's the thing, Yasmine." He leans in slightly, "You don't have to. That's what I'm here for." His gaze assesses me, but not in the way my students look at me during a session. No, this is different, more possessive.

I shift my weight, keeping my smile easy. "It's kind of you to offer, Ethan. I really appreciate it."

"Just think about it," he says, flashing another smile, though something in his tone suggests he's already decided for me.

As we step into the dining area, I exhale, letting the conversation settle in my mind. Ethan is brilliant, successful, and undeniably charismatic. But something tells me that he doesn't let go easily when he sees an opportunity. And right now, for whatever reason, he sees one in me.

I glance around the table and my gaze instinctively halts when it meets Alex's. I swear he's looking at me like I hung the moon. Every time our eyes lock, the rest of the world seems to fade into some blurry, irrelevant backdrop. It's unnerving in the most infuriatingly magnetic way.

We haven't spoken since yesterday, when he caught me off guard at the beach. I'd managed to keep my composure then, but now I can't help but wonder how his session went today. Has he unraveled some hidden truth about himself? And, more importantly, why do I even care this much?

As these thoughts swirl, I try to convince myself this is just part of my job. Being attentive, caring, and invested is how I treat all my clients, right? There's nothing special about Alex. I'm just dedicated to their journeys. That's all.

But another thought sneaks in, uninvited. *Am I just lying to myself?*

I glance at him again, quickly, like I'm trying not to get caught. He's listening to Sophia from across the table but doesn't seem remotely interested in what she's saying. His body language looks like he's deep in thought. About what? Or maybe… about *who?*

Great. Now I'm reading his microexpressions like I'm some emotional detective. I take another spoonful of soup and tell myself to focus on *anything* else. But I can't. Maybe I'm not as unaffected by Alex as I pretend to be. And that thought? It's as annoying as it is… exciting.

CHAPTER 37

ALEX

I'm walking to the ocean this morning, just like Emilio told me yesterday. The guy was so serene about it, like wading into salt water would magically fix my entire life.

I barely slept last night. Seeing Yasmine at dinner was like being hit by a rogue wave. I'm trying to keep it together, trying not to overthink, but she stirs *something* in me. Something big. Something I can't ignore, no matter how hard I try. She makes me feel… alive. Lighter, somehow. Our next session is tomorrow and the thought of seeing her again is enough to make my stomach do flips like some overgrown puppy in love.

After I royally screwed up and ghosted her all those years ago, she probably thinks I'm the textbook LA-walking-redflag she needs to dodge at all costs. And honestly? She wouldn't be wrong. I've done nothing to prove otherwise.

But Yasmine isn't the kind of person to hold grudges. She's not like anyone else I've met. There's not a mean or judgmental bone in her body, which, frankly, only makes me feel worse. I don't deserve her kindness or her patience.

I step into the ocean and the water is warm. The morning is quiet, with only a few early risers dotting the beach. I can see why Yasmine loves this place. It's peaceful and calming—or at least, it should be.

Focus, Alex. This is about healing. Not her. *You.*

I wince as something sharp jabs the sole of my foot. A seashell? A piece of coral? Who knows. I shuffle forward, only to feel something slimy and slithery wrap around my toes. Seaweed? Plastic trash? Fantastic.

The sun's already heating my shoulders, and I'm starting to regret this whole cleansing ritual. Emilio made it sound so profound, but right now, I just feel… annoyed.

"Yeah, real transformative," I mutter under my breath, glaring down at the water as if it personally betrayed me..

As I wade a little deeper, I can't help but let my mind drift back to Yasmine again—her laugh and how she looks at the world like it's full of endless possibilities. I shake my head, trying to banish the thought. This is about me. My journey. My redemption arc or whatever. But deep down, I know the truth. No amount of salt water will wash her out of my mind.

I groan, throwing my hands up in defeat. So much for the mystical, soul-cleansing powers of the ocean. Apparently, all it's cleansed me of is my patience and the skin on my foot. I trudge back to shore, the squelch of seaweed and sand between my toes adding insult to injury. Saltwater drips off me like a sad, soggy caricature of enlightenment as I head straight to my room.

After a quick rinse to banish the lingering smell of brine and defeat, I towel off and start getting dressed for my sound bath session with Gabriela.

And of course, my mind drifts back to Yasmine, again. The way her eyes sparkled across the dinner table last night like she was lit from within. For one ridiculous, earth-shattering moment, she made me feel like the only man in the world.

I pause, staring at my reflection. This is… new. *Borderline obsession*, if I'm being honest. And I'm not a guy who obsesses. Ever.

Her face flashes in my mind again, like some enchanting screensaver, and I can't help but smile. My reflection smirks back like it knows exactly how screwed I am. Great. Now even my mirror is in on it.

I approach Gabriela's setup back on the beach. A soft mat rests on the sand, surrounded by an intricate arrangement of crystals that glint in the sunlight. Each one, I'm sure, has a purpose I don't understand.

"Good morning, Alex," she greets me warmly. "How are you feeling today?"

I shrug, offering a small smile. "I took Emilio's advice and went swimming in the ocean earlier. It was refreshing, but… a bit rocky."

Gabriela chuckles knowingly, gesturing for me to sit on the mat. "Ah, the rocks. A reminder that even in beauty, we must tread carefully. But it's good that you went in. Small steps toward connecting with this place."

As I settle onto the mat, she kneels beside me and picks up a vibrant pink rock. "These crystals hold a special place in our healing journeys. This one, the rose quartz, represents love, not just romantic love but self-love and compassion for others. It represents opening up your heart." She places it gently back down and then picks up a smoky-looking rock. "This one is for grief, grounding, and release. It represents letting go; letting go of the pain you carry." Finally, she holds a sparkling yellow crystal. "And this," she smiles, "Yellow citrine is for gratitude and abundance. Today, we'll focus on the beauty and blessings in your life, even the ones you may overlook."

I'm not sure how much stock I put in the power of these stones, but I'm intrigued all the same. Gabriela's voice carries a calm conviction that's hard to ignore. "You're in one of the world's most mystical and healing places, Alex. The Riviera Maya has a vibration unlike anywhere else. The ancient Mayans believed this land was sacred and that a higher power blessed its waters and earth. Before entering the ocean, they would offer gratitude."

Her words sink like a tide pulling at the shore. "That's… interesting. I didn't know that."

She gestures to the horizon. "Look around you, Alex. Embrace your fortunes; to be here, on this stunning beach, with the privilege of dipping into one of the most beautiful, healing waters on earth."

I glance at the shimmering waves and the turquoise sky above. Suddenly, everything feels different, like someone turned up the brightness of the world.

And yeah, I feel ashamed for how I grumbled through the morning, too distracted by my thoughts to appreciate what was right in front of me. Gabriela's right, this place *is* special. And maybe there's something to say about stepping into it with more gratitude.

"Lie back," she instructs me gently. I stretch out on the mat and she begins to play a series of crystal bowls, the resonant tones filling the air like an otherworldly symphony. It's surprisingly nice.

"Close your eyes," she continues, her voice like honey dripping into the quiet. "Take a deep breath. Feel the sand beneath you. Let the sound wash over you, let the waves carry your tension away."

I try—I really do. I focus on the vibrations and slowly, her words start to pull me into a state of relaxation.

"Think of one thing you're grateful for," she says. "It can be as small as the sunlight on your face or as big as the people who bring meaning to your life. Hold it in your mind and let gratitude fill your chest."

Predictably, my brain resists. Gratitude? Sure, let me just flip that switch. But then, like some traitorous slideshow, Yasmine flashes through my thoughts—the way she makes me feel like I'm uncovering some hidden part of myself I didn't even know existed.

My chest tightens, not in a bad way, though. It's… unfamiliar, almost like stretching a muscle I haven't used in years.

As the sound waves ripple through me, I start to understand. Maybe gratitude isn't about the things you have or the stuff you've checked off some list. Maybe it's about letting yourself feel the messy, complicated, beautiful truth of it all.

CHAPTER 38

YASMINE

It's the fifth day of the retreat, and to say I'm overwhelmed would be putting it mildly. Not by the work itself; I love what I do, but by the sheer weight of the traumas that everyone is unpacking. It's like being surrounded by emotional suitcases, and they just keep getting heavier.

Honestly, I'm counting down the minutes until the weekend. No more shadow work or deep dives into inner pain? *Yes, please.* And, okay, I'll admit it, I'm also kind of looking forward to spending more time with Alex. Not that I'd say it out loud. But let's face it, the guy has a gravitational pull.

I'm in Pablo's yoga pavilion, setting up for today's session, when Alex walks in. My breath catches and I swear his does too. Is this tension just in my head? Because it feels thick enough to cut with a butter knife. My pulse didn't get the memo that I'm supposed to be the calm, grounded yoga instructor.

I want to ask him a million things. *How are you finding the retreat? Did you sleep well? Do you feel like a new man yet?* But I reel myself in and settle for the simplest question. "How are you doing, Alex?"

He flashes a smile that's both sincere and devastatingly charming. "I'm doing great now that I see you."

And just like that, my composure goes flying out the window. I can feel the blush creeping up my cheeks. Of course, Alex notices because his smile grows even wider. There's something in his expression that makes it hard to feel embarrassed. It's like he doesn't just see the blush; he finds it endearing.

I take a deep breath and remind myself to stay professional, but if he keeps this up, I might need a yoga session for myself after this.

"Today, we're going to do a meditative yoga practice," I say, calm but purposeful as I look at Alex. He's already sitting on his mat, giving me his full attention.

"We will connect your breath and movement to release stuck emotions," I explain, gesturing gently. "There's actually some fascinating science behind it. This practice activates your parasympathetic nervous system—basically your body's 'rest and digest' mode, and reduces stress to create space for healing."

Alex tilts his head, a sly smile playing on his lips. "I've never done anything like this before, but if anyone's going to bend me into emotional and physical shape, I'm glad it's you."

Oh, he's good. I pretend not to notice the playful glint in his eyes as I focus on my props. "You might hate me halfway through, but you'll thank me later." I say, keeping my tone light.

I've curated this flow specifically for him. Every movement and every breathwork exercise is designed to address grief, healing, and gratitude.

"Let's begin by opening up your heart chakra," I say softly. His movements are tentative at first, as if he's not entirely sure he's doing it right. "It's about letting go of the weight you've been carrying, the grief, the pain, and creating space for joy, for lightness. With every inhale, welcome in that possibility. And with every exhale, let go of what no longer serves you."

His chest rises and falls in time with my words. His expression shifts to something almost vulnerable, like he's standing at the edge of an uncomfortable truth he can't turn away from.

The air feels charged, as if the room itself is holding its breath. There's a gravity to it that I wasn't expecting. The tension he wears like armor slowly melts away. He's really giving this his all, and I realize just how much he's ready, maybe even desperate, to heal.

Seeing it stirs something in me. A quiet awe at the courage it takes to face yourself. For all his charm and confidence, this is the real Alex—vulnerable, searching, and human. He's letting the cracks show and it's beautiful.

"Now, we'll move into a twist," I say, demonstrating the movement with care. "Like wringing out a sponge, physically and emotionally, this will help release what no longer serves you." My voice softens, inviting him to trust the process.

Alex watches me momentarily, his brow furrowed in concentration as he mirrors my posture. At first, there's resistance—his shoulders tight, his form a little hesitant, but as he breathes through it, I notice a shift. His body surrenders and the tension that clung to him unravels.

The air in the room changes with him as if the weight he's been carrying is no longer pressing down so heavily. "This feels…" Alex pauses, his voice low but steady, like he's searching for the right words. "It feels like I've been holding on to something I didn't even realize was there. And now, it's like I can finally let go." His breathing has deepened, as though with every exhale, he's shedding layers of invisible weight.

"That's exactly it," I say reassuringly. "Sometimes we hold on without realizing it. But the body remembers. It always remembers."

He nods, his gaze distant but focused inward like he's sifting through pieces of himself. "I didn't think something so simple could feel this powerful," he admits, his voice softer now, edged with wonder.

By the time we finish, he's lying in *Savasana*, completely still, and for a moment, I can see it—the vulnerability, the courage it takes to be here, to face whatever he's been running from.

I give him a few moments of silence before I speak. "Take your time coming back. Notice how you feel. Let yourself sit with it, whatever's changed, even if it's subtle."

When he finally sits up, there's a quiet sense of calm that wasn't there before. He looks at me and there's something in his eyes. Gratitude, yes, but also something deeper, something unspoken.

"Yasmine," he says, his voice filled with a sincerity that makes my heart stumble. "I think I get it now. I think… I'm actually healing."

The way he says it, the way his gaze lingers on mine, makes the air between us feel electric. I should say something grounding and professional, but the intensity in his expression holds me captive.

"You've done the work, Alex," I manage, despite the flutter in my chest. "I'm just here to guide you."

He grins and there's something undeniably flirty in his smile. "No, Yasmine. It's more than that. You didn't just guide me, you created this space and made me feel safe enough to let go. I don't think anyone else could've done that."

His words hit me like a wave and I can't tell if it's the energy of the session or just him. I return his smile, feeling something shift within myself, too. This moment is his, but somehow, it's mine as well.

There's a beat of silence. Alex shifts his weight slightly, his gaze locking on mine with an intensity that makes my stomach do a little flip. "I was wondering," he starts, his tone casual but laced with something deeper, "after dinner tonight… do you have time… to hang out for a bit?"

There's an edge to the question that sends my pulse racing. I hesitate, caught between the part of me that wants to keep things professional and the part that… well, doesn't. After a moment, I respond, "I can make some time."

I swear the temperature in the pavilion rises by a few degrees. "Great," he says, his voice low. "I'll see you later."

I start clearing the room after he leaves, but my mind is nowhere near my task. Our conversation replays in my head, every word, every glance. It feels as if we're standing on the edge of something neither of us fully understands yet. And I let myself wonder where this might lead.

—

By the time I retreat to my room, a bubbling excitement stirs within my calm exterior. I draw a bath, letting the warm water embrace me like an old friend. I reach for my favorite sea salt scrub—there's something therapeutic about the act, the way the roughness of the salt transforms into softness, like polishing away the weight of the day.

When I step out of the tub, every inch of me is alive with an electric anticipation. I catch a glimpse of my reflection in the mirror. My long, dark waves tumble down my back, still damp and curling softly, framing the sharp green of my eyes. My lips curve, a hint of color against the golden flush of my skin.

On the chair nearby, my short taupe dress hangs in a casual drape, its simplicity almost deceptive. Tonight, it feels like more than just an outfit; it's an intention. Maybe even temptation. I slip it on and take a moment to smooth it against my curves. When my gaze returns to the mirror, my reflection answers with a knowing smile. Something about tonight feels like it's going to be the start of something I can't quite name. When was the last time I felt this kind of excitement? This flutter of nerves? There's no denying it, the pull I feel towards Alex is more than attraction. It's an ache, a curiosity, a fire. Yes, he's breathtakingly handsome, let's not pretend I don't have eyes. But that's not what's making my heart race. It's watching him lean into his vulnerability, choosing to face the messy, uncomfortable truths of his grief and healing. In a world where so many people run from their emotions, Alex walks straight toward his. And that? That's the kind of bravery that's impossibly, undeniably sexy. And then there's the way he confides in me, like he trusts me to hold the parts of himself he's still figuring out. It feels intimate and sacred. He's offering me a glimpse into something no one else sees.

I glance down and notice my hands trembling. Not from fear, this is something else entirely. Thrill. A glowing gratitude that I get to be here with him, walking alongside him on this path.

It's been years since I've allowed myself to feel this way about anyone, to let this kind of warmth creep into my guarded heart. And you know what? It feels… good. Really, really good.

As I make my way toward the dining room, I feel ready. Whatever tonight holds, I'm open to it.

—

Everything about the moment feels golden. The light, the laughter, even the faint hum of the waves in the distance. If this were a movie, I'd be rolling my eyes at how over-the-top dreamy it all is.

Sophia grins at me, her tone teasing as she leans closer. "So, Yasmine, I heard Ethan gushing about you earlier."

I arch an eyebrow, already suspicious. "Oh? That's… concerning," I reply half-jokingly.

She laughs. "No, seriously! He's been raving about the retreat. Apparently, he's so blown away that he's considering opening some wellness center in Portugal. And get this, he mentioned you as someone he'd want to partner with!"

I blink, caught completely off guard. "Portugal? Ethan? Me?" I laugh, shaking my head. "This sounds like the setup for one of those reality shows where everything goes horribly wrong."

Gabriela's eyes widen, her excitement palpable. "Would you actually consider moving there? I mean, it's Europe! Think of the cuisine, the aperitivo…"

"Tempting," I say, wrapping my head around the idea. "But can you picture me running a retreat in Portugal? I'd be the only one teaching yoga while stuffing my face with pastel de nata."

Sophia snorts. "That's called balance."

I laugh. "Honestly, I've never really thought about it. Suppose the opportunity felt right and came with a strong enough call, then maybe. But it's a big maybe."

Gabriela practically vibrates with enthusiasm. "Yasmine, this is huge! You should absolutely consider it. You've already built something incredible here. Who says you can't create something even bigger somewhere else?"

I smile at her but my mind is spinning inside. Portugal. A new life. Ethan's mystery proposal. It's overwhelming, exciting, and completely absurd. But then again, isn't that how some of the best stories start?

Before I can respond, a deep voice cuts through our conversation. "Ladies."

I look up, and there he is. Alex, standing by the table, his gaze locked on me like I'm the only person here. "Yasmine," he says, "you look beautiful tonight."

My pulse quickens despite myself, and I'm hyper-aware of how Sophia and Gabriela exchange quick, knowing glances. Traitors.

I muster a smile, trying to keep things casual. "Thanks, Alex. You clean up pretty well yourself."

He smirks as if he knows he's gotten to me. He pulls out a chair and settles in at the table. The chef arrives with the first course, but it's hard to focus on anything other than the occasional glances Alex throws me.

The conversation flows around me like background noise. Every time I feel his gaze, I find myself pausing. When our eyes finally meet again, it's like time slows down. There's something disarming about how he looks at me, like he's taking me in piece by piece.

Before I can even unpack the charged air between us, Alaina's bright voice cuts through the moment like a splash of cold water. She's seated next to Alex, her hand casually resting on his arm. "You've been hiding these muscles, Alex," she teases, her fingers brushing his sleeve. "What's your gym routine? Because clearly, it's working."

Her laugh rings out, the kind that says *look at me, only me*. Alex chuckles, polite but unaffected, the glint in his eye suggests he's aware of the game she's playing.

I focus intently on my plate, trying to tune them out, but the sight of them together needles at me. The way she's drawing out his easy charm stirs something in me. A longing, maybe, or the ache of wishing *I* was the one pulling those smiles from him.

I take a steadying breath, grounding myself in the mantra I've come to rely on: *What's meant to be will be*. If there's something real here, something worth exploring, it'll grow in its own time.

CHAPTER 39

ALEX

Dinner finally winds down. It's not that the meal wasn't great—everything was perfect. I just spent most of it half-distracted, stuck in small talk with Alaina when all I really wanted was to be near Yasmine.

I scan the table and catch sight of her quietly walking away. I rise, trying not to look too eager. Alaina says something but I don't hear it. I politely excuse myself before rushing off. I'm not trying to be rude—I just need to know where Yasmine's going. I want to talk to her. Be with her. Without anyone else in the way.

I catch up with her and my heart races a little faster. "Hi," I manage to say, which is honestly a miracle, considering just being near her scrambles my brain like eggs on a hot skillet.

"Hi," she breathes back, her voice soft and light, but there's a slight hesitation in it. She seems just as unsure of what to say as I am, which is oddly comforting. "How was the rest of your day?"

I can't help but smile. Yasmine's sweetness is effortless, like everything she does comes from a place that's honest and unfiltered. It catches me off guard every time—in the best way.

"It was fine," I respond, "But it's better now that I'm with you."

Her eyes flick up to mine, and for a split second, there's something there that makes my chest tighten. Is that desire? My heart stumbles over itself, and just as I'm trying to figure out if I imagined it, she grabs my hand.

"Come with me," she says, like she's made up her mind and expects me to follow.

Her hand is small in mine and the moment we touch, it's like a jolt of electricity shoots through me.

"Where are we going?" I ask, letting a playful smirk tug at my lips.

"It's a surprise," she says with a mischievous spark in her mesmerizing green eyes.

I let her lead me. The retreat center fades behind us as we walk, and the sounds of the night grow clearer.

"You're not planning to kidnap me, are you?" I tease. My tone is light, but there's an edge of humor in it, to cover up how intensely I'm feeling.

She laughs, like a melody I'd happily get stuck in my head. "If I were, you wouldn't even know until it was too late," she quips, glancing back at me with a grin.

Her hand tightens slightly around mine, and I feel an overwhelming sense of comfort. I look up to find us standing before a small oceanside cave, its entrance barely visible in the moonlight. As we approach, the low light spills in, casting a soft, ethereal glow.

"Sometimes I come here to meditate," Yasmine says almost reverently. I don't respond, because honestly, I'm so lost in her eyes that I completely forget to speak. She misreads my silence, glancing away with a hint of uncertainty. "If it's not your thing, we can totally go somewhere else—"

"No," I cut her off a little too quickly. "This place is beautiful. Like you." The words spill out before I can stop them. Normally, I'm smooth; hell, AJ and Mark practically crown me the king of rizz. But with Yasmine? She messes with my head in ways I didn't even know were possible. Am I actually *nervous?*

Even under the faint glow of the moonlight, I can see the blush creeping into her cheeks. It's the most endearing thing I've ever seen, and before I can think better of it, I lift her chin gently with my finger.

"Thank you for bringing me here and sharing this place with me," I say, my voice quieter now, matching the intimacy of the moment. "I can tell it's special."

It feels like the entire world has gone silent for a moment except for us. Her eyes pull me in deeper than I thought possible.

"You've done such an amazing job in this retreat so far, Alex," she says, her voice laced with sincerity. "You've come such a long way. And… I'm so proud of you."

Her words hit me like a tidal wave. Hearing her say she's proud of me makes me feel massive, like I could take on anything in the world.

And suddenly, I see her quiet strength, her kindness, the way she seems to carry this light wherever she goes. It's not just her beauty, though—let's be honest—she's the most stunning woman I've ever seen. It's something deeper. Or maybe it's everything all at once.

All I know is that standing here with her, I feel like I'm exactly where I'm supposed to be.

CHAPTER 40

"That means so much to me..." Alex says, like he's letting himself truly feel the weight of the moment.

Something stirs inside me—a need to comfort him. Before I realize what I'm doing, I tell him something I've never told anyone.

"You know," I begin, my voice quieter now, "when my mom died, I felt completely lost. Like the world had cheated me somehow; she was such a light, you know? One of those people who makes you believe in the goodness of the world, and then... life dimmed her. Life just... took her."

Alex watches me intently. "I was stuck in that same darkness for a long time," I say gently. "What pulled me out wasn't just time. It was finding people who were committed to healing others. Spiritually. Emotionally."

My voice softens even more. "And honestly, Alex... I've always felt this strange connection to you. Even back then—before you told me about your mom—it was like we shared a kind of knowing." I let out a quiet breath. "And now it makes sense."

The silence between us stretches but it doesn't feel awkward.

Alex's eyes hold so much adoration, pain, and maybe even gratitude, but I can't quite piece together what's going through that fascinating mind of his. Then he speaks, and his words hit me like lightning. "You know, the day we first met, I was convinced you were a literal angel sent from God to pull me out of whatever hole I was in. And you did." His voice cracks just slightly, the emotion spilling through. "And I'm so fucking sorry I blew it."

The sincerity in his voice is so raw, so unguarded, that I can't help but believe every word. "You didn't, Alex," I say softly, smiling at him. "Everything is exactly as it's meant to be."

For a moment, neither of us speaks. The world around us feels distant and blurred, like we're the only ones standing in this strange, uncharted territory of vulnerability.

The need to comfort him overwhelms me, pulling me forward before my mind can catch up. My hand finds his jaw, my fingers brushing against the slight stubble, and I tilt his face toward mine. When our eyes meet, I'm caught in the depth of his gaze. Those gorgeous hazel eyes seem to hold so much pain, hope, and something that feels dangerously close to longing.

Alex leans into my touch, his eyes closing briefly like he's grounding himself in the reality of this moment. His lips part slightly and I realize we're both breathing harder now. His hand lands on my waist, firm but hesitant, as if testing whether I'll pull away. I don't. Instead, I feel a jolt of electricity rush through my body, lighting up every nerve ending. He must feel it, too, because his grip tightens, anchoring me closer as though he's afraid I'll disappear. Then his eyes open, locking onto mine with an intensity that makes my heart stutter. It's too much. Too raw. Too… unprofessional. What am I thinking? This is *his* retreat and journey, and I almost risked derailing it.

Alex's expression falters as if he can sense the turmoil written all over my face. I fumble for my words, trying to explain the mess swirling inside me. "I'm sorry… I…"

He cuts me off, his voice low and rough, almost like a growl.

"I'm not."

That stops me in my tracks.

"Fuck, Yasmine—" He rakes a hand through his hair, and I swear the sheer sexiness of that move makes my knees weak. It's distracting. I want to be the one to mess up his hair, to make him look this undone. "No one's ever gotten under my skin like this." His voice sends a shiver down my spine. There's so much emotion there, so much vulnerability that it takes all my strength not to close the distance between us again. But I can't. I won't. "Alex," I say softly, my heart breaking with each word, "you're going through so much right now. You're sorting through all of this pain, this grief, and I don't want to be the reason you lose focus. We're not thinking clearly."

He steps back, and the absence of his hand on my waist is immediate, like someone snatched away a blanket on a cold night. The air between us feels colder now. He nods, staring at the sand, his hands sinking into his pockets as if trying to hold himself together.

"Right, yeah." He says quietly. He clears his throat but it doesn't quite mask his disappointment. He doesn't meet my eyes and that sliver of distance feels like a chasm. I hold out my hand, hoping he'll take it and see this isn't rejection; it's me trying to protect him and do what's right. He hesitates, but then his hand slips into mine, and the small connection is all I need.

CHAPTER 41

ALEX

I've knocked out the first week of this retreat already, which, to be honest, feels like a miracle. Surprisingly, it hasn't been so bad. Somehow, I actually feel like I've grown. A lot. Like real emotional growth. And the craziest part? I haven't even felt the need to check on work. *Me.* The guy who once took a Zoom call during a heli-skiing trip. If that's not character development, I don't know what is.

It's Saturday, which means group bonding activities are on the agenda. I'm not sure what surprises Pablo has in store for us, but leave it to him to know what we need, even before we do.

Honestly, I couldn't care less about what we're doing. None of it matters. What does matter, *who* matters, is Yasmine. Just the thought of seeing her again makes my chest feel electric. That moment yesterday was a shift in the axis of my universe. It unraveled me in ways I didn't know were possible, like she found all the carefully sealed cracks in my armor and slipped right in. And the way it felt so easy to get lost in her, to let everything else—time, place, and reason, fade into nothing… that scares the hell out of me. Yet I can't stop wanting more. But here's the thing: I've built my entire life on control. I don't fall and I don't trust. I don't do *feelings* I can't manipulate, package, and file away for later. But with Yasmine? She's breaking every rule I've ever written for myself and I don't even think she knows she's doing it. Slowly, steadily, she's slipping under my skin, and I'm not sure whether I should fight it or let myself drown.

All I know is that she's changing me, piece by piece. And I don't know if I've ever been more terrified or alive.

CHAPTER 42

YASMINE

Everyone is gathered in the courtyard. The early sun paints the ground with a warm, golden glow, and everything feels calm, as if the universe itself is smiling down on us. Pablo stands at the center, his hands folded, radiating his usual serene yet mystical energy. Honestly, the man could announce a tax audit and still make it sound like an invitation to enlightenment.

"My friends," he begins, his voice calm but carrying just enough drama to hook us. "Words cannot describe how proud I am of all of you." His gaze sweeps over us like we're his kids at graduation, and he pauses for effect. Classic Pablo. "In just five short days, I've seen incredible transformation. Whether it's learning to let go of fear and guilt…" His eyes land on Alaina, who looks like she might cry. "…rediscovering yourself after separation," a kind smile toward Ethan, "or standing proud in your identity," a nod to Sophia, who beams. Then, he turns to Alex, and I swear, the air feels different. "Or opening your heart to the love you deserve."

Alex shifts ever so slightly, like the spotlight is uncomfortable for him, and my heart does this annoying little flutter thing. *Ugh.*

Pablo clasps his hands together. "Now, for the next phase of our retreat, each of you will embark on a spiritual journey paired with one of our healers. These experiences have been carefully chosen to align with your paths and individual healing needs."

His gaze sweeps over the group like he's the host of a reality show about to reveal who's getting sent home. "Emilio and

Sophia, you'll head to Bacalar. Sophia, I strongly believe the lagoon's beauty will help you embrace transformation and renewal. Gabriela and Alaina, you will visit the mountains of Michoacán, where millions of Monarch butterflies will take flight—a reminder of rebirth. Ethan and I will explore Chichen Itza to connect with the ancient energies of the Maya civilization."

My heart is pounding by this point. He hasn't called my name yet, but I'm already bracing for impact.

"And finally…" Pablo's eyes land on me, and he smiles like he knows something I don't. "Yasmine, you'll be traveling to Holbox. And you'll be joined by Alex." He turns to Alex. "The island's peaceful aura is the perfect place to open your heart and embrace love without fear."

I blink. Holbox. With Alex. The words tumble around in my brain, and for a moment, I can only focus on how Alex's gaze settles on me. I try to play it cool, but my pulse is causing an embarrassing samba in my chest. There's something about this, about *him*, that feels like stepping onto a path I didn't even realize I wanted to take. And as much as I want to pretend this is just another part of the retreat, I can't shake the thought running through my head. If I'm going to explore a tiny island off the coast of Mexico, there's no one else I'd rather do it with.

—

The journey to the ferry station has been a blur of sunshine and laughter. From the moment we left Pablo's retreat center, Alex has been in rare form—quick with his dry wit and even quicker to toss those boyish smiles that I swear could disarm just about anyone.

We wind through sleepy towns and open stretches of road. The salty breeze whips through my hair while Alex pretends not to care that his perfectly messy look is getting even messier. At one point, I catch him singing under his breath to the local music station. When I laugh and call him out, he just smirks, unfazed. "I'm a man of many talents, Yasmine. Singing just isn't one of them. Consider yourself lucky you only got a preview."

I chuckle, leaning back into my seat. "I don't know, I think I'm ready for the full show."

He glances at me, eyes sparkling. "Maybe one day."

By the time we pull up to the ferry station, I'm grinning so much it actually hurts a little. Alex grabs both of our bags before I can even reach for mine. At first, I think it's just him being polite, but his subtle glances toward the ferry crew, who've been slightly too apparent with their lingering stares in my direction, tells a different story. I bite back a grin, pretending not to notice the possessiveness in his gesture.

The sun is high in the sky, bouncing off the turquoise water like diamonds scattered across the surface. It's almost blinding but so breathtaking I can't bring myself to look away. Alex stands beside me, gazing at the horizon with this quiet focus. For a second, I wonder if he's lost in some deep, philosophical thought.

Then he leans toward me, "Hey," he whispers, nodding subtly toward one of the ferry conductors. "Do you think his hat's big enough, or do you think he's compensating for something?"

I glance over, and sure enough, one of the ferry conductors is wearing a straw hat so comically oversized it looks like it was stolen from a giant scarecrow convention. The hat dips down over his ears, almost completely eclipsing his face. To make matters worse, he's paired it with neon green Crocs and a Hawaiian shirt so loud it's practically audible. I bite down on a laugh, leaning into Alex as I whisper back, "I think he's trying to send a signal to passing satellites."

Alex's shoulders shake with laughter. "Or maybe it's his version of SPF 100. No sunburn, no problem."

I can't help but dissolve into giggles, doubling over as the sound bursts out of me. "You're awful," I say, shaking my head, though I'm grinning too hard to mean it.

"Awful but accurate," he counters with a smug look.

The conductor, blissfully unaware of our antics, saunters past us, the brim of his hat flapping in the breeze like a kite barely tethered to his head. Alex leans in again. "If that thing flies off, I'm not chasing it."

"I don't think you'd have to," I whisper back. "It'd probably sail itself to Holbox." We both dissolve into laughter again. With Alex, even the ridiculous moments, *especially* the ridiculous moments, become something unforgettable. This trip is already shaping up to be one of those memories I know I'll treasure forever.

The ride isn't long, maybe thirty minutes, but it's filled with so much laughter and sweet little moments. When we dock, Holbox greets us with such tranquil charm. There are no cars, just golf carts and bikes, and life on the island moves at its own dreamy pace.

"Okay, this might actually be paradise," I say, my voice tinged with awe.

"Don't tell Pablo," Alex jokes. "He'll take credit for the whole vibe."

I laugh as we walk barefoot along a sandy path, the sun warm on our shoulders and the breeze keeping the heat at bay. "I feel like we've stepped into another world," I say, looking around at the pastel-painted buildings and palm trees swaying lazily.

Alex glances at me, his expression softer now. "Yeah," he says quietly, his thumb brushing against my hand. "But honestly? You're kind of stealing the show."

I roll my eyes, but my cheeks flush anyway. "You're such a flirt."

"Can you blame me?" He shoots back, flashing that handsome grin of his. And just like that, I'm reminded how dangerous it is, how dangerously *good* it is, to be in his presence. Because while this island feels like paradise, being with Alex is starting to feel like something even better.

CHAPTER 43

ALEX

One thing I've learned about Yasmine on this trip is that she should never, under any circumstances, be trusted with directions. We've gotten lost three times already, and usually, I'd be fuming by the second wrong turn. But with her? It's impossible to be annoyed. Every detour turns into an adventure. We've laughed so hard that my stomach is genuinely sore, and I'm starting to think I should count this as an ab workout. I can't remember the last time I'd had this much fun with someone. Maybe I never have. Everything Yasmine does, no matter how chaotic, is… alluring. It's unfair, really.

When we *finally* reach our bed and breakfast, Yasmine throws her hands up in the air like she's just conquered Everest. "We made it! See? I told you we'd find it," she says, panting as if our accidental half-marathon through the streets was intentional.

I chuckle. "Sure, if by 'find it,' you mean stumble onto it by sheer luck." She swats my arm, but she's grinning. "Come on," I say, tugging her toward the entrance. "Let's get checked in before you decide to navigate us somewhere else."

Inside, the place is immaculate, with the kind of charm that makes you feel like you've walked into someone's home rather than a business.

"We're here to check in," I say, smiling at the elderly woman behind the counter. She beams at us like we've just made her day.

"Well, aren't you two just the most beautiful couple!" She exclaims, clasping her hands together. Before I can correct her, and honestly, I'm not even sure I want to, she continues, "You know what? We're going to upgrade you to the honeymoon suite."

Yasmine's eyes go wide. "Oh, no, that's not ne—" she starts, but the woman waves her off like she's swatting a fly.

"Ah, no protests! It's on the house," she says firmly, her voice brimming with grandmotherly authority. "You can call me *Abuela* and my husband here, *Abuelo*." She nods at the elderly gentleman sitting next to her before turning back to us. "While you're staying at *Casa Sol*, you're family. Anything you need, you just ask."

Before either of us can say another word, Abuela is already leading us to our room. Yasmine looks at me, like, '*what just happened?*' and I shrug, amused.

When we step into the honeymoon suite, I must admit, it's impressive. The room is spacious but cozy, with fresh flowers on the nightstand and a balcony that opens up to an ocean view. The whole place feels like it's been touched by magic. Yasmine spins around, taking it all in, and her smile lights up the room. "Wow," she breathes.

Abuela rattles off a list of local restaurants with the enthusiasm of someone personally responsible for their online reviews. "*Casa Marina* has the best ceviche on the island. At *El Faro*, you have to try the lobster tacos. And *Don Pepe's*? Oh, his mole will make you believe in miracles." I nod along, trying to commit the names to memory while Yasmine is already scribbling them down on her phone like the diligent overachiever she is.

Just when I think she's wrapping up, Abuela leans in, lowering her voice like she's about to let us in on the island's best-kept secret. "And tonight," she says, her eyes sparkling, "there's a turtle hatching event on the beach. You *must* go."

She points a finger at both of us, her tone leaving no room for negotiation. It's less of a suggestion and more of a command, the kind only a grandmother figure can pull off without sounding overbearing. I'm about to ask what a turtle-hatching event even is, but before I can, she claps her hands together, grins, and walks off, leaving us standing there, oddly compelled to do exactly as she says.

I glance over at Yasmine, who's already grinning like she's imagining us surrounded by a sea of baby turtles flopping their way toward the ocean. Her enthusiasm is contagious, so much so that I find myself thinking, *yeah, okay, I can get emotionally invested in tiny turtles.*

"You heard the boss," I say, shrugging. "Guess we're doing this."
 "Obviously," she says with a laugh. "Who could say no to baby turtles?"

And just like that, I realize I'm kind of looking forward to it. Or maybe I'm just looking forward to spending the evening with Yasmine. Either way, I'm in.

"I'm going to freshen up, and then we can head out to explore," Yasmine says casually. I stare at her as she makes her way toward the bathroom. And, look, I try to be a gentleman, but the way she sways her hips at me is practically hypnotic. I'm just a man, okay? A weak, flawed, and thoroughly captivated man. Shame? *Zero.* Regret? *Also zero.* I mean, surely she knows by now the kind of hold she's got on me. It's not exactly a secret.

Ten minutes later, she walks out of the bathroom, and all coherent thought exits the building. She's swapped her travel outfit for a hot pink bikini top and jean shorts, and I'm not proud of the noise that escapes my throat—it's somewhere between a gasp and a wheeze. Subtle, I am not.

Her cheeks flush just a little, and I swear she notices. Of course, she notices. How could she not when I'm standing there like a deer caught in the headlights? "I, uh, I'm gonna get changed too," I stammer, scrambling for the bathroom like it's the last lifeboat on a sinking ship. The second the door clicks shut, I take a deep breath, which does absolutely nothing to help the situation. My body has betrayed me. Fully and completely. I glance down, glaring at the very obvious problem. Seriously? Why, of all times, does my cock decide *now* is a great moment to revisit my teenage hormones? I'm throbbing like I'm sixteen again and just saw my first Victoria's Secret catalog. Except, instead of a lingerie model, there's someone even more breathtaking on the other side of the door, someone so stunning she might as well be a real-life angel.

For a fleeting second, I consider the logistics of, well, handling the situation, but there's not enough time for that, not with Yasmine waiting for me. I splash some cold water on my face instead, muttering a pep talk to myself. "Rein it in, man. You're a grown-ass adult. Get it together."

Easier said than done when the woman just outside the door is custom-designed to ruin me. God help me…this is going to be a long weekend.

CHAPTER 44

We take Abuela's advice and head to the little beachfront spot she insisted had the best lobster tacos on the island. Let me just say she was *not* exaggerating. The tacos are so juicy and savory, they might as well have been made by the taco gods. Each bite is pure bliss, the kind of food that makes you close your eyes and moan without realizing it.

Alex, of course, teases me for it. "Are you having a moment with your taco over there?" he asks, smirking as he pops another bite into his mouth.

"Don't act like you're not doing the same thing," I fire back, pointing at him with my half-eaten taco. "I saw you close your eyes for that last bite. Admit it, it's a religious experience."

He holds up his hands in mock surrender, grinning. "Fine. Best tacos I've ever had. You happy?"

I lean back in my chair, smiling at him. "Very."

As we sit there, finishing off our meal and sipping on fresh lime sodas, I realize how completely at ease I feel with him. There's no one else I'd rather be with right now. Alex has this way of turning even the simplest moments into something unforgettable. Does he have any idea how much of a catch he is? I doubt it. For a guy who seems like he should ooze arrogance, he's shockingly modest. It's... refreshing.

After dinner, we wander along the shoreline toward the spot Abuela told us to meet for the turtle hatching event. The sun is dipping lower on the horizon, painting the sky in streaks of pink and gold, and the soft crash of waves fills the silence between us. It's peaceful, but there's this unspoken energy between us that makes my pulse flutter.

"Do you think the turtles know how dramatic this is for us?" Alex asks, breaking the quiet.

I laugh, nudging him playfully with my shoulder. "I'm pretty sure they're just focused on not getting eaten."

"Fair," he says, chuckling. "But still, I feel like we should give them a little pep talk. Something motivational. Like, 'Hey, buddy, the ocean's waiting for you. Don't let that seagull ruin your dreams.'"

I snort. "You're going to be that guy, aren't you? The one giving a TED Talk to a baby turtle."

"Don't act like you wouldn't join in," he fires back, his grin widening.

When we finally spot the group, a small cluster of people gathered near the shoreline, we're greeted by a young man named Mateo, who looks like he just stepped out of a surfer movie. He's tanned, tousled, and brimming with enthusiasm as he explains how the evening will unfold.

Alex leans closer to me as Mateo talks, his shoulder brushing against mine. "You think the turtles are ready for this level of fanfare?" he murmurs, his voice low and warm.

I glance at him, trying not to smile too much. "I think they'll manage." At this moment, when the world feels calm and light and a little ridiculous, I realize just how much Alex has started to mean to me. And I have a feeling these turtles aren't the only ones on the verge of something life-changing.

"Welcome, everyone!" Mateo says enthusiastically, breaking me out of my thoughts. "Tonight, we're helping these baby turtles take their first steps, well, crawls, into the ocean. It's a special moment, and we're here to ensure they get there safely."

Mateo locks eyes with me as he speaks, holding my gaze just a little longer than necessary. "And you," he says, pointing at me with a grin. "You have such good energy. I can feel it already. The turtles are going to love you."

I laugh, brushing a strand of hair behind my ear. "Well, I hope they don't judge me too harshly if I'm not very coordinated."

"You'll be perfect," he assures me, flashing a dazzling smile that makes it clear he's laying it on thick. I can feel Alex shift beside me, and when I glance at him, his jaw is tight, his arms crossed over his chest. His usual laid-back vibe has been replaced by something a little sharper, and it doesn't take a genius to figure out why. He's jealous. The realization sends a little thrill through me, though I keep my expression neutral. *Jealous Alex.* Who knew it could be so ridiculously attractive?

As Mateo continues to explain the logistics—how to stand back so the turtles can find their way and what to do if one looks stuck—I can feel Alex's gaze burning into the side of my head. When Mateo hands me a flashlight, Alex immediately steps forward. "I'll take that," he says as he grabs it before I can.

I raise an eyebrow, biting back a smile. "I think I can handle a flashlight, Alex."

"Just being helpful," he says, shrugging, though the slight edge in his tone makes me want to laugh. It's cute, honestly, watching him try to play it cool while clearly bristling over Mateo's extra niceness. Mateo, oblivious to the subtle shift in dynamics, hands Alex another flashlight. "Teamwork, right?" he says brightly, clapping Alex on the shoulder. Alex's answering smile is tight, his grip on the flashlight a little firmer than necessary.

I nudge him gently with my elbow as Mateo moves to the next group. "You okay?" I ask, my voice low, teasing.

"Fine," he says, glancing down at me. His expression softens slightly, but there's still a flicker of something territorial in his eyes. "Just making sure we're all prepared for the turtles."

I bite my lip to keep from grinning. "Right. The turtles. Definitely the priority here."

He narrows his eyes at me, his lips twitching like he's trying not to smile. I feel my heart skip a beat. Because this side of Alex—protective, a little possessive, but still *him*—is something I didn't know I wanted to see until now. And, truthfully, I kind of love it.

CHAPTER 45

I take Yasmine's hand without a second thought and lead her toward the farthest viewing point, as far away from Mateo as humanly possible, without leaving the beach entirely. It's not exactly subtle, but I don't care. I saw how he looked at her; like she was the main event and the turtles were just the opening act. And, honestly, who could blame him? Yasmine has that kind of beauty that stops you in your tracks. The type of beauty that makes it impossible to look away.

What's messing with me, though, is how much it bothers me. I don't even have any claim over her, yet seeing how every guy, and let's be real, some women too, look at her like that? It drives me *insane*. I've never been the possessive type before. With my exes, it was always easy to keep things light, detached, and casual. But with Yasmine? Everything feels different. It's like she's completely rewritten the rulebook in my head and I'm just trying to keep up. I shove that thought into the back of my mind and as we settle on the sand.

It's starting to get dark now, the kind of darkness that sharpens your other senses. And then, as if on cue, the ocean begins to glow. It starts subtly, almost like a trick of the light. At first, I think my eyes are playing tricks on me, adjusting to the darkness, but then it spreads. Soft, shimmering blue-green waves that light up the water like something out of a dream. For a moment, I sit there, completely frozen, as the ocean comes alive before my eyes.

"Bioluminescence…" Yasmine whispers, her voice full of awe. She grabs my arm gently as if needing to make sure I'm seeing this, too. "Alex, look at it. It's so beautiful."

And it is. The kind of beauty that hits you in the chest. The kind that makes you realize how small you are in the grand scheme of things. Here we are, two tiny specks in this vast, unknowable universe, watching something so simple yet extraordinary unfold right before us. Nature has this power, this overwhelming energy, and in this moment, I feel it all.

But then I turn to Yasmine, and suddenly, the glow of the ocean isn't the only thing that's breathtaking. Sparks of light reflect in her wide, astonished eyes, catching on the curves of her face like she's part of the magic herself. Her pouty lips are slightly parted, her expression unguarded and full of wonder, and she's so utterly, completely present in this moment that it's impossible to look away.

"So beautiful," I murmur. The words come out low and reverent, and I'm unsure if I'm talking about the bioluminescence or her. Probably both. Definitely both.

She turns to me then, her gaze soft and curious, and for a second, we're just sitting there, close enough that I can feel the warmth of her beside me. The glow of the ocean dances around us, but all I can see is her. And for the first time in my life, I feel like everything—the stars, the waves, the universe itself—has aligned to bring me to this exact moment.

The thought hits me like a wave. Somehow, in all the beauty this world has to offer, this moment feels like it matches up to all of it. Maybe even surpasses it.

She turns closer to me, and suddenly, we're so close our thighs brush. My cock reacts immediately; of course, it does because that's exactly what I *don't* need right now. Thank God it's dark. A strand of her hair falls across her face, and before I can stop myself, I reach out and tuck it behind her ear. My fingers linger for just a second too long, and when our eyes meet again, the rest of the world fades away. The moment stretches, charged and intimate. I stare at her pink lips, and for a brief, insane second, I wonder what they'd taste like if I just leaned in.

The next thing I know, I'm closing the gap. My lips meet hers, soft and deliberate, testing the waters, savoring the moment. And she doesn't pull away. No, she leans into me, her lips moving against mine, slow at first, as if she's exploring the weight of it, the meaning of it. It's gentle and unhurried, yet it sends a jolt through me. Our kiss deepens, a quiet surrender on both sides, and all the tension and unspoken words come crashing to the surface. It's like we've opened a floodgate we didn't even realize we'd been standing behind, and now there's no turning back.

I lose myself in her. Completely. My hand moves to her waist, pulling her closer until there's no space left between us. A fire spreads through me that I can't contain or explain. It's overwhelming but in the best possible way. The world around us disappears. No ocean, no glow, just us. At this moment, she's the only thing that exists, and I don't want to hold back. I don't want to think. I just want *her*.

Just as I'm completely lost in the kiss, wrapped up in the soft press of her lips and the way her hands feel so perfect against mine, that douchebag Mateo's voice cuts through the moment like an uninvited mariachi band.

"They're coming! It's happening!" he yells. I swear, the guy has the timing of a drunk karaoke singer.

Yasmine pulls back, her lips still so close I can feel her breath against mine. Then she grins a radiant, unfiltered smile that makes my chest feel like it's about to burst. "Alex! Did you hear that?" she says, her voice practically vibrating with excitement. "The turtles are hatching! Let's go!"

Before I can even process what's happening, she grabs my hand and yanks me to my feet. Honestly I could care less about the turtles right now. All I can focus on is the feel of her hand in mine, soft and warm like it was made to fit there. I'm a grown man, and yet, at this moment, I find myself thinking, *never let go.* How ridiculous is that?

As she pulls me along the beach, I can't help but laugh, even as I stumble over the uneven sand.

"You know," I say, trying to keep up with her pace, "for someone who spends most of her time meditating and breathing deeply, you run like someone's chasing you."

She looks back at me, her eyes bright with excitement, her laughter spilling into the night air. "This is important, Alex. *Baby turtles!* Keep up!"

"Right," I mutter, grinning despite myself. "Priorities."

We slow down as we approach the crowd, careful with each step to avoid accidentally squashing one of the tiny hatchlings. And then we see them—the most incredible sight—hundreds of tiny, determined little babies flapping their way toward the glowing ocean, each fighting against the odds to make it to the water. I feel something shift inside me as I watch these fragile little beings navigate their way through the vastness of the world. It's humbling, in a way I didn't expect. For a moment, I stand there, taking it all in, completely awestruck by the sheer magnitude of the universe and its quiet beauty. Yasmine squeezes my hand and I glance over at her. She's watching the turtles with this pure, childlike wonder that makes my chest ache in the best way. I can't help but smile because, as amazing as this moment is, nothing compares to experiencing it with her.

"Pretty incredible, huh?" she whispers, her voice soft but filled with emotion.

"Yeah," I say, my voice quieter than usual. My gaze drifts from the turtles back to her, and I realize, without a shred of doubt, that there's no one else I'd rather be here with. "It really is."

At this moment, I am utterly, completely, spectacularly screwed. One kiss and I'm a goner. A single taste and I'm starving for more. It's like she flipped some hidden switch in me and now there's no going back. Then, as if the universe hasn't already thrown enough at me tonight, I look down at these tiny baby turtles flapping their way toward the ocean, and my brain decides *this* is the perfect time to short-circuit. Suddenly, I'm having thoughts—wild, terrifying, ridiculous thoughts. Thoughts about Yasmine, about the future, about her… pregnant. With *my* baby. What the hell is happening? Who am I right now? I'm not this guy. I don't fantasize about futures or families or babies. I'm in so deep I may as well be at the bottom of the ocean.

I take a shaky breath, willing myself to pull it together. *Reel it in, Alex. For the love of God, reel it in.* The last thing I should do right now is blurt out something insane like, "Hey, Yasmine, I know we just kissed, but have you considered raising a family of tiny humans with me?" Yeah, that's not happening. All I can do is hold her hand and keep these wild thoughts locked up tight. Out of respect for her, for this moment, for the delicate balance we've just started to find.

CHAPTER 46

YASMINE

Alex and I are laughing so hard that I'm wiping tears from the corners of my eyes. He's just finished some absurd story about an overenthusiastic cryptocurrency pitch gone wrong, and I haven't cracked up this much in years.

But the laughter stops as soon as the door clicks shut behind us. Our honeymoon suite is gorgeous, sure, but the centerpiece, the elephant in the room, is the massive, plush bed. Just one. It is the kind of bed you'd expect in a honeymoon suite, complete with fluffy pillows and a soft duvet that practically screams intimacy. My eyes flick to the two chairs in the corner. They're tiny, decorative things that no human should attempt to sleep on.

I glance at Alex, who's shifting awkwardly and rubbing the back of his neck. "Uh, I can sleep on the floor," he offers, his voice casual, but the tension in his jaw says otherwise.

I shake my head quickly. "No, Alex, come on. We're adults. I'm sure we can manage to share a bed," I say, trying to sound practical, even though my heart is pounding. Who am I kidding? The idea of sharing a bed with him, especially after *that* kiss, feels like some sort of cosmic joke.

He hesitates for a second, his eyes searching mine, then nods. "If you're sure."

"Totally," I reply, my voice a little too high-pitched to sound convincing. I grab my bag and excuse myself to shower and change to escape the sudden tension. Except, of course, once I'm in the bathroom, I realize I've made a rookie mistake. I forgot to pack pajamas. The universe really is testing me. After staring at my limited options, most of which are swimwear, none of which include modesty, I wrap myself in a towel and step out of the bathroom, cringing at how awkward this is about to be.

"Uh, Alex?" I say, my voice light and casual, like I'm not standing there in nothing but a towel. "Do you have an extra shirt I can borrow?"

He looks up from where he's sitting on the edge of the bed, and the smirk that spreads across his face nearly makes me combust. "Yeah," he says, standing and walking to his bag. He pulls out a worn Stanford t-shirt, and the moment I see it, my breath catches. It's *that* shirt. The one I stole from his closet all those years ago.

"Alex…" I say softly, holding the shirt in my hands. "You brought this with you?"

He looks a little sheepish, which is such a contrast to his usual confidence that I feel something twist in my chest. "I, uh…" He rubs the back of his neck, that boyish grin making another appearance. "It kind of became my favorite shirt."

And just like that, I'm completely undone. He's adorable, infuriating, and I can't even bring myself to tease him. Instead, I smile softly and take the shirt. As our fingers brush, that familiar spark shoots through me, sharp and electric, leaving me momentarily breathless. I retreat to the bathroom, my heart pounding, and pull on the shirt. It smells like him—clean, warm, and comforting, and it feels far too intimate like I'm stepping into something I can't take back. The soft fabric hangs loosely on me, brushing against my skin, but the thought of him having worn it so many times makes my cheeks flush. How does something so simple feel so heavy?

When I finally return to the room, I freeze, my breath catching in my throat. Alex is now completely shirtless. And *holy hell.* I don't know what I expected, but it wasn't *this.* His broad shoulders and chiseled chest look like they belong on the cover of a fitness magazine. His abs—sharp, defined, and infuriatingly perfect, catch the soft glow of the bedside lamp, casting shadows that make him look like a freaking Greek god. Every muscle is taut, sculpted, and so distractingly perfect it's a miracle I'm still standing. My brain can't seem to form a coherent response. "Uh… I…" I stammer, my voice embarrassingly breathless.

His biceps flex in a way that makes my pulse do the Macarena. "Hope you don't mind, but I couldn't get the AC working, so unless you want to sleep next to a human sauna, I'll have to go shirtless tonight," he adds. His tone is light, but his eyes… his eyes are dark and intense like they're taking in every inch of me in his shirt and savoring it.

I swallow hard, trying not to let my gaze linger on the way his boxers sit just low enough on his hips to make me dizzy. "No… I don't mind," I manage to squeak out, though I'm lying to myself because I *do* mind. This is bad. Really, really bad. Because now, not only am I supposed to share a bed with him, but I'm supposed to do it while he looks like every forbidden fantasy I've ever had come to life.

After brushing his teeth, he finally comes to bed, and I'm already curled up at the very edge, pretending to be asleep like my life depends on it. Maybe, just *maybe*, if I lie still enough, I can convince myself that I'm not totally losing my mind over the fact that Alex—shirtless, sculpted, and smelling stupidly good, is about to lie down next to me. I hear him shuffle around for a moment, then the bed dips, and suddenly, his warmth radiates toward me, like it's got a mind of its own. I clench my eyes shut tighter. *Breathe*, Yasmine. *Just breathe. You're a grown woman. You can handle this.* Except my body is not on the same page as my brain because every nerve feels like it's on high alert. Even the slightest movement from him sends a jolt straight through me. I try to focus on literally anything else—my yoga training, the baby turtles from earlier, the sound of the waves outside. *It's just proximity,* I tell myself. *It's science—body heat or something.*

And then he sighs and I hear the sheets ruffle. "Yasmine," he murmurs, his voice low and husky, like he knows I'm faking sleep and is calling me out without actually saying it. My heart does a full-blown somersault. I don't move. *Don't take the bait,* I think. *Play dead.* He chuckles softly, and I swear I can hear the smile in his voice. "Goodnight," he says, and it's so simple, so innocent, yet somehow it sends my pulse racing all over again.

"Goodnight, Alex," I manage to squeak out. His warmth, so close yet untouchable, wraps around me like a challenge, and all I can think is, *how the hell am I supposed to survive the night?*

A sliver of sunlight sneaks through the curtains. I sigh contentedly, sinking further into the plush bed. Everything feels so perfect, so dreamlike, the kind of comfort that makes you never want to wake up. My body is wrapped in warmth, pressed against something firm and unyielding, yet somehow impossibly soft. It's… chiseled. Solid. *So solid.* A large hand wraps around my waist, holding me tightly, and I snuggle back into it instinctively. A small moan slips from my lips before I can stop it. Then I hear a low, gravelly groan behind me that rumbles through my back like thunder. And just like that, the hazy bliss evaporates, replaced by a sharp, startling clarity.

This isn't a dream. It's Alex. And the very real, very hard steel rod pressing against my ass? That's Alex, too. Oh God. I don't breathe. I don't move. I'm completely paralyzed by the realization that I've not only been grinding against him like a hormone gremlin but that also it feels *perfect*. Like we were made to fit together, puzzle pieces clicking into place. I should move—I *have* to move—but I'm frozen. And, worse, I'm wet—so, so wet. A new horror dawns on me, I didn't wear underwear to bed. The only thing between us is his thin pair of boxers. And his cock, his *huge* cock, as I remember so vividly, is pressing insistently against me, like it knows exactly what it's doing. I try to convince my body to inch away, to wiggle out of his hold without waking him, but every slight movement only makes things worse. His grip tightens, pulling me even closer. And then, as if the universe is determined to test my self-control, he growls softly and buries his face in the crook of my neck. The low, primal sound sends a shiver down my spine, and I bite my lip to stifle the moan threatening to escape. His hand moves slowly under the hem of my borrowed shirt, his fingers rough and warm as they trail up my stomach. When he cups one of my breasts, squeezing it with a firm, possessive grip, a soft cry escapes me before I can stop it.

 "Alex," I whisper, but it's not a protest. It's a plea—a surrender. He groans against my neck, his lips brushing my skin, lazy and unhurried as they move to my shoulder. I feel his breath, hot and ragged, as his hand strokes over my nipple, teasing it into a tight, aching peak. My hips move before I can stop them, grinding back against him with a mind of their own, and the friction is electric. It's as if my body is on autopilot, responding to him in ways I can't control. His free hand moves to my upper thigh, holding me firmly in place, and the low, tortured sound he makes nearly pushes me over the edge. "Fuck," he moans, the word spilling out like it's been dragged from the depths of him.

And that does it. I can't hold back anymore. A moan escapes me, full and breathy, and just like that, he freezes. Everything stops—the kisses, the touch, the heat, and suddenly his hand retreats from my body like it's been burned. I instantly miss the warmth, the weight, and the pressure of it.

"Shit," he breathes, his voice hoarse and panicked. "I'm sorry, Yasmine. I thought… I thought I was dreaming." I turn my head just enough to meet his eyes, wide with shock. I don't know what to say, but my body hasn't gotten the memo because it's still buzzing and aching for the connection he just pulled away from. He shifts slightly, putting more space between us, and I swallow the disappointment tightening in my chest. "It's… it's okay," I manage, though my voice wavers. It's not okay. None of this is okay because now that I know what it feels like to have him touch and hold me again, I don't know if I can go back to pretending that I don't want him just as badly.

CHAPTER 47

ALEX

What the hell is wrong with me? I'm standing under this freezing cold shower, hoping, praying, it'll do something about the situation between my legs. My cock is still raging, like it didn't get the announcement that we've moved on from this morning's little… incident. Or maybe I should call it what it was—me unconsciously groping Yasmine in my sleep like a complete caveman. God. She must think I'm an animal. But then, she didn't seem freaked out. Not in the slightest. In fact, she seemed…*turned on*. I don't think I'll ever forget the way her body pressed into mine, the heat of her bare ass against my boxers. That feeling is seared into my brain now. And if she had any doubts about her effect on me, she sure doesn't anymore. It's humiliatingly obvious. I'm completely whipped for her, and my body is fully on board with that fact.

I step out of the shower, quickly towel off, and wrap it low around my hips. When I walk back into the room to grab my clothes, I catch her staring. Her eyes flick down over my chest, following a bead of water as it rolls down my abs. Her lips part slightly and the look of desire on her face makes it nearly impossible for me to turn away. I clear my throat, trying to cut through the tension. "So, uh, Abuela said something about setting up a picnic for us today. You up for it?"

"That sounds lovely," she breathes, her voice a little unsteady. She's still reeling from this morning. I can see it in the flush of her cheeks and the way her hands fidget in her lap. I need to address what happened, even though it's the last thing I want to discuss.

"Listen, about this morning—" I begin, but at the same time, she blurts out, "I'm sorry I was grinding up against your cock." My brain short-circuits. My eyes widen, and she winces, looking like she wishes the ground would open up and swallow her whole. It's so painfully adorable I can't help the grin tugging at my lips. I rub the back of my neck, trying to play it cool, but when I glance back at her, the desperation in her eyes nearly floors me. She's looking at me like she wants something, something we both want, and it's taking every ounce of my self-control not to close the space between us and finish what we started this morning. But I can't. If I let myself give in and scare her off, I'll never forgive myself. So instead, I rein in the wild storm of emotions clawing at my chest, and force myself to focus on her words.

"You don't have to apologize," I say, my voice quieter now, softer. "If anything, I should be the one apologizing. I didn't mean to… well, you know."

She laughs nervously, tucking a strand of hair behind her ear. "We should probably get ready for that picnic. Abuela will hunt us down if we don't show up."

I nod, but my gaze lingers on her, not quite ready to let the moment go. When we finally make our way downstairs, Abuela greets us with a smile so warm it could melt butter. "Ah, *Mi Hijo*, come! Let's prepare for your picnic! Today, we're going to make tamales, *Abuela style*," she announces, with the kind of enthusiasm that leaves no room for argument.

Wait. *We're* making the picnic? I glance at Yasmine, and she's already looking at me with a mix of confusion and amusement, her eyebrows raised slightly. It's one of those moments where no words are necessary. Her expression says it all: *Are we really doing this?* And mine replies, *I guess we are.* How are we already communicating without speaking? That should be strange, right? But with Yasmine, it feels natural. Easy. Like we've been doing this for years.

Abuela ushers us into her kitchen, which somehow strikes the perfect balance between cozy and professional. There's a long counter, every inch covered with ingredients: piles of peppers, bowls of fresh meats, and a neat little mountain of masa flour. "First, we prepare the sauce," she explains, motioning to at least ten different types of peppers. Then, we will make the masa dough."

I glance at Yasmine again, and she's already rolling up her sleeves, her face lit with curiosity. "How hard could this be?" she grins as she picks up a pepper and inspects it like a rare artifact.

"Famous last words," I tease, grabbing an apron from the hook. She sticks her tongue out at me and I can't help but laugh. God, she's so effortlessly cute that it almost hurts. We quickly fall into a rhythm, chopping, mixing, and laughing as Abuela guides us through each step with the patience of a saint. Yasmine starts blending the sauce, her brows furrowed in concentration, and I catch myself watching her more than I should. She has this way of being completely in the moment, completely present, and it's magnetic. And that's when it happens again. The little voice in my head, whispering *I could do this with her every day for the rest of my life.* The thought stops me cold, the knife in my hand hovering mid-chop. I glance at her again, and suddenly, I can see it. Us. In a kitchen like this, cooking side by side, waking up together and laughing, teasing, just *being.* And the idea doesn't terrify me the way it should. No, it excites me. It makes me feel like I'll do whatever it takes to make that vision real. But then reality creeps back in. Yasmine isn't a business deal I can seal with a handshake or a well-placed offer. She's not something I can "secure." She's her own person—wild, free, beautifully complicated, and if this is ever going to happen, she has to choose me.

"Are you okay over there?" her voice cuts through my thoughts. She looks at me with a playful smile, her hands covered in masa dough. "You're staring," she says.

"Am I?" I ask, trying to play it off, but I can feel the corner of my mouth twitching into a smile.

She narrows her eyes at me. "What's going on in that head of yours, Mr. Cryptic?"

"Just wondering how you managed to get masa everywhere," I tease, gesturing to the flour smudged on her cheek. She swipes at her face, missing the spot completely, and I step closer, wiping it away with my thumb. The moment lingers too long to be casual, too charged to be ignored, and I have to step back before I lose all sense of control.

Abuela interrupts, clapping her hands together. "Perfect! Now we assemble the tamales!" Her cheerful voice breaks the spell, and Yasmine moves to grab a handful of corn husks, her cheeks a little rosier than before. I focus on the task at hand, but my mind is racing. This woman is wrecking me in the best way. I'm falling for her, hard and fast, and the crazy thing is, I don't even care to fight it anymore.

CHAPTER 48

The tamales are steaming in Abuela's kitchen, filling the entire building with a warm, savory aroma, but instead of letting us enjoy the fruits of our labor, she sends us off to pick up a flan from her *amiga's* bakery. Apparently, this is how things work here. Guests prepare their own meals and run errands too. At first, I thought it was strange, but honestly? I'm not complaining. Every second of it is fun because I'm with Alex. He makes every moment better in all the ways that matters.

I can't help myself, I decide he deserves to know how much I've been enjoying this. "Alex," I say with sincerity, "you've made this trip really amazing so far. I hope you're enjoying it as much as I am."

He stops mid-step, turning to look at me with surprise. "It's funny," he says, his lips curling into a sideways grin that makes my stomach flip. "Because I could say the same thing." And just like that, I'm smiling too. We keep walking, falling into an easy rhythm of teasing banter and light-hearted conversation. He makes me giggle so much that my cheeks start to ache, and it's honestly the best kind of ache I've ever felt.

When we arrive, the bakery is exactly what I'd imagined: a tiny, colorful little shop with trays of fresh Mexican pastries displayed behind the glass window. The woman behind the counter greets us with a friendly smile, her apron dusted with flour.

"Uh, hi," I say a little awkwardly. "Abuela sent us to pick up a flan?" *Does she even know who 'Abuela' is?* Neither Alex nor I know what Abuela's actual name is, and now I'm questioning everything. But the woman doesn't miss a beat. Her face lights up with recognition and she ducks behind the counter to retrieve a perfectly golden flan. "Of course!" she says, handing it to me with a proud smile. And then, as if it's the most natural thing in the world, she adds, "You two are the most beautiful couple I've ever seen. You'd make such beautiful babies."

I choke. Full-on cough, sputter, try-not-to-die choke. Alex, on the other hand, smiles at her like she's handed him a compliment he's been waiting his whole life to hear. "*Muchas gracias*," he says smoothly, and there's an unmistakable amusement in his eyes when he glances my way.

I stare at him, unsure of what to make of his casual acceptance of her statement. "That was… pretty bold of her," I manage to say, clearing my throat as we step out of the bakery.

He looks down at me, his eyes dark and intense, his smirk nothing short of wicked. "Well, she's not wrong," he says, his voice low and teasing. "We would make pretty amazing babies, don't you think?"

I stop walking. "I—what?" The words barely come out as my brain trips over itself.

He chuckles, watching me like he knows exactly what kind of effect he's having on me. "Relax, Yasmine. I'm just saying what everyone's thinking."

"Yeah, sure," I mutter, rolling my eyes to cover how hot my face feels. I start walking again, my heart racing, but his smirk lingers in my mind, making it impossible to calm down.

When we get back to *Casa Sol*, Abuela greets us with the kind of enthusiasm only she can pull off. "Ah, my lovebirds! You did such an amazing job today. Your picnic is all packed up and waiting for you on the beach. I'll bring out the flan and some tea shortly."

I blink. There it is again, that assumption that Alex and I are a couple. It's becoming a trend. And, weirdly, neither of us ever corrects it. In fact, I kind of like the sound of it, a lot more than I probably should.

When we arrive at the beach, we stop in our tracks, completely stunned. It's not just a picnic; it's a whole *experience*. There's a white linen tipi tent with wooden stakes, fluttering gently in the breeze, giving us just the right amount of shade. A beautifully patterned Peruvian-style blanket is spread out over the sand and there's a perfect arrangement of hand painted plates, cutlery, and a proper picnic basket filled to the brim with what can only be described as Abuela's culinary magic. In addition to the tamales Alex and I made together, there are *elotes* sprinkled with chili and lime, a bowl of freshly made tortilla chips and guacamole, a platter of vibrant tropical fruit, and two premade margaritas waiting for us in chilled glasses. It's stunning and thoughtful, the kind of setup that could grace the cover of a lifestyle magazine.

"Wow," I breathe, taking it all in. "This is… perfect."

But when I glance at Alex, he's not looking at the picnic. His gaze is fixed on me, warm and unrelenting. He smiles, his voice low. "Yeah, it is."

I roll my eyes, laughing softly. "You haven't even looked at the spread."

"Don't need to," he says, his grin widening. "The view's already pretty amazing."

My cheeks flush despite the cool ocean breeze, and I busy myself sitting down on the blanket, pretending that his words don't make my heart race. But then he sits down next to me and suddenly I can't think about anything else. The space between us is practically nonexistent. Our knees brush lightly and that faint contact sends a thrill through me.

We dive into the food, but there's no rush, no pressure. It's just easy. We mesh effortlessly and naturally like we've been doing this for lifetimes. He teases me for how much lime I squeeze onto my corn and I fire back about the way-too-sensual-way he licks guacamole off his finger. At one point, he leans forward to grab a slice of mango and his knee presses fully against mine, lingering there. He doesn't move it and neither do I. The slight touch feels intentional, sending a slow warmth through me, settling low in my stomach.

"You know," he says, his voice quieter now, "I don't think I've felt this relaxed in… I don't even know how long."

I look at him, caught off guard by the shift in his tone. "Really?"

He nods, his gaze meeting mine. "Yeah. It's… you."

The way he says it, soft and earnest, leaves me breathless. I open my mouth to respond, but nothing comes out. For a moment, we sit there, the waves filling the space between us. "I mean, the margaritas help," he adds, smirking again, breaking the tension just enough to make me laugh.

"Sure, let the margaritas take the credit," I tease, nudging him with my shoulder. There's no awkwardness anymore, no walls, no pretending. It's just us, sitting on this beautiful beach, sharing food, laughter, and moments that feel like they've always belonged to us. As I glance at Alex, his face lit with the soft glow of the sun, I realize that I've never felt more at peace than I do right now with him.

We're in the middle of a playful argument about whether tamales count as finger food (I say yes, he says no because he insists you can't eat them without a fork) when suddenly, a gust of wind sweeps across the beach. Before we even realize what's happening, the edge of our picnic blanket starts to flutter. In a split second, it takes flight like it's auditioning for *The Sound of Music*, sending napkins, cups, and a rogue tamale into the air.

"Shit! The tamales!" Alex shouts and laughs simultaneously, lunging forward to grab the blanket.

I burst into laughter as I scramble to catch a cup rolling toward the waves. "Forget the tamales! Save the drinks!"

Alex makes a run for the bag containing our tamales. His long legs move fast and I can't help but laugh again over how he looks like an action hero in a summer blockbuster. He catches the bag just as it's about to be carried out to sea, spinning around and jogging back toward me with a proud grin. "You're lucky I have reflexes like this," he says, plopping down on the blanket again.

"Oh, sure. You're my hero," I tease, laughing as I reach out to brush sand off his shoulder.

He raises an eyebrow as he sits back down next to me. "So I saved the tamales; I think I deserve a reward."

Suddenly, everything else fades away and it's just him and me again, caught in this moment that feels too big to ignore. We're not smiling anymore. The teasing is replaced by something raw. My heart pounds as I look at him, really look at him, and the space between us feels impossibly small. I can feel his presence pulling me closer without either of us moving. If I leaned in, even just an inch, our lips would touch. We're already so close, practically sharing the same breath, and my body screams for me to close the gap. His eyes flicker down to my lips, and without thinking, I wet them, my tongue darting out on instinct. His gaze darkens, his jaw tightening just slightly, and when his eyes lift back to mine, they're full of heat and want, something that makes my pulse race. The tension is unbearable, coiled so tightly around us that it feels like it will snap at any second.

And then it does.

He closes the distance, or maybe I do. I can't tell because when our lips crash together, it's everything. It's fire and need and desperation rolled into one perfect, overwhelming kiss. His hands find my face, holding me like he's afraid I'll pull away, but there's no chance of that. My hands are in his hair, tangling, pulling him closer because suddenly, close isn't close enough.

Our kiss deepens, all softness giving way to something hotter, hungrier. His lips move against mine with a purpose, like he's trying to tell me something he can't put into words. My body presses against his and the world tilts, heat flooding me in waves. It's dizzying and consuming, like everything I've been holding back is pouring out in this one moment. I don't care what it means or where it's going. All I know is that right now, with his heart beating just as wildly as mine, I've never felt more alive.

CHAPTER 49

ALEX

We barely make it through the hallway before we're slamming the door open, our bodies colliding like we've been starved for each other. My mouth crashes against hers, raw and hungry, teeth and tongues in a chaotic, perfect mess. Her hands tangle in my hair, pulling me closer, and mine are everywhere… her hips, her back, her ass, trying to memorize every curve, every inch of her. We're finally back in the sanctuary of our room and I don't waste another second. I press her against the wall, my hands gripping her ass hard, and I lift her up effortlessly. Her legs wrap around my waist, her long skirt riding up, and the feel of her heat pressed against me is enough to make my cock throb painfully in my shorts. One of my hands slide up her thigh, and that's when I realize, "Fuck," I groan, my voice rough and low as my fingers find her wet, needy pussy. "You're not wearing panties?"

Her only response is a soft moan. She's already so slick, so warm, and I grit my teeth, my control slipping with every second. "You're already so wet for me, angel," I rasp, my cock straining desperately against the fabric of my shorts, aching for her. In one swift motion, she pulls my shirt over my head. The look in her eyes, so hungry and full of need, makes my chest tighten. My girl likes what she sees. I kiss her neck, finding that spot I know drives her wild, and when she moans my name, it's the best sound I've ever heard. I want to drown in it, to hear her say it over and over again until the world disappears.

Flashes of the first time we did this race through my head—vivid and overwhelming. This is so much better than any dream, any fantasy I've tortured myself with over the years.

I've imagined this moment so many times, in a world where she was always mine to mark, love, and keep.

I push my middle finger into her and she clenches around me instantly. My palm presses against her clit as I work her hard, my movements precise and deliberate. I remember exactly how to drive her over the edge. She gasps, her head falling forward against my shoulder, her breath hot and uneven against my skin.

"Alex, oh my God," she cries out, her voice breaking out a moan that sends a shiver through me. She's close, so close, and I push her further, curling my finger inside her while continuing to massage her clit with my palm. Her thighs tighten around me, and her pussy clamps down on my finger.

"That's it, good girl," I growl, my lips brushing against her ear. "Look at you, coming all over my finger. You're so fucking tight I can barely fit a second one in." Her moans grow louder, desperate, and she reaches for my shorts, her hands tugging at my waistband with a kind of urgency that makes me throb. I step back just enough to shove them down, and the second my cock springs free, her breath hitches audibly. I'm thick, hard, and dripping with precum, and the way her eyes widen sends a rush of heat straight to my core. "You remember how tight you were for me all those years ago, angel?" I murmur, my voice low and teasing. "I can't wait to see if you still feel the same."

Her eyes meet mine, filled with so much desire that my chest aches. "Alex, *please*," she whispers, her voice trembling. "I need you."

I press my forehead against hers, my hand sliding up her thigh again, positioning myself at her entrance. "You have me, angel," I tell her, my voice soft but firm. "You've always had me."

CHAPTER 50

With a slow, deliberate push, Alex slides into me, inch by inch, stretching me in ways I haven't felt in so long. The memory of how big he is flashes through my mind, but now, with the sheer hardness of him, it's almost overwhelming. The deep, consuming stretch burns in the most delicious way, a sweet ache that sends waves of pleasure through me. His jaw clenches as he buries himself deeper, his body trembling like he's holding on by the thinnest thread of restraint. There's nothing but raw need in his demeanor, like he's trying hard not to lose control, but I don't want him to hold back.

"Give me everything, Alex," I whisper, my voice firm yet breathless. "Fuck me hard." A guttural growl escapes him, low and primal, and whatever restraint he was clinging to snaps. He slams into me with a force that has my head tipping back against the wall, a moan ripping from my throat. His hair falls messily over his forehead, his eyes dark and full of unrelenting need as his body moves with a pounding rhythm that feels both wild and perfect. The air between us is hot and charged, our bodies slick with sweat as the sound of skin meeting skin fills the room. Every thrust sends waves of pleasure over me, building and building until I feel like I might shatter.

"Alex," I cry out, my voice breaking as his movements push me closer to the edge. My nails dig into his shoulders as the tension coils tight in my core. And then it hits harder and deeper than anything I've ever felt. My body clenches around him as I orgasm, my cries echoing in the air, the pleasure so intense it borders on pain.

"Fuck, yes," he groans, his voice strained as he slows just enough to let me ride out the waves of my orgasm. As the haze starts to clear, reality creeps in. My voice is hesitant, almost shaky. "Alex… I'm not on birth control."

He stills, his forehead falling against mine as he takes a deep, ragged breath. For a moment, I worry I've ruined the moment, but then he cups my face, his thumb brushing my cheek. "It's fine, angel," he pants, his voice low and steady. "I'll pull out." Before I can respond, his lips are on mine, capturing me in a kiss so intense it makes my head spin. I shift my hips, taking him deeper, and the growl that rumbles from his chest sends a fresh wave of heat through me. His hand grips my ass even tighter as he thrusts faster and harder, the wall behind me trembling with each movement. My legs stay locked around his waist, my hands tangled in his hair as I meet his rhythm. His body is taut, his muscles flexing with every move, and I can feel his raw power as his breathing grows heavier. When I sense he's close, his movements becoming erratic, I untangle myself from him, sliding down to my knees. He groans as I take him in my hands, his cock thick and throbbing. Without hesitation, I take him into my mouth, swallowing him deep enough that he curses under his breath.

"Yasmine," he gasps, his voice hoarse. I hollow my cheeks, moving with purpose, and the way his body tenses is intoxicating. He mutters something unintelligible, his control slipping entirely as he tips over the edge, spilling into me with a strangled cry. The heat of him, the rawness of the moment, leaves us both trembling. When it's over, he pulls me to my feet, his hands gripping my waist as he presses his forehead to mine, a soft smile playing on his lips.

"You're going to be the death of me," he murmurs, his voice filled with something deeper than just lust. And I can't help but wonder if I already feel the same about him.

We just had sex, two more times. Once in the shower—it started innocently enough with Alex washing my body, but of course, it didn't stay innocent for long. One heated look, one brush of his lips against my neck, and suddenly, we were pressed against the tiles, lost in each other all over again.

And then, again, here in bed. The softness of the sheets and the warmth of his body against mine made everything feel more intense, more consuming, like we're sinking into something deeper than just the physical. Now, we're tangled together, our limbs entwined, completely spent, and unwilling to move. The world outside doesn't matter; it barely even exists. All that exists is this moment that feels like a sanctuary of safety and warmth. It's quiet and perfect. Tomorrow, we will go back to Tulum. "Pablo never ceases to amaze me," I murmur, my voice soft against the steady rhythm of Alex's heartbeat.

He lets out a low chuckle, his hand running lazy circles up and down my back. "He knew exactly what he was doing," he says, his tone somewhere between amused and thoughtful.

I tilt my head to look at him, and let out a small laugh, nuzzling closer into him, my cheek pressed against his chest. "Do you think he orchestrated all of this?"

"Oh, absolutely," Alex replies without missing a beat. "The man's been playing 4D chess while we've been clueless pawns." I laugh, my body shaking slightly against his, and he tightens his hold on me. "Well," I say, my voice quieter now, "I'm not complaining."

"Me neither," Alex says softly, his lips brushing the top of my head. I lean into him and drift off into the best sleep of my life.

CHAPTER 51

ALEX

We just arrived back in Tulum, and the entire journey felt like a dream, not because of the views or the smooth ride but because of Yasmine. Everything with her is better. She makes the world brighter and sharper. Honestly, I feel like I'm on cloud nine. Scratch that, I feel like I'm on cloud nine with a cocktail in hand and zero turbulence. I've never been this happy. She's perfect for me in every way, but a little voice in the back of my head, the one that's always been there, keeps whispering, *This is new territory. Danger ahead. Exit now.* Every instinct I've spent years honing is screaming at me to run. But here's the thing: I don't want to. For the first time in my life, I want to stay. I want to be wherever she is for as long as she lets me.

We agreed to meet again after dinner when we returned to the retreat center. Back in my room, I flop onto my bed and stare at the ceiling, trying to get my shit together. But it's impossible because all I can think about is her. The way her laughter still echoes in my head. How she looked at me during the ride back, making me feel like I'm the only person in the world to her. The way, now that she's not here, it feels like something's missing. Like *I'm* missing.

I glance at the clock. Dinner is hours away, but I'm already counting down. God, what is happening to me? Is this what falling feels like? Because if it is, I'm not sure I ever want to land.

—

Time moves in slow motion and dinner feels like absolute agony. I'm across the table from Yasmine, as far away from her as I can possibly get, and it feels like some kind of cruel punishment. We both agreed to keep things professional, not to let anyone here know what's been happening between us, but this? This feels like torture.

I try to focus on the conversation, the food, anything, but it's useless. My eyes keep drifting to her like she's some magnetic force I can't resist. She's sitting there, smiling at something Pablo's saying, and it's unfair how effortlessly stunning she is. The way her cute little nose crinkles when she laughs and how she lights up the entire table make my chest ache in a way I don't even want to analyze.

For her sake, I'm doing my best to keep my distance. I'm holding it together, *barely*. Because I know if I sit near her, all bets are off. My hand would be on her thigh under the table, my lips would be brushing her ear, and before I know it, I'd be dragging her out of this room like some raged, needy caveman. So I stay put, gripping my fork like it's the only thing tethering me to sanity. I'm done for. I'm sitting here in the middle of dinner, surrounded by people, and all I can think about is how much I want to touch her, kiss her, pull her into my arms, and remind her exactly how crazy she makes me. Instead, I take a sip of my water and try not to look like a man unraveling by the second.

As soon as dinner ends, I'm on my feet, making a beeline for Yasmine like a man on a mission. Subtlety? Entirely out the window. I stop in front of her, ignoring the curious looks from everyone else at the table. "Yasmine, can I, uh, talk to you about a yoga question I have?" The lie is half-baked at best, but it's all I can come up with in my desperation to get her alone.

Pablo arches an eyebrow at me, clearly amused, and I give him a look that says, '*You started this; don't judge me now*'. He chuckles, shaking his head like the puppet master he clearly is. Yasmine, ever polite and perfect, smiles sweetly. "Of course," she says, excusing herself from the table. As soon as we're out of sight, I grab her hand and practically pull her toward the beach, my steps hurried, my pulse pounding.

"Alex!" she says, laughing as she struggles to keep up with my pace. "You're so impatient! What's the rush?"

I glance over my shoulder, a sly grin tugging at my lips. "The entire dinner," I say, my voice low and rough, "all I could think about was you. All the dirty, filthy things I need to do to you. And now, I'm going to do every single one of them."

Her steps falter, her eyes widening slightly. "Alex…" she starts, her voice a little breathless, but there's no protest. If anything, there's anticipation. I stop walking for a moment, turning to face her, my hand still wrapped firmly around hers. I step closer, just enough that she has to tilt her head back to meet my gaze. "You've been driving me insane," I murmur, my thumb brushing over her knuckles. "I can't get you out of my head. And now that I finally have you alone…" I lean in, my lips hovering just above her ear. "I'm not wasting another second."

"You're insatiable," she murmurs, but there's no denying the heat in her voice.

"Completely," I say with a smirk, tugging her hand. We continue walking, and as the moonlight reflects off the water in the distance, I see the moment she realizes where I'm taking her.

"Wait," she says, slowing her steps. "Is this…" I stop in front of the cave she brought me to last week. The one where we almost kissed, where the tension between us was so thick it could've set the place on fire. But we didn't let it go any further then. Tonight, that's going to change. I got here before dinner to set everything up—blankets, pillows, the works. It had to be perfect. Romantic, but not trying-too-hard romantic. Thoughtful, but not *desperate guy who's been low-key obsessed with you for years* thoughtful. Her eyes widen slightly and I can see the realization flicker across her face. She looks at me, her lips parting, and I can't help but smirk. "This is… beautiful. You're unbelievable, you know that?"

"I've been called worse," I tease, stepping closer. My hand tightens around hers as we walk inside. "But this place isn't just for sightseeing tonight."

She raises an eyebrow, her laughter soft and warm. "Oh, so we're christening caves now, are we?"

"Absolutely," I say, my voice dropping to a whisper as I lean in closer, my lips brushing her ear.

"This place deserves better memories."

Her breath hitches, and when she looks up at me, there's a mix of humor and heat in her gaze. "You're impossible," she says, but she doesn't pull away.

CHAPTER 52

The moment Alex's hands pull me closer, the world fades away. He guides me until I'm straddling him on the blanket he laid out, its cool surface a sharp contrast to the heat building between us. He grabs my waist and the energy between us is electric and undeniable. My body moves instinctively with his, and before I realize it, my hips are grinding down against him. He groans into my lips, like he's barely holding on to his restraint. The sound is primal, sending a thrill through me. I feel him harden even more, his cock pressing against my core, and the heat pooling in my stomach becomes unbearable. Alex looks up at me, his messy hair falling over his forehead, his eyes dark and burning with intensity. God, he's so handsome, so utterly captivating. My body aches for him. I lean forward and we kiss, slow and deliberate, the kind of kiss that sends sparks through me. I've longed for this kind of connection for so long, for *him*, and now, having him here with me is almost overwhelming. Under the moonlight filtering through the cave, it feels like the universe itself has conspired to bring us back together. I stop fighting it. I let myself fall completely, wrapping myself in the intimacy of this moment.

"You don't know how long I've been wanting to do that," Alex says, his voice low and rough, with the slightest hint of a laugh. It's been less than twenty four hours since we last had each other, but I feel the same way.

I drop my forehead to his, closing my eyes. "I think I might have an idea," I whisper, smiling softly against him. His hands roam down my back, resting on my ass before squeezing firmly. The sensation sends a surge of desire through me and I gasp.

"I love how sensitive you are," he murmurs, his voice dripping with want. My hands slide to his hair, tugging gently as I lean in for another kiss. This one is deeper, hotter, and filled with all the pent-up longing we've both been holding back. His hands trail up my thighs under my skirt and he groans as his fingers find my center. "Fuck, angel," he whispers, his breath warm against my ear. "You're so wet for me, aren't you?"

The heat of the moment, the way he calls me 'angel'—like it's a name meant only for me—is all too much. My body feels wild, desperate, and completely untethered. "Yes," I breathe, my voice trembling. Just for you." I sit up and tug his shirt over his head, revealing his toned chest and broad shoulders. He chuckles, low and sexy, before doing the same with my dress. I'm not wearing a bra, and when his eyes land on my bare body, he hisses through his teeth.

"Yasmine..." he groans, his voice breaking on my name as he palms my breasts, squeezing and kneading. The way he touches me, with such hunger, makes me moan. My head falls back as the pleasure builds.

"I need you, Alex," I pant, my hands fumbling to undo the buttons of his pants. I tug them down just enough, not bothering to get them off completely. His cock springs free, hard and big, and he lets out a sharp exhale as I wrap my fingers around him.

"Holy shit," he groans, his grip on my hips tightening. "Let me take care of you first. I'm going to explode otherwise."

"No," I whisper, aligning him to me, meeting his intense gaze as I hover above him. "I don't care. I need you. I've missed you... *this*, so much." Even though it's only been a day, if I don't count waking up with Alex in between my legs this morning, it still feels too long without his touch.

I slowly sink down, his thick length stretching me inch by inch. The pressure is intense, a mix of pain and pleasure that makes me bite my lip to stifle my cry. He's so big, almost too big, but it feels perfect, like my body was made for him.

"Oh God," Alex groans, his voice strained as his head falls back. His fingers dig into my hips, but he doesn't rush me, letting me take him at my own pace. "You're so fucking tight, Yasmine." Fully seated on him, I moan, my body trembling as I adjust to the overwhelming fullness. He's gripping onto every last shred of restraint, jaw clenched and breathing labored. "Slow, angel," he rasps, his voice hoarse. "You're going to have to go slow, or I'm not going to last." I nod, because words can't escape me right now, as I start to slide up and down along his length, each plunge sending ripples of pleasure through me. The connection between us is so much more than physical. It's all-consuming. I lean down, pressing my chest flush against his, and he captures my lips in a kiss that's both soft and demanding. His tongue teases mine as I grind harder, losing myself in the rhythm of our bodies. He's groaning now, wild and unrestrained, pushing me further.

"Yasmine," he grits out, his voice rough and desperate. "I need to pull out. I'm close."

But I'm right there with him, the tension in my core coiling tighter and tighter. "No," I gasp, grinding harder. "I'm almost there. Don't stop. Oh God, Alex—" The orgasm hits me like a wave, flooding over me with an intensity that leaves me breathless. My body shudders and I cry out his name again and again as the pleasure consumes me.

"Fuck," he growls, his hips jerking beneath me as he follows, his release hot, hard and deep. His grip is so firm I know I'll have marks tomorrow, and I love it. All I can think about is how incredible it feels to have all of him with me. We collapse together, tangled and breathless, our bodies still connected as we come down from the high. His arms wrap around me tightly and I bury my face into the crook of his neck, inhaling his scent as realization dawns. His warmth is still inside me, and I know there's no taking back what just happened.

CHAPTER 53

Fuck. Fuck. FUCK.

I just came inside her.

And the worst part? I want to do it again. And again. For the rest of my goddamn life.

The fact that we both let it happen, knowing exactly what we were doing, proves how utterly, completely, and hopelessly out of control we are for each other. And I have *never* been out of control in my life. But with Yasmine? She obliterates every single rule I've ever lived by. I don't know what I'm getting myself into, and it should terrify me. But you know what's even scarier? The thought of a life without her. It doesn't make sense. None of this does. My life used to be about restraint, deals, and empire-building. Now? My only goal is her.

We're still tangled together, our bodies flushed from the aftermath, the cool night air doing nothing to settle the fire between us. The moonlight catches the gold in her eyes as she stares up at me. Then— "Oh no..." Yasmine breathes, voice laced with realization. No. Nope. Not happening. I don't let her finish, crushing my lips against hers before she can start overthinking. Because if she starts thinking, she might panic. And if she panics, she might regret it. And if she regrets it...No. No, absolutely the fuck not.

She sighs into my mouth, her fingers curling into my hair like she doesn't want to stop. Good. Maybe if I keep kissing her, we can avoid this whole "processing what just happened" thing altogether. But Yasmine isn't stupid, and she's definitely not someone who can be distracted for long. When I pull back, her lips are swollen, and her breath is uneven. I'm considering diving in for round two when she says softly, "Alex… we didn't use protection."

I swallow hard. "I know." She blinks up at me, waiting. So, I do the only thing I know to do in moments of sheer existential crisis. I make a wildly inappropriate joke. "If I have it my way, you'll be running around with eight of my babies pretty soon."

Yasmine snorts—a full-on, unfiltered, beautiful laugh. And just like that, the knot in my chest loosens. "You want eight kids?" she asks, amused.

"Not particularly," I smirk. "I've never thought about kids before. But I gotta figure out a way to keep you." Her smile falters, just for a second, like she's trying to figure out whether I'm being serious. I am. And that alone should scare the fuck out of me. Instead, I lean in, brush my lips over hers, and give her a kiss full of confessions I don't know how to admit yet. A silent promise. A plea. At this moment, I would do anything for this woman, because, for the first time in my life, I know what was missing in my life and who will make it complete.

—

My mind is still spinning from last night as I step into my one-on-one session with Pablo. I swear I woke up feeling… different. Lighter. Like someone cracked open my chest, scooped out all the bullshit, and replaced it with something terrifyingly real. I even caught myself humming in the shower. What the hell is happening to me?

Pablo's already seated on a cushion near the open window, the scent of sage and ocean breeze wafting through. Classic.

Always in his mystical, all-knowing, too-wise-for-this-world era. He lifts his head when he sees me and smiles. "Alex, you look brighter today."

I scoff, but there's a tug at my lips. "You mean I don't look like an insufferable asshole for once?"

His laugh is calm, knowing. "I meant what I said. It suits you."

I drop onto the cushion across from him, rubbing a hand over my jaw. "Yeah, well… I feel good. Really good." Too good. So-good-it-must-be-a-trap good. Pablo stays quiet, just watching me with those wise, uncomfortably knowing eyes that always make me feel like he's reading me like an open book. I exhale, tapping my fingers against my knee. "But there's something else I need to get off my chest."

He nods, encouraging. "Go on."

I hesitate, then just say it. "I want to talk about the vision I had during my reiki session with Emilio."

Pablo's expression shifts, curious but still calm. "I'm listening."

I clear my throat, suddenly unsure why this feels so hard to say out loud. "I saw my mom." The words are quiet and careful. "She told me… not to be afraid to love freely. That she wants me to live without holding back."

His face softens, like he already knows how much that shook me. "That sounds like a beautiful reassurance."

I let out a humorless laugh, running a hand through my hair. "Yeah. You'd think that, right? But it's me we're talking about. My immediate reaction was to question whether I was having some kind of emotional hallucination." Pablo chuckles but doesn't interrupt. I shift, suddenly feeling on the edge of something big. Or maybe I'm already in free fall. "I... I think I love Yasmine." There. I said it. Holy shit, I said it. Pablo's smile widens slightly, but he doesn't rush to respond. He waits, letting me sit in the moment and own it. "But I'm afraid," I admit. "I don't want to use her as some emotional crutch. What if I'm latching on to the first person who's made me feel... whole? What if this is just misplaced gratitude or some post-trauma rebound?"

Pablo studies me for a moment before speaking. "I understand your hesitation." His voice is steady. "But what if that's exactly what love is? A form of healing. You're not just attaching yourself to someone because they helped you. Yasmine isn't a crutch, Alex. She's *proof* that you're healing. She's part of the journey, not a distraction from it." I blink. Okay, *damn*. That was... a lot. And it's probably entirely too accurate.

Something buzzes beneath my skin, a strange mix of nerves and relief. "So you're saying... it's okay to let myself be this happy? This quickly?"

Pablo exhales a small laugh. "Alex, time is relative when it comes to love. If your mother's message was to love freely, and you've found someone who makes you feel that kind of joy, why fight it?" He tilts his head slightly. "Healing isn't a finish line you cross. It's something you allow yourself to experience again and again." I stare at him for a beat, letting it all settle. And surprisingly, I don't feel the need to argue.

Instead, a slow grin tugs at my lips, and I feel it again. That ridiculous, completely unearned spring in my step. "You're good at this, you know that?"

Pablo chuckles. "I've been told."

I shake my head, exhaling. "I guess I'm just not used to opening up like this."

"None of us are," he says, eyes glinting with something wise and frustratingly accurate. "Until we find the right person. Don't let fear hold you back."

I nod, letting out a slow breath. Finally, I don't want to run..

CHAPTER 54

YASMINE

This final week is packed with activities, leaving me no time to talk to Alex since our passionate night in the cave. But something between us has shifted. I feel it in the way my heart hums like a tuning fork whenever his name crosses my mind. It's different now. *Better.*

Luckily, I track my cycle religiously, and despite our little… accident, we should be in the clear. The universe is merciful.

The door opens, and just like that, he's here. Alex walks into our final yoga session, and *ugh*, seriously? How does he look even better today? It's honestly offensive. Tall, chiseled, fresh, with just the right amount of scruff. He moves like he owns the space without even trying.

Our eyes meet, and there's that undeniable spark again, sizzling between us like an exposed wire. Then he smiles. *Oh*, I'm in trouble. I scramble for composure, but my voice still comes out a little too breathy. "Hi."

Alex's smile deepens, his eyes soft but knowing. "Hi." Why does he say it like that? My insides melt into actual soup, and I must be looking ridiculous because my face definitely feels like it's doing something embarrassing.

I gesture to the mat across from me, desperate for normalcy. "Sit, please." He obliges, sinking down onto the mat with effortless grace while I clutch onto my last remaining shred of professionalism. "How are you feeling today?" I ask, keeping my tone light and casual as if my entire body isn't currently on fire.

He tilts his head then flashes me that devastating smirk. "Better now that I'm with you." Oh. *Oh*, we're playing that game today? I arch a brow, determined to stay unfazed, or at least pretend to be.

Alex chuckles, shaking his head. "And before you start overthinking it, no, I'm not using any pickup lines. I've only ever been honest with you." Well, great. Now, I'm definitely blushing. My entire body betrays me as heat rushes up my neck, setting me ablaze like a human lantern. I clear my throat, waving away the warmth creeping over me. *Focus*, Yasmine. You are an enlightened, spiritually grounded woman. Act like it.

"This is our last session together," I remind him, ignoring the pang that realization brings. "So I want to focus on anything you still need to work on. Are there any areas we haven't fully addressed yet?" A beat of silence stretches between us.

Alex doesn't answer immediately. Instead, he looks at me. Deeply and intensely. Unnervingly real. I shift slightly, suddenly hyper-aware of how he's staring into my soul like it holds the answers to everything. I've never let another man go this deep, but Alex has a way of slipping past every barrier as if he was always meant to be there.

Finally, he looks down, exhaling as if steadying himself. When he lifts his gaze again, it's serious. "Well… Yasmine," he begins, hesitating for just a second. Then, with all the weight of the universe behind it, he confesses, "I've fallen in love with someone."

My breath? Gone. *Vanished.* Stolen straight from my lungs.

His expression is raw. "And I want to love that person freely, completely, without hesitation. But…it's something I've never done before. It's unfamiliar territory for me. So I might need a little guidance." Then, with a small, almost teasing tilt of his lips, he asks, "Do you think you can help me with that today?"

The room tilts. Or maybe it's just my heart throwing itself against my ribs. I blink at him, my brain doing backflips to process what's happening. "Alex…" I say slowly, choosing my words carefully, but I can't think.

Luckily, he cuts me off before I can spiral. "Before you start overthinking," he says, lips quirking as if he knows exactly what's happening in my head, "just know, I'm not expecting anything from you. I just wanted to tell you how I feel. That's all." His smile is so reassuring, so achingly open, that all my nerves evaporate.

Just like that, I'm at ease. As Alex settles onto the mat, I take a deep breath, centering myself before guiding him through what might be our most meaningful session yet. If there's one thing I've learned on this journey, it's that love, like yoga, is a practice—a daily commitment—a willingness to breathe through the discomfort and open up, even when it's terrifying.

I kneel beside him, keeping my voice soft but steady. "Love, true, unguarded love, requires trust." I guide Alex into *Ustrasana*. He kneels with his hands resting on his lower back for support. His muscles are tense and resistant.

"Go slow," I instruct, placing a gentle hand on his chest. "Lift through your heart. Breathe." He exhales, arching his back as he leans into the stretch. "This pose is about opening up," I continue. "Physically, yes, but emotionally too. Love requires the same thing, exposing the parts of us that we usually protect."

Alex glances at me as I press my palm lightly against his sternum. His breath deepens. "Surrender. Let yourself be open, even if it feels scary." I gently tell him. He exhales again, this time sinking deeper. I feel his resistance softening, his chest expanding.

Next, I move us into Tree Pose but with a twist. We do it together, standing side by side, pressing our palms together in the air for balance. Alex wobbles immediately. "Okay, this is a terrible idea."

I giggle. "Your balance is terrible. The idea is fine." He glares at me, but he's smiling. "This pose is about trust," I explain. "Balance isn't just about strength; it's about knowing when to lean on someone else. Love works the same way."

Alex stills, absorbing my words. I press into his palm just enough for him to feel it. "You don't have to do everything alone," I say softly.

His fingers twitch against mine. After a long moment, he exhales. "Yeah," he says. "I think I'm starting to get that."

For the final part of our session, I have Alex lie on his back in *Savasana*. I sit beside him, lowering my voice to a soothing murmur. "Close your eyes and place one hand over your heart, the other over your stomach." He does. I wait a beat before continuing. "Now, imagine love, not as something you have to chase or control, but as something already inside you. Like breath. Like warmth. Something that exists freely, without conditions." His chest rises and falls. "Now," I say, "ask yourself, what would it feel like to love without fear?"

Silence. Then, so softly I almost don't hear it, Alex whispers, "Like coming home."

I swallow past the lump in my throat. After a few moments, I gently touch his shoulder. "Come back when you're ready."

His eyes flutter open, and when they meet mine, everything shifts. It's not just a look. It's a pull, like the entire universe just narrowed down to this moment. His gaze is deep and unguarded, in a way that makes my stomach tighten. Somewhere in this tangled mess of whatever we are, I realize he isn't alone in this. He isn't the only one afraid. He isn't the only one learning how to love without running. I am, too. I thought I had it all figured out—what it meant to be open, surrender, and trust. But now, staring at him, feeling the weight of everything we are and could be, I see the truth. Without thinking, I cup his face in my hands and kneel in front of him. His breath stills, his body going perfectly still beneath my touch like he's been waiting for this. And I have, too.

The moment our lips meet, something inside me unfurls, something terrifying and inevitable. This isn't just a kiss. It's an understanding, a silent acknowledgment of everything we've been too scared to face. It's love. The kind that sneaks up on you. The kind that doesn't ask for permission.

When we finally pull apart, Alex exhales, resting his forehead against mine like he's grounding himself. In a voice so low I barely hear, he whispers, "Thank you." He doesn't explain. He doesn't have to. I already know.

Thank you for helping me love.
Thank you for seeing me.
Thank you for healing a part of me I didn't even know was broken.

I smile, brushing my fingers through his hair. My heart is completely, utterly ruined for this man. "See me after dinner?"

His lips curve, and I swear the entire universe shifts around us for a second. "Yeah," he murmurs, nodding. "I can't wait." Then, before I can move away, he pulls me back in for one last kiss, like he's committing it to memory.

CHAPTER 55

ALEX

Soft sheets. Glowing sunlight. And her. Curves that could ruin a man. The scent of jasmines and gardenias mixed with Yasmine is something uniquely hers. Warm skin and a hint of sea salt, something I've become utterly addicted to. I pry my eyes open to make sure I'm not dreaming. She's draped across me, her long, wild hair spilling over my chest, her lips brushing lazy kisses along my neck. Her body is pressed against mine, so soft and perfect, and I swear, I could lay here forever. I smile like an absolute idiot. Because she does that to me. She makes me feel things I've never let myself feel before—the kind of happiness that makes me forget I've once built walls around my heart.

"Good morning, baby," she rasps sexily. Her eyes spark with something wicked as she starts to slide downwards, and she licks her lips like she's still hungry for me, even after last night. *God*, last night. We practically had a marathon. The bed, the bathtub, then twice more in the middle of the night, somewhere in that hazy, half-awake, half-dreaming state where our bodies somehow found each other again and again. And now she still wants more. *Fuck*. I'm just as insatiable as she is.

"Angel," I manage to groan, my voice hoarse, wrecked from everything she does to me. She grins that mischievous, beautiful, knowing smile that tells me I'm about to die in the best way possible.

"Lay back," she coos, her voice low, sultry, full of promise. "Let me take care of you."

I can't think. I'm already so hard it's borderline painful, my cock straining as Yasmine's warm breath ghosts over me. And then, *holy hell.* She licks the precum off my tip, her eyes flicking up to meet mine, and I nearly lose it right there. She's teasing. Playing with me like she knows exactly how much control she has over me. And she does. Her hands wrap around my base and she starts stroking me, slow and slick, using her spit and my own precum as lubricant. I hiss, my hips twitching involuntarily. I have no shame anymore. Not when it comes to her. Then her lips part, and she takes me into her mouth, deep, wet, and hot. I groan as my fingers grip the sheets. Her tongue swirls around me, teasing me with just the right amount of pressure before she takes me in deeper. My head falls back as I revel in this feeling of pure ecstasy. Her mouth is tight and warm, like silk, sucking me down inch by inch. It's almost sinful how good this feels, how something so beautiful between us can be so filthy at the same time. She works me deeper, bobbing her head, her tongue pressing against that perfect spot along my length, and when she tries to take me all the way, struggling just a little, I nearly break. I watch her, completely mesmerized at the way she gags slightly, her throat tightening around me, the tears glistening in the corners of her eyes, and the way she loves it. She smiles around me like she's just as wrecked as I am, like she was made to ruin me. She is my undoing.

"Fuck," I grit out, my hands tangling in her thick, wild hair as I start thrusting into her mouth. She takes it, deep-throating me without hesitation. Before I can lose control completely, I yank her up, dragging her onto my lap, crashing my lips against hers in a kiss that's deep, messy, and desperate. She moans into my mouth, her body soaked for me, ready, and I don't think I've ever wanted anything more in my life. I kiss down her neck, slow and wet, trailing lower, breathing her in, needing more.

"Alex…" she pants, gripping my shoulders. She's dripping for me.

I pull her over me and command, "Sit on my face." She does, shuffling upwards without hesitation. Her thighs cage me in, her hands gripping the headboard for balance, and the second her sweet pussy meets my mouth, I groan against her. I swear I could live here. Die here. Worship her forever. I devour her, my tongue dragging up her slit, swirling over her clit before plunging into her, tasting her everywhere. Inside, around, drinking her down, flicking, sucking, pulling every breathless whimper and moan from her lips like a prayer. She grinds down onto my face, her thighs tightening around my head, and I relish in the suffocation of her, my hands gripping her ass, pulling her even closer as I suck her clit into my mouth and flick my tongue against her in urgent, perfect strokes. Yasmine screams, her body shaking, breaking apart on my tongue.

But I'm not done. Before she can recover, I flip her beneath me, hovering over her, locking my gaze onto hers, and slamming my cock into her with one deep stroke, feeling the aftershocks of her orgasm around me. She cries out, gripping my arms, nails digging into my shoulders, and I fuck her through it, slow at first, making her feel it. I draw out every last ripple of pleasure before I start driving into her harder, faster, chasing something I never knew I needed until now. Yasmine is moaning like crazy, gasping my name, and I swear it's the most beautiful sound in the world. I want to record it and set it as my fucking alarm. Her body grips me so tightly and I'm losing it, losing myself, but I don't want this to end. I slow my pace, rolling my hips, making it deeper, torturing both of us, and when I rest my forehead against hers when our eyes lock, everything else disappears. I see her. And she sees me.

I whisper against her lips, my voice rough. "I love you. So fucking much, I could do this forever with you." And the way her breath catches and trembles beneath me tells me she feels the same way, too.

She pulls me down, her legs tightening around my waist, her hips tilting up, and fuck. I sink even deeper, and whatever last shred of control I had? Gone. Completely and utterly gone. Yasmine grinds up against me, squeezing my body in a way that makes my vision blur, my breath stutter, and my entire being shatter into hers. It's too much and not enough all at once. I can't think. I can't hold back. All I can do is feel. She takes me—all of me, meeting every deep, aching thrust with an urgency like she doesn't just want this; she needs it. *Needs me.* And I need her. So I give her everything. Every part of me I've ever kept guarded, every locked door, every inch of my body and soul that I didn't even realize belonged to her until this very moment. I make love to her like it's the only way I know how to tell her she owns me, *completely* now. Her nails dig into my back and I feel her start to unravel beneath me, tightening, trembling, her body begging me to fall with her. And I do. It hits us both, our orgasms crashing over us at the same time, tearing through me with unrelenting force, pulling me under, drowning me in her. It's the most intense, euphoric, earth-shattering release I've ever had. Because it's with her. The best sex of my life, with the love of my life.

I collapse beside her, both of us panting and completely wrecked. After a long beat of silence, she turns her head and smiles at me. Like a goddess, like she's mine. "That was…" she whispers. I grin, completely ruined for her, and brush my fingers over her cheek.

"…a great way to wake up." I finish her sentence, leaning in, capturing her lips in one last slow, deep kiss, trying to

memorize this moment because I don't want to leave it.
Because this? This is the closest to heaven I've ever been.

CHAPTER 56

YASMINE

Something changed between Alex and me this morning. I felt it in the way he said he loved me. But there's no time to unpack the weight of what just happened. Because right now, I have to meet Ethan for our final session. I don't exactly dread working with him, but something about him has always felt… off. It's like he's playing a game only he knows the rules to. He walks into the yoga pavilion with a sneaky smirk, making my instincts go on high alert.

"You look absolutely gorgeous today, Yasmine." His tone is too smooth, too rehearsed.

I offer a polite smile, keeping my energy calm and neutral. "Thank you." I move to steer the conversation toward yoga, our actual reason for being here, but Ethan, as always, seems far more interested in himself. He flirts and brags about his latest business ventures, barely pretending to care about the session. I'm used to it. But today, it grates on me more than usual.

Then, his tone changes. "Yasmine, I don't want this to be the last time I see you," he says, watching me too closely like he's already anticipating my answer.

I pause, wary. "Oh?"

"I have a proposal." He straightens, his voice taking on that boardroom confidence that's probably closed a thousand deals. "I want you to spearhead the opening of my retreat center in Portugal. My firm is expanding, and we're looking to conquer Europe. And this retreat has opened my eyes to the wellness world." He leans in slightly, flashing a charming grin. "I think we could make a lot of money together."

Ah. "That opportunity sounds amazing, Ethan." I say honestly. "But I'm not really in this for the money, if that's your goal." Portugal would be incredible. But something in my gut tells me to hesitate. And I tell myself Alex has nothing to do with this hesitation.

Ethan waves a hand as if brushing off my concerns. "Making money is a secondary reward for all the good you will bring there. These people in Portugal deserve the kind of healing you can offer, and I know it won't be the same without you." His words almost make sense, but something in how he says it suggests he's selling me an outcome that he's already decided. My first instinct is to talk to Alex about it. What's going to happen to us after this retreat is over? We never discussed it. But I shove the thought aside before I can read too much into it.

"I'll think about it," I say, keeping my tone polite.

Ethan's eyes flicker and smirks. "Don't think about it too long." There's an edge to his tone, as if he expects me to say yes, simply because he's not used to hearing no. I don't love it, but he's not wrong. Opportunities don't last forever. And Ethan is, above all else, a businessman.

"Let's begin, shall we?" I say, and with that, we move into our final yoga session. Ethan's words linger in the back of my mind. But so does Alex.

—

Dinner just ended and I barely wait for my plate to be cleared before I rush off to find Alex. I've been sitting on this conversation all day, and it's gnawing at me. I don't like playing games. I never have. I slip towards a quiet corner of the retreat center and Alex finds me before I find him. Strong arms wrap around my waist from behind, pulling me against a firm chest. I don't need to turn around to know who it is; his scent is unmistakable—fresh, clean, with the faintest trace of something warm and masculine—just *him*. A deep chuckle vibrates against my back as his chin settles in the crook of my neck. "I've been waiting all day to get my hands back on you." His lips brush against my skin, sending a shiver down my spine.

I exhale a quiet laugh, already melting into him. "Me too." He spins me around, and before I can say another word, his mouth is on mine. I loop my arms around his neck as he presses me close. The world disappears. Just the two of us, lips tangled, breaths mingling, like we're making up for every second we weren't touching today. But I can't get lost in this. Not now.

"Alex…" I murmur, reluctantly pulling back.

His brows furrow slightly, but there's patience in his gaze. "What's wrong?"

I swallow, suddenly nervous. "Ethan asked me to go with him to Portugal after the retreat. He wants me to help open a wellness center." I force the words out, wanting everything in the open.

Alex's expression doesn't change immediately. He just studies me for a beat. Then, finally, he murmurs, "I see." That's it? *I see?* His voice remains neutral, but there's something tight about it. "I mean, it's obvious why he'd want you. You're incredible at what you do." His jaw tenses slightly. "But I won't pretend I trust his intentions." I nod, understanding his meaning. Ethan and Alex never exactly got along. Still, his reaction feels… restrained. I can't tell if that's a good or bad thing. "What did you say to him?" Alex asks, his tone careful.

"That I'd think about it," I admit. "He mentioned it would be for at least a year. I…"

"Fuck," Alex mutters, cutting me off. He exhales sharply, rubbing a hand over his face. "I can't make this decision for you." His voice is firm, but his eyes look conflicted. "And you don't need to explain yourself to me."

I shift uncomfortably. "We never really talked about what happens to us after this retreat, Alex…" His gaze flickers and he slides away from mine. The air between us turns thick. For the first time tonight, I feel the distance between us. *Say something,* I silently plead. Give me something, anything. But he doesn't. So I force a smile, nudging him playfully. "Why don't we go back to your room? We can talk more there." He nods, but the way he clears his throat, a telltale sign he has things he wants to say but won't, makes my stomach twist.

We walk back quietly, hand in hand, through the moonlit courtyard. When we reach his room, he barely waits for the door to shut before pulling me into a fierce hug, as if anchoring himself. I close my eyes, sinking into him—so many emotions swirl in the air, but neither of us knows what to say. So, instead, we kiss. The tension, uncertainty, and frustration comes crashing over us as we stumble backward onto the bed. His body cages mine but there's nothing rushed about the way we touch tonight. No desperate hunger. No frantic urgency.

Just tenderness. Because this isn't just about lust. It never was. But a part of me is desperately afraid that this could be one of the last times we'll be together.

CHAPTER 57

ALEX

I'm on my way to Pablo's last session but my mind is somewhere else—or rather, with *someone* else. Last night flipped everything upside down. Before I saw Yasmine, I was ready to tell her I wanted a future with her. Not just some casual, undefined thing. A real future. One where she might come back with me to Los Angeles. It would've been a lot to ask, but after having her, knowing what it feels like to wake up next to her, I can't imagine my life without her.

"You seem deep in thought." Pablo's voice cuts through my haze, his ever-knowing smirk in place.

"Sorry. Hi." I shake my head, a little embarrassed to have been caught zoning out.

His eyes twinkle with amusement. "What's got you so wrapped up today, Alex? Or should I say… who?"

I glance down, debating how much I actually want to say. But this is Pablo. If there's anyone who can give me the clarity I desperately need, it's him. I exhale and go for it. "This retreat…It's probably been the most transformative experience of my life. And I need to thank you for that." Pablo nods as if he already knows. Of course, he knows. I swear the man is psychic. But I can't dance around it, so I just lay it all out there. "I thought I'd be leaving here with Yasmine in my arms, maybe not right away, but eventually." I let out a sharp breath, my fingers gripping the edge of my seat. "But she told me something yesterday. She's thinking about going to Portugal with Ethan. He's going to open a wellness center there…"

Pablo's expression flickers. He looks slightly taken aback but not entirely surprised. "If anyone can do it, it's Yasmine. She's incredibly gifted. Her light doesn't go unnoticed." I nod, because of course people want her. Of course, *Ethan* wants her. But knowing that doesn't make it easier. I hate that part of me. The ugly, possessive part that's fuming over the idea of her choosing him over me. I know that's not what she's doing. It's not about Ethan; it's about her, her career, and her dreams. But that doesn't stop the gnawing feeling in my chest, the burning need to have her. To claim her.

Pablo watches me closely, and just as I wonder if he can hear my thoughts, he says, "I'm going to tell you something from one of my favorite poets, Khalil Gibran. It's a quote you've probably heard before." He pauses, his voice steady. "If you love somebody, let them go. For if they return, they were always yours. And if they don't, they never were." I stare at him. I know there's truth in what he's saying. There's logic. There's wisdom. But when it comes to Yasmine, I am the least logical man alive.

I'd already started thinking about what it would take to restructure my entire company just so I could follow her to Portugal. Just so I could be wherever she is. But she didn't ask that of me. I swallow the lump in my throat and remain silent.

Pablo's voice softens. "I'm proud of you, Alex. The fact that you're here, talking about this instead of shutting down, shows how much you've grown." I look up at him and he smiles. "I want you to know, it's okay to feel what you're feeling. Love isn't just happiness and sunshine. It's facing the hard things, feeling the doubt, the fear… and still choosing to believe in it." He leans back, thoughtful. "It's the most powerful thing we get to experience as humans. And I'm happy you're experiencing it." His words hit me somewhere deep. I don't say anything right away. I just sit with it, letting it sink in. Because he's right, *I love her.* And now, I have to figure out what the hell to do about it.

—

It's the last day of the retreat and the past twenty-four hours have been a blur of activities, people saying their goodbyes, and moments slipping through my fingers before I can grab onto them. I didn't see Yasmine last night. Maybe it was intentional—maybe she needed space, or maybe I did. But now, with only hours left before we go our separate ways, I can't let this end like that. I need to see her.

I walk toward the beach and she's standing in almost the exact spot where I first saw her when I first arrived here. But everything is different now. I love her now.

"Hey, beautiful." My voice is careful, as if I don't want to pull her too harshly from her thoughts. She turns, those deep green eyes locking onto mine, and I feel it again—that gut punch of disbelief that someone this breathtaking, this extraordinary, even exists. That I got to have her, even for just a moment.

Her lips part slightly, forming a soft smile, but there's something bittersweet in it. "Alex," she murmurs, "I missed you last night." Her voice is laced with regret, as if she wishes things had been different.

I nod, swallowing down the lump in my throat. "I missed you too." And God, I did. Every second. "But I figured we both needed a night to think." Her gaze drops to the sand, and I hate this. This distance, this weight between us. The ache in my chest that's telling me I'm about to lose something I can't bear to lose. I step forward, gently tilting her chin up so she has no choice but to look at me. "Listen, Yasmine," I say, my voice rougher than intended. "I want you to know… I'll wait for you." Her breath catches. "I've fallen madly, deeply, and completely in love with you." I continue, the words leaving me like an exhale I've been holding for weeks. "And I don't take that lightly. You're it for me, Yasmine. I think a part of me always knew that. I'll be here when you're ready to come back to me." I'm handing her my heart on a silver platter with no shields or defenses. Whether she wants it or not, it's no longer mine. It's hers. Her eyes brim with tears and I feel my stomach twist because I'm terrified this isn't going to end the way I want it to. She steps forward and wraps her arms around me, pressing herself into my chest like she's trying to memorize me. She feels it too—this love, this impossible pull between us. I shut my eyes, tightening my hold, breathing her in, praying this isn't goodbye. But it is. And for the first time in decades, my eyes sting with something I refuse to name.

The ocean stretches out endlessly in front of us, the sound of the waves crashing against the shore echoing the chaos in my chest. My heart feels like it's been ripped open, crushed under the weight of everything left unsaid. I would have moved oceans for her. I would have followed her to the ends of the earth if she asked me to. But she didn't, and her journey isn't mine to take. I try to remind myself that she's chasing her dream, that this is the kind of opportunity she's worked so hard for. I want to be happy for her, but the parts of me I've kept locked away for so long are breaking free, no matter how hard I try to hold them back. She's opened something in me I thought I'd buried. A wound I've spent years trying to heal but never truly could. The loss, the sense of abandonment, is a scar that runs deep. It's the shadow of loss from when I was too young to understand, but old enough to feel the ache of being left behind.

My mind circles back to that familiar, haunting refrain—the

fear of history repeating itself, the fear of losing someone I love all over again. And this time, it feels even harder, because Yasmine isn't being taken away; she's choosing to leave. I feel hollow as the waves mock me with their relentless rhythm, and all I can think is that I should have seen this coming. I should have known that no matter how much I love her, it won't be enough to keep her.

CHAPTER 58

YASMINE

I hold onto him, my arms wrapped around his solid frame, and for a moment, it feels like time has stopped. The love I feel for Alex is vast and boundless, so powerful that if I let myself, I might hold on forever. But love isn't about possession or fear. It's expansive. It's freedom. He's letting me go, and in the same way, I'm letting him go, too. Because if we are meant to find each other again, we will. I trust that. I trust us.

My voice is soft when I murmur against his shoulder, "I don't expect you to put your life on hold for me, Alex." I mean it. Or at least, I want to. Alex pulls back just enough to look at me, and instantly, I miss the warmth of him. His hands settle on my shoulders, anchoring me in place as his stormy eyes pierce into mine.

"Yasmine," he says, his voice rough with emotion, "you're it for me. And I'm sorry, but I'm not a generous man. I don't share. And in the same way, I hope you know I won't be able to even breathe in the same direction as another woman." My breath catches. Every word and syllable is laced with so much sincerity it almost knocks the air from my lungs. I don't need promises. I don't need declarations. I feel the truth in him. I hold his gaze, my fingers tracing lightly over the sharp angles of his jaw, memorizing him at this moment. Then, I rise onto my toes and press my lips to his in a soft, reverent kiss—a quiet vow that doesn't need words. He pulls me closer like he's trying to imprint himself onto me. Like maybe if we kiss long enough, we'll never have to say goodbye at all.

I know this isn't the end. Love like this doesn't end.

CHAPTER 59

ALEX

8 weeks later.

It's been two months and it still feels like someone reached into my chest, ripped out my heart, and forgot to stitch me back up. I wanted to ask Yasmine to try long-distance, but I didn't want to push her. So now, I'm stuck in hell. It takes everything in me not to book a flight to Portugal right now. I tell myself I have work to do, deals to close, and people who need me, but none of it matters. Every day without her feels like torture. I only had her for a handful of days, but now that I know what it's like to fall asleep with her tangled in my arms, waking up alone without her scent or warmth is unbearable.

My phone buzzes and I grab it immediately, my pulse spiking. Just AJ. I groan and answer. "What do you want?"

"Damn, is that how you greet your bestie?" his voice is obnoxiously cheerful, which only makes me more annoyed. "Listen, man, I need to pull you out of this funk. You're bumming us out. I'm coming over in twenty minutes, and I'm taking you out."

"I'm not in the mood."

"Too bad, I'm already on my way." And with that, he hangs up.

—

The club is loud. The bass thumps through my chest, the air thick with alcohol, perfume, and a haze of desperation that I used to thrive in. We're in the VIP section of this club, the table cluttered with expensive bottles I've barely touched. The crowd below moves in waves, bodies pressing against each other, and I can feel eyes on me—women who would have had my full attention before. Now, I don't give a damn.

"Man, this is like old times," Mark says, raising his glass. "Except now we're richer and better looking."

AJ smirks, tipping back his whiskey. "Speak for yourself. I've always been better looking."

Poppy laughs, curling into Mark's side. "You guys are insufferable." She kisses him, and I look away, my stomach twisting—not because of the PDA, but because my brain goes to the one place it shouldn't. I start imagining Yasmine with someone else. Some fruit fly in Europe, looking at her the way I do. Touching her. Kissing her. My jaw tightens. I can't. I fucking can't.

My friend Josh, oblivious to my downward spiral, rolls his eyes. "Pierce, what's with you? You've been quiet all night. I expected you to already have some girl's number by now."

I shrug, swirling the whiskey in my glass. "Not in the mood."

AJ raises a brow. "Not in the mood? Since when have you not been in the mood?"

Mark leans forward, studying me like a puzzle he's just figured out. "Wait a second… this isn't still about Tulum, is it?" His smirk grows. "You're still thinking about her, aren't you?" I don't respond, which is an answer in itself. "Yasmine," he continues, leaning back. "Isn't she the one you met all those years ago? The mud-splash girl?"

And just like that, I'm back there—driving home from a failed one-night stand, frustrated and tired, when my car sprayed mud all over her. She stood there, dripping in dirt, and somehow, that moment tilted the entire axis of my world. She became my aphrodisiac in every sense of the word. Yasmine pulled me out of a funk I didn't even realize I was in, and now, like all those years ago, she's ruined every other woman for me.

Josh snaps his fingers in front of my face. "Pierce, you good? You've got that faraway look, man."

I shake it off, setting my glass down. "I'm fine." It's a lie, and they all know it.

AJ leans in. "If this Yasmine girl still has you in knots, why haven't you done something about it?"

Mark nods. "Yeah, what's stopping you?"

Josh lifts his glass. "You've got women throwing themselves at you, and you're here, brooding like a lovesick idiot. That's how you know it's real. Go get her."

I exhale, rubbing a hand over my face. "I'm trying to be the bigger person here. You know, 'if you love someone, set them free' and all that shit."

AJ rolls his eyes. "Yeah, yeah, real poetic. But also? Fuck that." He leans forward. "You can't let this one go. She's not like the others. You know it. You've said it yourself a hundred times."

I close my eyes, trying to block out the truth in his words. But I can't, because he's right. "She's destroyed all other women for me." She's it. She's the only one I want.

Mark grins and claps me on the back. "Then what the hell are you waiting for?"

AJ smirks. "I gotta agree with Mark. I know you're trying to be all enlightened and noble with your 'letting her go' bullshit, but the Alex Pierce I know has never let anything slip through his fingers if he really wanted it." His eyes narrow. "And you really fucking want her."

My pulse picks up. They're right. I've been torturing myself for what? To prove I can do the honorable thing? Fuck that. Yasmine isn't just a fleeting thought. She's not some phase. And it's time I stopped running from that truth.

Josh shakes his head, laughing. "Man, we should be the ones getting paid thousands for this therapy session."

CHAPTER 60

The *Serra Zen Retreat Center* rests in the rolling hills of Sintra, surrounded by lush forests that feel almost enchanted. Ancient trees line the cobblestone paths, and from the highest point, I can make out the shimmering Atlantic ocean. The main building is a restored 19th-century villa with stone walls, vibrant Portuguese tiles, and arched ceilings. The yoga hall overlooks the entire mountain, offering a breathtaking view. Just beyond the villa lies the meditation garden, where stone benches are tucked among fields of lavender, perfect for solitude.

It feels like things couldn't be going more smoothly. My yoga center in Tulum is flourishing, and Alyssa is fully managing it now. On the surface, everything is perfect. And yet, there's this ache in my chest I can't shake, no matter how hard I try. A part of me wishes Alex could see all of this, too. It's been two and a half months since I left Tulum and ten weeks since I saw Alex.

But today, I'm not letting myself dwell on it. Sami is visiting from Italy, where she's been studying abroad. She's staying with me for a week and brought her friend, Chan, along. When I walk in, the two of them are already chattering away in the kitchen, their laughter filling the air. Chan is leaning against the counter, wearing a wildly patterned shirt, bright orange pants, and velvet loafers with rhinestones. He gestures dramatically with a wooden spoon in hand, pretending to stir an invisible pot as he regales Sami with some story.

"So there I was," he says, his voice rich with flair, "stuck in the middle of this tiny coffee shop, holding a cappuccino that costs more than my rent, and the barista is giving me *that* look. You know the one."

"What look?" Sami asks, her eyes sparkling with amusement.

"The judging-you-but-still-flirting-with-you look," he replies, waving the spoon. "And I'm thinking, 'Sir, I'm flattered, but unless you're planning to comp my drink and pay my tuition, I don't have the bandwidth for this conversation.'" He tosses the spoon into the sink with a flourish. "So, naturally, I tipped him anyway. We're all starving for validation, aren't we?"

I laugh as I pour myself some coffee. "Chan, you are impossible."

"Darling," he says, spinning around to face me, "Every moment of my life is impossible. You're welcome."

Sami rolls her eyes fondly. "Ignore him. He's been like this since we left the airport."

"Lies," Chan says, placing a hand dramatically on his chest. "I was actually restrained for the first twenty minutes. You're lucky to know me in my fully blossomed state." We all burst into laughter, and for the first time in weeks, I feel a genuine lightness in my heart. The three of us spend the rest of the morning wandering the retreat grounds. Chan offers unsolicited, over-the-top critiques of everything, from the color of the cushions in the dining hall ("They're giving me serene, but could they give me serene and fabulous?") to the placement of the fountain in the meditation garden ("You've got symmetry, but where's the pizzazz?").

Sami, ever the grounded one, nudges me as we walk. "This place is amazing, Yaz. I'm so proud of you."

Her words hit me harder than I expect and I blink away the

sudden sting of tears. "Thanks, Sami. It means a lot."

Chan interrupts, draping an arm around both of us. "Group hug moment! I live for this wholesome energy." As we stand there, laughing in the middle of my retreat center, I feel a flicker of something I haven't felt in a while. Hope. Maybe I'll figure everything out after all.

We're standing by the fountain in the meditation garden, the soft trickle of water filling the air as Chan delivers another one of his dramatic critiques about the lack of "disco ball energy" in my retreat. I'm laughing, Sami is rolling her eyes, and for a moment, everything feels light. Then I hear footsteps behind me, purposeful and steady. I turn instinctively, and my breath catches my throat.

Alex.

He's standing there, looking like he's just stepped out of a dream, or maybe a movie about impossibly handsome men who always seem to know the exact moment to appear. His dark hair is slightly mussed, his shirt unbuttoned just enough to reveal a hint of his broad chest, and his sharp eyes lock onto mine with an intensity that makes my heart pound. He shoves his hands into his pockets, looking both confident and, somehow, a little unsure.

I can't speak. My brain struggles to process how he's standing here, in Sintra, at my retreat, when the last time I saw him was in Tulum. Chan, ever quick on the uptake, leans toward Sami and whispers, loud enough that I can just barely hear him, "Who is this, and did he step straight out of Big Hot Man Monthly? Because *wow*." Sami stifles a laugh, her eyes darting between Alex and me like she's trying to piece together what's happening.

Alex's gaze never wavers, even as he takes a small step closer. "Yasmine…" he murmurs, his voice steady but softer than I expect. I feel my heart hammering in my chest, my palms suddenly clammy. Chan's quip echoes faintly in the back of my mind, but right now, all I can focus on is Alex—how he's looking at me like he's been carrying the weight of something he's finally ready to set down.

"Alex," I manage, my voice barely above a whisper. "What… what are you doing here?" He stands there, his eyes fixed on me like I'm the only thing in the world that matters.

"You look beautiful," he says softly. His gaze sweeps over the space around us. "And this place… it's incredible. I mean it, Yasmine. I'm so proud of you." His words hit me harder than I expect, and for a moment, I just stand there, blinking back the emotion rising in my chest. I've worked so hard to make this place what it is, and hearing him say that feels like something I didn't even realize I needed.

"My family's in town for a European-wide charity foundation gala. It's being held in Portugal this year. I don't usually go to these kinds of things unless it's for work, but…" He pauses, his eyes meeting mine, "I made an exception."

"Why?" I ask, even though I already have a suspicion.

He give a boyish, almost mischievous grin that makes my stomach flip. "Because there's a pretty girl here I wanted to see."

"Oh?" I say, arching a brow, trying to sound light. "Should I be worried?"

Alex laughs, the sound rich and warm. "The pretty girl is you, obviously."

I can't help but laugh, too, my cheeks heating despite myself. His expression softens, and his voice drops a little. "It's always been you, Yasmine. Only you." The words land like a punch to my heart.

I swallow hard, trying to steady myself as my emotions threaten to overwhelm me. "Alex…"

"Come with me to the gala," he says, his tone almost pleading but still confident. "Friday night. Say yes."

There's something about the way he asks, the way he's looking at me, that makes it impossible to say no. "Okay," I say softly, nodding. "I'll go." The smile that breaks across his face is pure relief and sends a warmth to my chest. He leans in and presses a kiss to my cheek. It's brief, almost just a peck, but the tenderness of it, the way his lips brush my skin and the faint scent of his cologne, sends a shiver down my spine..

"Friday," he says again, his voice low and soft as he pulls back, his eyes lingering on mine for a moment before he steps away.

I nod, watching him walk away, my heart still pounding. Even as I stand there, trying to process everything, I feel the heat from his kiss lingering, like a promise of what's to come.

It's finally Friday night and my apartment is a whirlwind of
activity. Sami and Chan are here, buzzing with energy, as they
help me prepare for the gala. Well, help might be a modest
word. Sami practically takes over my wardrobe while Chan
hums to himself, setting up his makeup kit like a painter
preparing for a masterpiece.

"I'm telling you, Yasmine," Sami calls from my bedroom as she
rummages through my closet, "you don't have anything
remotely hot enough for tonight. This is a gala, not a yoga
class!"

I roll my eyes, adjusting my robe as I sit at the small vanity in
the corner of my room. "I have plenty of dresses, Sami. They're
just... understated."

"Understated is code for boring," Sami quips, emerging from
the closet with a dramatic sigh. "Good thing I went shopping
today." She smirks and pulls out a sleek garment bag.

I narrow my eyes. "What's in there?"

"Your salvation," she says with a grin, unzipping the bag to
reveal a dress that makes my jaw drop. It's stunning—deep
emerald green with a plunging neckline, a thigh-high slit, and
just enough shimmer to catch the light. It's sexy, glamorous,
and completely out of my comfort zone.

"I can't wear that!" I exclaim, staring at the dress like it might
bite me. "It's... it's too revealing!"

Sami arches a brow, unfazed. "It's perfect. And you're wearing it."

Chan, busy setting up his brushes and palettes, glances over and lets out a low whistle. "Oh, honey, she's not wrong. That dress is a moment."

I shake my head, feeling the beginnings of panic. "I can't pull that off. What if—"

"Nope!" Sami interrupts, holding the dress out towards me. "No arguments. You're putting this on. Alex is going to lose his mind."

Chan steps in, taking my shoulders and gently guiding me toward the bathroom. "Trust us," he says, his voice soothing but firm. "We're turning you into the woman of the night. Not just glamorous. *Iconic.*"

I groan but take the dress and close my bathroom door behind me. My breath catches when I slip it on and see myself in the mirror. The fabric hugs my body in all the right places, the green makes my skin glow, and the cut is daring enough to feel bold but not over the top. I step out, and the look on Sami's and Chan's faces says it all.

"See?" Sami says triumphantly. "I told you."

Chan waves me over to the vanity, pulling out a chair. "Alright, sit. We're just getting started." He works magic with my hair, twisting it into a sleek updo with soft tendrils framing my face. Then comes the makeup, bold, smoky eyes, perfectly contoured cheeks, and a nude lip that somehow ties everything together. When he's done, he steps back, hands on his hips, admiring his work. "Perfection," he declares. "You're a *goddess.* A vision. A gift to mankind." I look in the mirror and barely recognize myself. I look… stunning. Sexy. Confident. Exactly how I want to feel tonight.

Sami beams at me, grabbing my hands. "Yaz, you're going to knock him dead. He's not going to know what hit him."

I laugh nervously, butterflies fluttering in my stomach. "I just hope I can walk in these heels."

Chan grins, handing me a clutch. "Honey, you're not just walking. You're floating. Now go give Alex a night he'll never forget."

Bubbles tickle my nose as I take another sip of champagne. Sami, Chan, and I are lounging in my living room. The bottle of champagne sits proudly on my coffee table.

"Cheers to fabulous men and even more fabulous nights," Chan declares, raising his glass dramatically.

Sami snickers, clinking her glass against his. "Cheers to Yasmine for actually letting us spoil her for once." I laugh and take another sip. I usually don't indulge like this, but tonight, I'm allowing myself to celebrate. Two and a half months of hard work, endless planning, building, and perfecting my retreat center—and it's perfect. I'm so proud of what I've built, proud of myself. If there's ever been a reason to let loose, this is it. The thought of seeing Alex tonight makes my stomach flip. I haven't been able to stop thinking about him since he showed up earlier this week. He came to Portugal to see *me*. If that doesn't mean something, what does?

"You're thinking about him, aren't you?" Sami teases, breaking into my thoughts.

"No," I lie, though the heat in my cheeks betrays me.

Chan gasps dramatically, pointing at me with his glass. "She is! Look at that blush. Yasmine, darling, if you get any redder, you'll set the room on fire."

I shake my head, laughing as I set my glass down. "Alright, fine. Maybe I am. Is that a crime?"

"Absolutely not," Chan says, leaning forward with a gleam in his eye. "It's delicious. Alex Pierce, international billionaire heartthrob, chasing after you across continents. This is what dreams are made of."

"Seriously, though," Sami says, her tone softening. "You're excited to see him, aren't you?"

I nod, the smile on my face growing despite myself. "Yeah, I am. I don't know what will happen, but… he came here. That has to mean something, right?"

"Of course it does," Chan says, raising his glass again. "To Yasmine, to making him fall hopelessly in love with you all over again."

I laugh and clink my glass against theirs, letting the warmth of their support fill me. Whatever happens tonight, I'm ready. A knock cuts through the moment like a sharp inhale, and my stomach twists with nerves. It's *him*. I set my champagne glass down and my heart races as I glance at the mirror by the door, giving myself a final once-over. Chan and Sami exchange a look behind me, but I don't have the energy to decipher it. I can only think about Alex standing on the other side of this door.

I take a deep breath and open it. And there he is. Standing there in a black tuxedo, the epitome of sexiness and success as if he had just walked off the cover of a magazine. The sharp lines of his suit hug his frame perfectly. His dark hair is tousled effortlessly and his piercing eyes lock onto mine. He looks devastatingly good, better than any man has a right to look.

"Hi," I manage, my voice softer than I intended.

"Hi," he replies, his voice low and steady. At that moment, it's like the world stops. Everything fades. My body responds to him instantly. My skin warms and my heart beats so loudly that I'm sure he can hear it.

CHAPTER 61

ALEX

The door opens, and for a moment, I forget how to breathe. Yasmine stands in front of me and it feels like the world is tilting. She looks… breathtaking—her dress clings to her perfectly, showing off her curves in a way that's almost sinful. The slit in the fabric reveals her long legs, tan and sculpted, and the plunging neckline draws my eyes straight to her cleavage, bringing flashbacks of the nights when my hands, lips, and tongue had been there. My pulse quickens. She looks up at me, her eyes meeting mine, and for a second, I'm completely tongue-tied. Her beauty has always hit me like a freight train, but tonight, she's something else entirely. Absolutely irresistible.

"Wow," I manage, my voice lower and rougher than intended. "Yasmine, you look incredible."

Her cheeks flush slightly, and she smiles. "Thank you," she says softly.

I step closer, drawn to her by an invisible magnet. "Seriously," I say, more deliberately this time, "you're stunning. Completely mesmerizing."

A flicker of relief and confidence crosses her face and it's like watching a flower open in fast-forward. She has no idea how powerful she truly is, and I'm more than happy to be under her spell.

"Oh! Alex," she begins, turning with a radiant smile, "I want you to meet my sister, Sami, and Chan."

Sami steps forward first with a warm grin. "Ciao, Alex. We've heard *so* much about you."

Chan chimes in, "Yeah, it's great to finally put a face to the name. Yasmine's told us *all* the best stories."

I laugh softly, returning their smiles. "Hope she only told you the flattering ones."

Sami nudges Yasmine, eyes darting between us. "Well, you two look like you've got plenty to catch up on. Don't let us cramp your style."

Chan nods in agreement, adding, "Have a blast at the gala, don't get into too much trouble, kids!"

Yasmine and I share a soft laugh and I send them a quick nod of thanks before turning back to her. My lips curve into a subtle smile. "Ready?"

She meets my gaze. "Yeah," she murmurs, a quiet confidence radiating from her. I focus on steadying my breathing and ignore how her presence pulls at me like gravity. Her hand slips into mine and it feels as natural as breathing, like something I'm meant to do without even thinking.

Raul is waiting by the limo. As soon as we approach, he steps forward and opens the door for Yasmine. "It's nice to see you again, *Miss* Yasmine," he says with a grin, with just a little too much emphasis on the word representing her unmarried state.

Yasmine smiles back, and it's a little too bright for my liking. "Raul! I didn't realize you travel with Alex. It's really good to see you, too."

Jealousy spikes in my chest like a flare, sharp and immediate. It's ridiculous, I know. Raul is my driver and happily married for twenty years, but the way her smile lingers at him makes something primal twist inside me. I don't want her smiling like that at anyone else. Not him, not any man. That's for me. *Only me.* I force myself to keep my expression neutral as I guide her into the limo. Raul closes the door behind us, and the second we're alone, I roll up the divider without a word.

Before she can ask what I'm doing, I reach for her and pull her into my lap so she's straddling me. She gasps, her hands instinctively landing on my shoulders. "Alex—" she starts, but I cut her off.

"I've missed you," I murmur, my voice rough and thick with everything I've been holding back. My hands grip her waist like she might disappear if I let go, my eyes searching hers, desperate to make her understand. "Yasmine…you belong with me. You always have."

Her breath hitches. At this moment, with her so close, her body pressed against mine, I know there's no going back. She's mine, and I'll do whatever it takes to make her stay. I pull her down and press my lips to hers. Our kiss is soft and tentative at first—like we're relearning the shape of each other. But it doesn't stay that way for long. The heat between us builds and before I know it, it grows hotter, hungrier, more urgent. Her body shifts closer to mine, feeding the fire that's been simmering inside me since I saw her tonight.

I have to remind myself to hold back and not mess up her dress and perfect hair. But her lips—those luscious, pouty lips, are fair game. They're mine to ruin, and I do exactly that, kissing her harder, tasting her like I've been starving for weeks. And God, I have been. The need to consume her, to make her feel everything I can't put into words, is overwhelming. I know she feels it too—that electric charge between us, it's impossible to ignore. This is everything I've been missing, everything I can't live without. I can feel her start to grind on my lap, and with the way her dress is pooled at her waist right now, I can feel the heat of her bare pussy through the thin panties she's wearing.

I swipe my thumb over the lacey fabric and she's soaking. "Fuck, Yasmine, you're dripping, angel."

"Only you can do this to me, Alex," she murmurs back, her voice clouded with anticipation. And, as usual with Yasmine, I lose all sense of logic and control. I set her back on the leather seats and slip to the floor, bent in front of her, with her legs propped over my shoulders. I press a gentle kiss to her ankle and lick her leg up to her inner thigh. She groans as I slide her panties to the side. Yasmine is panting, and her arousal coats my seats. I'm so fucking turned on.

She looks down at me with smoldering hooded eyes. "I need you, baby." I'm done for. I dive into her pussy like it's my last meal. I'm ravenous for her. She tastes so sweet and juicy. My thumb rubs her clit, slowly at first, until she lets out an agonizing moan, and I smile against her entrance. My face must be coated right now and I've never felt so turned on. My cock is rock hard, testing the confines of my pants. Yasmine's fingers find my hair in the way I love; she tugs and scrapes with her nails. I groan in pleasure and lick her hard, fucking her with my tongue as deeply and intensely as I can.

"Oh, Alex, oh my God, YES!" She cries out.

That undoes me. I fuck her like that with my mouth until I feel her inner muscles squeezing my tongue. If that's not the hottest thing ever, I don't know what is. She's completely unraveling on my face.

As she comes down from her high, she cups my face and smiles at me with the most beautiful smile. She pulls me up and says, "My turn, baby."

I want to tell her she doesn't have to, but I don't have the resolve. Maybe I'm a selfish prick, but nothing else matters when it comes to Yasmine. She pulls me up onto the seat and reverses our positions. "God, you're so fucking beautiful, Yasmine," I say as I try to restrain myself. She gives me the sexiest grin and undoes the buttons of my pants, sliding them down to my ankles. She inhales and pauses, almost reveling in what she sees. "Miss my cock, angel?" I smirk at her. She bites the bottom of her lip and licks my tip, and I buckle. *Fuck* I'm sensitive.

"Mmm I missed the way you taste," she mutters before opening her mouth again and taking me deep. I let out a guttural sound and it takes every ounce of my restraint to avoid grabbing her hair hard. She slides me in, all the way deep down her throat, and works me like that harder and faster until I'm close to coming. As if she knows, she slows her movements, wraps her fingers around my base, and starts pumping me. I'm breathing so hard and uncontrollably right now. This feels like my every dream, but even better.

"You like that baby?" she asks me.

"Fuck yes, Yasmine, only you can do this to me," I grit out.

That must have triggered her, in the best possible way, because she dives full in again and deep throats my cock hard, so fucking fast. She's choking and gagging, and her eyes are watering, and I'm making a royal mess of her face, but this is the most beautiful site I've ever seen. She swallows while my cock is down her throat, and that undoes me. I feel a deep urge build up and rush out as my balls tighten. My cock jerks so hard I don't know if I've ever come so much before. I'm shooting out so much cum that I'm worried I'm going to choke her, but she's swallowing me down like an absolute champ. The way her throat moves makes me want to do dirty things all night long.

And like that, I'm well and truly addicted to Yasmine Sepehr all over again.

CHAPTER 62

YASMINE

Alex slowly pulls his pants back on, like he's savoring the aftermath of what just happened. "You're incredible, you know that?" he murmurs, his voice full of warmth as his fingers trail down to fix one of the straps on my dress. "I don't think I'll ever get enough of you." He smiles, his thumb brushing lightly over my lips. "And these lips…" His grin turns into something wickedly playful. "Yeah, they're completely ruined. Not that I regret it for a second."

I groan, swatting at his arm, but his rich, unrestrained laughter fills the space. He sits back, watching me with amusement as I reach for my compact to fix my makeup. "Do you think people will know?" I ask, my voice tinged with genuine worry. "I mean… they'll know, won't they?"

"Absolutely," he says, grinning shamelessly. "Your lips are thoroughly ruined, and we smell like… dirty deeds."

"Alex!" I groan, covering my face with my hands, but I can't help laughing as he leans forward, his grin wider than ever. He reaches for my hand, threading his fingers through mine and pulling me closer. His expression shifts, the teasing giving way to something unshakable.

I focus on fixing my makeup. "You're lucky I like you," I say, but there's no denying the smile tugging at my lips.

He grins, his lips brushing my temple in a tender, lingering kiss. "I'd be luckier if you told me you're mine."

Suddenly, the limo eases to a stop. "Ready to do this?" Alex asks with an irresistible tilt of his lips.

I return his grin, heart pounding. "As ready as I'll ever be." The second we step out of the limo, I'm blinded by flashing lights and a flurry of cameras shoved in our direction. The air buzzes with excitement, reporters' voices cutting through the commotion. "Alex, over here! How does it feel being named one of *Economy Time's* top venture capitalists of the year?"

"Alex, is this your new girlfriend?"

The questions come rapid-fire, blending into a chaotic symphony of curiosity and urgency. I instinctively tense, my hand tightening around Alex's arm as the crowd surges closer. His presence here is clearly a massive deal, the kind of publicity that has everyone clamoring for a piece of him. But he doesn't flinch. Instead, he straightens, radiating an effortless confidence that makes him so magnetic. He places his hand over mine, a subtle yet protective gesture, and leans in slightly. "You good?" he murmurs, his voice low enough that only I can hear.

I nod, even though my heart's pounding. "Yeah, I'm fine."

He glances down at me, his eyes softening for a moment before he turns back to the cameras. He doesn't answer any of their questions, but his body language says enough. The way he stands close to me, the way his hand stays firmly on mine—it's all deliberate—a silent declaration. The paparazzi eat it up, the flashes intensifying as they continue shouting over one another. "Alex, is Portugal your next investment opportunity?" "How long are you staying in the country?" "Is your girlfriend part of your plans?"

Alex just chuckles under his breath, steering me toward the entrance. As overwhelming as it is, I can't help but marvel at how he handles it all like he was born for moments like this. The ballroom is buzzing with energy, all elegance and sophistication. Alex leads me through the crowd, his hand resting lightly on the small of my back.

"I forgot to mention, you're about to meet my entire family," he says like it's the most casual thing on earth.

"What?" I ask with a slight panic. I see them before we even reach the table—four striking men whose presence immediately commands attention.

"Here we go," Alex says, leaning close to my ear. "Yasmine, meet Dad and my brothers."

The first to stand is an older man, handsome with a rugged face that speaks of years spent under the sun. He wears a bolo tie and a tailored jacket that feels distinctly cowboy. "Well, now," he says, his eyes crinkling at the corners as he smiles. "Ain't you a sight for sore eyes. Name's Clint, but call me 'Dad.'" Clint says, his voice carrying the unmistakable drawl of the Midwest.

I smile, charmed immediately. "It's so nice to meet you."

"The pleasure's mine," he replies, tipping an imaginary hat before stepping aside to introduce Alex's brothers.

A dashing man, looking like a slightly older, rougher, version of Alex, stands up and reaches his hand out to me. "Lucas," he says, "It's great to meet you finally. I mean, Alex doesn't bring women around often, so…" His voice trails off as he glances at Alex with a knowing grin. "You're clearly special."

Alex rolls his eyes but doesn't deny it, and my cheeks warm under Lucas's kind words. The woman sitting next to him is stunning, and before I can say hi to her, she boldly introduces herself first as '*Tammi, the hottest influencer of the year.*'

Alex and I give each other a look as I quirk one of my eyebrows. He responds with a smirk and an eye roll. Then I look over to a young man, a glass of champagne lazily balanced in his hand. He doesn't bother standing, instead offering me a lazy grin. "So this is the legendary Yasmine," he drawls, his tone teasing. "I was starting to think Alex was making you up."

"Zane," Alex says with a sigh, though there's no real heat in it.

Zane shrugs, his grin widening. "Nice to meet you," he says, raising his glass in a mock toast. "Welcome to the circus."

Sitting next to Zane is up-and-coming actress Scarlett Stone, and she seems hooked on him—head over heels, in fact. I can barely contain my excitement at the sight of a real celebrity at our table. Zane, however, looks distantly disinterested. Finally, a man who also bears a striking resemblance to Alex, save for the early traces of salt and pepper in his hair, rises abruptly. He extends his hand in a calm, almost brooding manner. "Cole," he says, his voice clipped. His movements are polished, his phone buzzing on the table beside him. He silences it with a swipe that feels almost dismissive. He's handsome, no doubt, but there's a seriousness to him that makes it clear he doesn't have time for frivolities.

Clearly, good looks and confidence runs in Alex's family. As the conversation flows, I can feel them warming to me, and I'm warming to them. And Alex? He's watching me with that look of his like I'm the only person in the room. It doesn't take long for the Pierce family's presence to draw attention. A man approaches our table, leaning down to whisper something to Alex and Lucas. I catch snippets of words—"potential venture," and "partnership." Alex's brow furrows briefly before he gives me an apologetic look.

"Excuse us for a second," he says, his hand brushing mine briefly before he stands.

"Go ahead," I say with a smile, and I mean it. I'm not bothered. This is his world—people vying for his time and attention, eager to pitch their ideas or secure his involvement. It's part of who he is, and I understand that. I'm not here to compete with it or feel slighted by it. I'm here because I want to be.

As Alex steps away, another man quickly trails after him, and soon, a small group surrounds him, all talking animatedly. I watch momentarily, marveling at how he commands attention before I decide to excuse myself.

"I'm going to grab a drink at the bar," I say to Clint, who's just finished regaling the rest of the table with a story about the time he wrangled a bull that had escaped during a county fair.

He pauses to nod at me, his smile warm. "Go on, darlin'. Don't let us keep you tied down." I chuckle and rise from the table, smoothing my dress as I make my way across the gala. The room is stunning, bathed in warm light reflecting off the crystal chandeliers above. The bar is sleek and polished, a small oasis in the middle of the bustling event. I slide onto a stool, catching the bartender's attention.

"What can I get you, miss?" he asks, his Portuguese accent thick and friendly.

"Just a glass of white wine, please," I say, offering a polite smile. As he moves to pour the drink, I take a moment to breathe. It feels good to step away and take in everything from a distance. The conversations, the laughter, the music—it's all a beautiful swirl of energy, but being here, alone for a moment, gives me a chance to center myself. As I glance back toward the table, I spot Alex in the middle of a group gathered around him. His gaze meets mine, and for a moment, all of time stops. Once again, it's just me and him. Suddenly, a slender hand comes up to his arms, breaking our spell. A sleek blonde woman vies for his focus, and he turns to her, his expression polite as he listens to her enthusiastically explain something. I smile to myself. Even with beautiful women trying to drape themselves all over him, I can read Alex's heart, which has me written all over it.

As I sip my wine, savoring the quiet moment, a deep voice pulls me from my thoughts. "Excuse me," the man says, and I glance up to see someone tall and striking standing beside me.

"Mind if I join you?" he asks, gesturing to the stool beside me.

I give him a polite smile. "Sure."

He slides into the seat next to me and offers his hand. "I'm Rafael," he says, his Portuguese accent subtle and undeniably charming.

"Yasmine," I reply, shaking his hand.

"Yasmine," he repeats, rolling the name off his tongue like it's exotic. "Beautiful name for a beautiful woman."

I laugh softly, taking another sip of my wine. "Thank you."

"So," he says, leaning in just enough to signal interest, "What brings you here? Besides catching the attention of everyone in the room, of course."

I raise a brow at him, amused by his boldness. "I'm here with someone."

"Oh?" His smile widens, playful. "Let me guess. Is he the lucky guy over there?" He points to a man near the corner of the room, a portly older gentleman with a bright purple bowtie who's animatedly discussing something at his table.

I can't help it; I burst out laughing, nearly choking on my wine. "Absolutely not," I manage, shaking my head. "Not even close."

Rafael grins, clearly enjoying himself. "Okay, okay. Let me try again." He scans the room dramatically, his finger poised as if he's narrowing down suspects. "That one." He points to a short man with slicked-back hair who's currently shoveling cocktail wieners into his mouth like it's his last meal on Earth.

"Nope," I say, laughing again. "Wrong again."

He leans back, feigning defeat. "You're not making this easy, Yasmine."

"That's because you're not even close," I tease, setting my glass down.

Rafael rests his chin on his hand, studying me like a puzzle he's determined to solve. "Alright, I give up. Tell me, who is the man lucky enough to be your date tonight?"

I smile, feeling a little thrill at the chance to say it out loud. "Alex Pierce."

His eyebrows shoot up in surprise, and he blows a low whistle. "*The* Alex Pierce?"

"That's the one," I say, unable to hide the slight pride in my voice.

Rafael chuckles, shaking his head. "Well, now I know why he's always in the center of the room. He's not just brilliant; he has excellent taste." I smile politely, my heart warming at the thought of Alex.

CHAPTER 63

ALEX

I'm standing in the middle of a small crowd, people vying for my interest left and right. Everyone wants something—an investment, a partnership, advice on scaling their next big idea. I nod, smile, and respond where I need to, but my focus isn't on them. It's on *her*.

Yasmine.

She's across the room, perched elegantly at the bar, turning heads without even trying. I'm mesmerized by the way she carries herself, her effortless grace. She doesn't even realize the effect she has on people. She's so oblivious to her beauty, unaware of the chaos she stirs just by existing. That's what I love most about her. Her power isn't in her looks, though they're enough to stop traffic; it's in who she is. My gaze locks onto her, and for a moment, the noise of the room fades entirely. My chest tightens, everything else forgotten. For just a second, it feels like the world shrinks down to only the two of us.

Then, someone steps into her space—a man leaning in too close, his smile too charming. I watch as he says something to her, his body language clear. He's flirting. Yasmine responds but I can tell she's not interested even from across the room. That doesn't stop him, though, and it's not long before another guy swoops in after him, trying his luck.

Over the next fifteen minutes, though it feels like hours, I watch as one man after another approaches her. Each time, she handles it with poise, but it's maddening. My blood simmers, jealousy sparking in my chest. Finally, I've had enough. I end the conversation I'm having, offering some half-hearted excuse I don't bother to remember, and start making my way toward her. My steps quicken as I push through the crowd, the distance between us feeling unbearable. I'm almost sprinting by the time I reach her, my heart pounding with a mix of frustration and determination.

Yasmine deserves better than this circus, and I'm not going to stand idly by while she's surrounded by men who don't realize she's already taken. By me.

CHAPTER 64

YASMINE

The man currently in front of me, Rory, was it? He was charming at first, but his attempts at flirting have quickly veered into uncomfortable territory. I take a step back, putting space between us, but he moves closer. "Not nice to touch another man's lady," I say firmly.

"Oh, come on," he leans in with a smirk. His hand grazes my waist, and I freeze for a moment, caught between anger and disbelief. "Don't be like that."

Before I can do or say anything else, a strong voice cuts through the noise, sharp and commanding. "Take your hands off my girlfriend."

I turn, relief washing over me as Alex steps between us, his presence like a shield. His expression is calm but deadly serious, his jaw tight, and his eyes locked on the man, who immediately stiffens. Recognition flashes across the guy's face as he realizes who he's dealing with.

"Mr. Pierce?" he stammers, his bravado crumbling in an instant. "I, I didn't know—"

"Now you do," Alex cuts him off. "Apologize to her. And leave."

The man mutters a hurried apology to me before scrambling off, his earlier confidence nowhere to be found. Alex doesn't even glance at him as he turns to me, his expression softening. "Are you okay?" he asks, his hand gently brushing my arm, his concern palpable.

"Yeah," I say, exhaling shakily. "Thank you. That guy was—"

"A jackass," Alex finishes for me, shaking his head. "I'm sorry I left you to fend off the wolves on your own." His lips curve into a small, self-deprecating smile. "I had a feeling it was dangerous to leave the confines of a bedroom with you."

Despite everything, I laugh, shaking my head at him. "You're impossible."

He grins, his fingers lacing through mine as he takes my hand. "Come on," he says. "Let's get back to our table." As we walk back together, hand in hand, I feel my tension start to fade. We're finally seated, the emcee takes the stage. The lights dim and all eyes turn toward the spotlight on him.

"Good evening, everyone," he says, loud and animated. "Thank you for joining us tonight at the *European Children's Fund Gala*, held this year in the beautiful Cascais, Portugal."

A ripple of polite applause moves through the room and I glance at Alex, who's relaxed in his chair, one hand resting casually on the table, the other holding my hand under it.

"Of course, we have to give a special shout-out to the Pierce table tonight, our biggest donor every year." The emcee gestures toward us and a spotlight briefly lands on the table. My cheeks heat as the attention falls on us, but the brothers seem unfazed. "I mean, come on," the emcee continues with a grin. "Is it just me, or did this family hit the genetic lottery?"

Laughter ripples through the room, and Clint glances around at his sons, his rugged features softened by the undeniable pride in his eyes. The sight of it makes my heart swell. It's rare to see a family dynamic like this, one filled with such different personalities but a clear, unshakable bond.

The emcee shifts gears, a sense of excitement building in his voice. "And now, let's get to the good stuff—the auction!" The crowd claps, leaning forward in anticipation as the first item is brought to the stage. A velvet tray is delicately placed on a pedestal under the spotlight. The emcee steps forward with a flourish, gesturing toward the display. "Ladies and gentlemen," he begins, his voice rich with anticipation, "our first item tonight is nothing short of extraordinary. A breathtaking 8-carat green diamond necklace, once owned by Isabella the Second of Spain, the Queen of Castile."

The centerpiece is an otherworldly rock, with deep forest hues and flecked with what look like tiny stars trapped within its depths. Surrounding the gem is a halo of smaller diamonds, each catching the light and creating a dazzling rainbow. It's not just a necklace, it's a masterpiece, an artifact of beauty and regality.

"A piece of history," the emcee continues, "A symbol of elegance and timeless beauty, worn by a queen who captivated an empire. Tonight, this treasure can be yours." My breath catches as I take in the necklace displayed on the screen behind him. Alex notices my reaction and smirks slightly but doesn't say a word.

"Shall we start the bidding at two hundred thousand euros?" the emcee announces. A hand shoots up almost immediately and the bidding begins. The price climbs steadily—three hundred thousand, five hundred thousand, then seven hundred thousand euros. I glance at Alex as his hand goes up smoothly, his expression unreadable.

"Eight hundred thousand euros!" the emcee calls, nodding toward Alex. "Do I hear nine?"

Another bidder raises their paddle and the war intensifies. One million. The numbers keep climbing, and I can feel the tension in the room building with each new bid. I glance at Alex, who remains calm, his hand going up every time the emcee looks his way.

I lean closer, lowering my voice. "You're really going for this, huh?"

He glances at me, his lips twitching into a small, amused smile. "It's worth it." I raise a brow, my curiosity piqued. The necklace is undeniably beautiful, but I can't help wondering who it's for. A gift for someone? A collector's item? My mind spins as the bidding soars past two million euros.

"Five million," Alex says smoothly, his voice carrying just enough authority to make heads turn. The room murmurs as the other bidders hesitate, finally shaking their heads. The emcee claps his hands together. "Sold! To Mr. Alex Pierce, for five million euros! Mr. Pierce, we will arrange to hand deliver this beautiful item with your assistant." Applause erupts and Alex leans back in his chair, completely unfazed. I catch the faintest trace of a smile tugging at his lips. Whatever his reasons for going all in on that necklace, he's not telling me.

The rest of the night is nothing short of spectacular. I can't take my eyes off Alex. The Pierce family's generosity leaves me in awe. By the end of the night, they'd donated over ten million euros to the cause, and their contributions were celebrated with a standing ovation. Watching Clint beam as the emcee thanks the Pierce family makes my heart swell. Generosity, it seems, runs deep in their blood.

As the gala winds down, Alex and I make our way back to his family's table to say our goodbyes. Clint stands, shaking my hand warmly. "It was a pleasure meeting you, Yasmine. Don't let this one mess it up." He throws a wink at Alex, who rolls his eyes but can't hide the faint grin tugging at his lips.

"It was so great to meet all of you," I say, meaning it. "Thank you for being so welcoming."

We leave the gala hand in hand, the cool night air wrapping around us as we step outside. My heart feels impossibly full, like it might burst from everything I'm feeling—pride, joy, and something much deeper. Tonight, I didn't think it was possible, but I've fallen even more in love with Alex.

Raul pulls the limo up to the curb. Alex's hand rests lightly on the small of my back as he guides me into the backseat. Before he can settle in, I lean in and kiss him, deep and unrestrained. My hands frame his face, and his lips respond instantly like they've been waiting for this. When I finally pull back, he blinks, slightly dazed, and grins. "Wow. What was that for?"

I smile, my fingertips brushing his cheek. "Because I'm so turned on by you tonight. Not just how you look, though that's definitely part of it, but your generosity. Your kind heart."

His grin softens, a flicker of something deeper crossing his face. "I'm connected to this charity in a way I don't usually talk about," he says, his voice dropping to a quieter, more vulnerable tone. "It was something close to my mom's heart. She was one of the original founding members. She believed in giving kids who've lost their parents a chance to rebuild their lives." He pauses, exhaling slowly as he glances out the window for a moment before looking back at me. "After I lost her, it became even more important to me. Like…continuing her work was the only way to keep a part of her alive. This charity is about honoring her."

His words hit me like a wave, and my chest tightens. "Alex, that's… that's amazing. Your mom would be so proud of you."

He gives me a small, almost shy smile but shakes his head. "You think so?"

"I know so," I say firmly. "You're an incredible person."

He looks away momentarily, his jaw tightening, before his eyes meet mine again, darker and heavier this time. "I'm not as great as you think, Yasmine. There are…a lot of things broken about me."

My heart aches at his words, but I don't let go of his hand. Instead, I hold on tighter. "We're all a little broken, Alex. But the way you care and the way you give shows the best parts of you. And those parts are enough. More than enough."

His gaze softens as he studies me, like he's searching for something in my eyes. For a moment, the limo is quiet, then he leans forward and presses his forehead to mine, his voice barely above a whisper. "You always know what to say."

And at that moment, I knew he was letting me see a side of him that no one else could see—my beautiful man.

CHAPTER 65

ALEX

The limo slows as we approach my hotel. It's so late into the night now that the only sounds around us are the Atlantic waves crashing against the shore just beyond the entrance. Raul gets out and opens Yasmine's door with a warm smile. "*Miss Yasmine*," he says, offering her a hand to step out. I shoot him a sharp glare, his lips twitching with a barely concealed smirk. It's an inside joke by now—his over-the-top chivalry with her drives me just enough up the wall to make it entertaining for him. Yasmine catches the look between us and laughs softly. "Be nice," she teases under her breath, her eyes sparkling with amusement. Raul winks at me before closing the door, and I shake my head.

As I leave the limo, the hotel doorman is already waiting, straightening his uniform. "Mr. Pierce," he says, his voice filled with reverence. "Welcome back, sir." He opens the grand glass doors with a flourish, bowing slightly as we walk past. It's like this every time—whether they know me by name or reputation, I expect the deferential treatment. But tonight, it barely registers. I focus entirely on Yasmine. The ocean breeze filters in through the open terrace doors, mingling with her scent, and I'm hooked all over again.

"Wow, this place is beautiful," she whispers to me. I smile but stay silent, because all I can think is, *nothing compares to you.*

CHAPTER 66

The door clicks shut behind us and I barely have a second to take in the room—it's massive, the grandest suite I've ever seen, with nearly 360-degree views of the ocean and the village beyond. But none of it holds my attention. It's not the view I'm focused on—it's Alex. The energy he radiates makes it seem he owns every inch of this space. It's impossible not to be drawn to him. Before I can take another breath, he's on me. His lips crash against mine, his kiss deep and consuming, stealing the air from my lungs. My heart races as his hands grip my waist, pulling me closer, and his body presses into mine with an intensity that makes me dizzy. We back up, step by step until my knees hit the edge of the bed. His hands are everywhere, guiding me down until I'm lying on the impossibly soft sheets, and he's hovering over me, all heat and raw power.

"I'm sorry, angel," he murmurs, his voice full of desire as his fingers trace the straps of my dress. "But this dress has to go." His hands find the zipper and slowly eases it down, like he's unwrapping a gift. He slips the fabric down, leaving me in nothing but my black lace lingerie. His eyes roam over me, dark and full of something that makes my skin flush even more. He exhales slowly, his gaze drinking me in. "Beautiful," he whispers, his voice full of awe. "I'll never get tired of this. Of you." His words make my heart skip. The vulnerability is intoxicating, and as he leans down, his lips brushing against my collarbone, I know I'm entirely his. He shrugs his tux jacket off and hovers back over my body, kissing me down my neck. I tug at his suit trousers, and he chuckles into my ear. "So needy, I don't even have my shirt off yet."

I smile into his embrace. I'm so turned on right now it's not even funny. I push his pants and boxers down and grab his thick cock, so hard, just for me. "Tell me, baby, do you only get this hard for me?" I don't even know who I am anymore, asking him so eagerly.

"Only you, Yasmine. Always you," he whispers back to me. I part my lips, inviting in the warmth of his deep, intoxicating kiss.An intimate part of my soul longs for him. I grip his big, thick cock and align him to my entrance. Staring into his eyes, I sink him into me, inch by inch, with parted lips and through hooded eyelids. My body now belongs to him, and I'm pulling him in desperately, claiming him with the same fire because we're lit from the same match. No matter how far away we are from each other and how different our lives can be, we burn from the same flame. He will always have a part of me with him.

He thrusts all the way into the hilt and I gasp. He feels incredible inside me. I'm filled to the max, and every bit of me, inside and out, is his for the taking. Alex shudders and pulls out slowly before pushing back in again, with more friction this time. I can tell he's already losing control. I love this about him—how he always loses control with me. He groans so deeply, and hearing him this way for me is such a turn-on.

"More, baby, yes," I whimper as I grip his shoulders in the way that drives him wild. Alex drops his forehead to mine and bites his lip to restrain himself. He pulls out and slams back into me over and over again. Deep, punishing, brutal hits, every thrust knocking the air out of my lungs. We both need this—a confirmation that everything was real between us.mI feel the incoming wave of pleasure deep inside. Seriously, how does he do it? Suddenly, the most overwhelming orgasm washes through me, so strong that I'm reverberating in an immense euphoria.

He slows his pace, teeth clenched in pleasure. "So fucking sexy," he rasps. In one swift motion, he shifts to kneel upright, never breaking our connection, and lifts my knees over his shoulders. The angle sinks him even deeper inside me, and I revel in the intense rush of fullness. His hands grip my hips, his biceps flexing, and I swear I've never been more turned on. A heady jolt of bliss courses through my entire body. I'm drowning in the sensation of how his thick, powerful cock completely fills me.

"Oh, Alex, yes!" I cry out. My breasts bounce with every erratic thrust, my mind reeling at the sight of him losing every shred of composure. It hits me all at once. I'm the one unraveling him, pushing him to the edge until there's no coherent thought left. And that knowledge sends a deep thrill through me. Suddenly, a new wave of pleasure sweeps through me, andI climax again—deep, intense, and all-consuming.

"Oh fuck, Yasmine, I'm gonna come," he warns.

I squeeze his shoulders tighter as I cling on and moan intensely, and I feel his hot cum course through me. His whole body is taut as he jerks hard, so deep inside me, and knowing that he knows I'm not on birth control makes me feel even closer to him. He lets out a guttural groan, and it's the sexiest sound I've ever heard.

Alex collapses on top of me, his breath ragged as it mingles with mine in the aftermath. My heart is still racing, my body buzzing from the intensity of what we just shared, but the look in his eyes completely undoes me. He brushes a strand of hair from my face, his fingers lingering against my skin. His voice is full of emotion. "You're everything to me, Yasmine," he murmurs. "I don't know how I got so lucky, but I'm not letting this go. I'm not letting *you* go."

The words hit me straight in the heart and my eyes sting with unshed tears, overwhelmed by the raw sincerity in his voice. "I love you, Alex," I whisper, my voice breaking slightly. "I love you so much."

His face softens, his lips curving into a small, almost vulnerable smile. "I love you too," he says, full of quiet conviction. "More than I thought I ever could." He shifts to his side, pulling me against him, his arms wrapping around me protectively. "Nothing will stand in our way. Not anymore."

I bury my face against his chest, and at this moment, I know it's true. Whatever challenges lie ahead, we'll face them together.

I wake up to the distant sound of crashing waves and the bed is soft and warm, but as I reach out, my hand brushes empty sheets. Alex isn't there.

The realization makes me pause, but it doesn't dampen the fullness I feel in my chest. Memories from last night flood in—dirty, beautiful, and unforgettable. A slow smile spreads across my face as I recall the way we lost ourselves in each other and how hot and intense it was. My cheeks flush, and I can't stop grinning.

A faint clanking sound pulls me out of my thoughts. It's coming from outside the bedroom door. Curious, I slide out of bed and spot Alex's dress shirt draped over the side of a chair. I grab it, slip it on, his faint scent still clinging to it. I walk barefoot to the door and slowly open it, peeking out. My breath catches when I see him.

Alex is standing in the suite's kitchen, his broad back to me, dressed in only boxers. His tan skin glows in the morning light, every muscle perfectly defined. There's something so effortless about how he moves, so unapologetically masculine. My eyes roam over him, taking in the strong lines of his body and the power in his build. It's impossible not to admire him. He turns around, holding a paper bag, and his eyes widen slightly when he sees me. For a moment, he looks surprised, but then a slow smile spreads across his lips. "Good morning," he says, his voice low and slightly raspy from sleep. "You're up."

I lean against the doorframe, my smile mirroring his. "I couldn't stay in bed, not when I heard all this noise. What are you up to?"

His grin widens as he holds up the bag. "Breakfast. I figured you'd be hungry after last night."

The way he says it, his tone teasing but laced with warmth, sends a wave of heat through me. I step closer, still wearing his shirt, and his eyes flick over me appreciatively, making me feel even more alive. "Maybe just a little" I say with a smirk. I step closer, my eyes falling on the paper bag in his hands. When I see the logo, I stop, blinking in disbelief. *Wayki Tacos.* The words are printed in bold, unmistakable letters, and I'm suddenly frowning and smiling simultaneously.

"How?" I ask, my voice a mix of confusion and delight as I look up at Alex. He smirks, setting the bag on the counter and pulling out a stack of neatly packaged ingredients. "I had my assistant arrange it," he says casually, like orchestrating a DIY breakfast taco kit from across the world is just another Tuesday for him.

I stare at him, completely floored. "You did that? For me?"

He shrugs, but the proud smile tugging at his lips gives him away. "Of course I did."

My heart swells and I wrap my arms around him, his scent enveloping me. "I love you, you know that?"

"Yeah," he says, grinning down at me, "and hearing it from you never gets old."

I laugh, my head resting against his chest, already excited to dig into what might be the best taco I've ever had because it came from him.

CHAPTER 67

ALEX

I watch her take a bite of her taco, wearing my shirt that goes down to her thighs, and I swear I can't look away. There's something almost hypnotic about how her lips curve around it, how she's savoring every bite. It's ridiculous how mesmerizing this moment is, but I'm completely under her spell. After everything we shared yesterday, something between us feels different, deeper. We've hit a new level and I feel it in every inch of me. The possessiveness I feel when I look at her, the overwhelming need to see her happy, to please her in every way possible, it's consuming. And then there's the simple truth that I just need to be near her, always. My friends back home would be laughing their asses off at me right now if they could see how truly whipped I am by this woman.

She licks a bit of sour cream from her lip, her tongue gliding out just briefly, and I can't help myself. My hand reaches out, sliding around her waist as I pull her closer. I can't keep my hands off her; honestly, I don't even want to try. "Alex," she says, laughing softly as she leans into me. "You're insatiable. I can't even eat a taco in peace."

I grin, brushing a strand of hair from her face, my thumb grazing her cheek. "Can you blame me?" I say, my voice low and unapologetic. "I'm obsessed with you." She laughs again, her eyes sparkling, and she shakes her head like she can't believe me. But I see how her cheeks flush and I know she loves it. My lips meet hers, soft and inviting, and everything else fades away. My hands cradle her face as I kiss her with purpose, with everything I'm feeling. She deepens our kiss and I feel the soft hitch of her breath as her body melts closer to me. She sighs and ignites something deep in my chest. I pull her closer, unable to help myself. There's no rush, no urgency. Just this raw, overwhelming need to feel her, to show her how much she means to me. Her fingers trace over my shoulders and down my chest, following the hard lines of my stomach. She moves lower, teasing, until they slip beneath the waistband of my boxers. She tugs them down, her touch deliberate, her eyes locked on mine. My breath shudders when her slender fingers wrap around me, squeezing just enough to make my vision blur. God, this woman. She's everything.

"I want to taste you, Alex." Yasmine's voice is soft, full of longing, and I swear it's the sexiest sound I've ever heard. I exhale sharply, my hands threading into her thick, dark hair as she kneels before me, her lips parting slightly. The way she looks up at me, eyes gleaming with heat, undoes me.

"You're so fucking beautiful," I murmur, my voice rough, raw. *Mine.* Her tongue flicks over the tip of my length before she drags it up and down, slow and torturous. Her fingers graze, stroke, and explore until she finally takes me in, deep and unrelenting. Fuck. My fingers flex in her hair, my body shuddering as she moves with perfect rhythm. Every slow pull, every deep push, every flick of her tongue sends pleasure crashing over me. I groan, my head tipping back, but just as I start to lose myself, she presses a firm palm against my stomach, steadying me. She looks up at me, my cock still buried between her lips, and shakes her head once before pulling back with a raspy, "Not yet." And then she takes me again. Harder. Deeper. Faster. I swear, my soul leaves my body. A strangled moan tears from my throat, my hands gripping the counter behind me, struggling for any sense of control. But there is none, not when it comes to Yasmine. She pulls away too soon, leaving me on the edge of something devastatingly good. Before I can beg for more, she tugs me down, pulling me over her as she stretches out beneath me on the cool floor.

Her arms wrap around my neck, pulling me down into a kiss that's desperate and consuming. I kiss her like I need her to breathe. My hands drag over her thighs, spreading them beneath me, teasing my way up to where my shirt, *my shirt*, rests high on her hips. The sight of her wearing only that, flushed and panting beneath me, has me gripping her waist harder, my control hanging by a thread.

Her body arches into me, her breathing ragged. "Alex," she gasps, pleading.

I smirk against her lips. "That desperate for me, angel?" She nods furiously, panting, her chest rising and falling in quick succession. Spellbound. I groan, dragging my cock up and down her slick heat before guiding myself to her entrance. Slow. Deliberate. Savoring this. I push in. We both moan at the same time, and fuck if that isn't the hottest sound I've ever heard. Her body welcomes me perfectly, tightening around me, pulling me in deeper as I sink all the way, claiming every inch of her. I hook my arm under one of her knees, lifting her leg, changing the angle just enough to make her breath hitch. I thrust, slow and deep at first, then faster, harder, taking her completely. We go at it like this for I don't even know how long. I'm too lost in this moment, in her. She grinds up against me, her body tightening, her pleasure building in waves I can feel.

"Alex," she gasps, her voice breaking as she clenches around me, her orgasm wrecking her. She's so tight, so perfect, so mine, and I can't hold back any longer. A deep, guttural groan rips from my chest as I let go, giving her everything, burying myself inside her as pleasure crashes over me like a tidal wave. I collapse over her, both of us heaving, spent and satisfied, tangled together on the cold kitchen floor.

A deep chuckle rumbles from my chest as I press my face into her neck, inhaling her. "We couldn't even make it to the bed."

She laughs, soft and breathless, threading her fingers through my hair. "You bring out the animal in me."

I lift my head, smirking. "Right back at you, angel." And as I look at her, blissed out and *mine*, I know this is where I belong with her.

CHAPTER 68

YASMINE

It's been two weeks since Alex came to Portugal and I'm starting to think he might actually be attached to me. Physically. Like a very tall, very possessive koala. Not that I'm complaining. Ever since we made things official, he's barely left my side. If I so much as shift in bed at night, he's awake, pulling me right back against him like I'm some human-sized security blanket. If I try to leave the room in the morning? Forget it. He's wrapping himself around me like an octopus, mumbling about wanting just five more minutes. The man is needy, and honestly? It's adorable.

We agreed to stay here in Portugal for now, at least until the opening ceremony of my retreat center, which, oh God, is tonight. No pressure or anything. Of course, Alex has taken on the role of overprotective bodyguard/boyfriend, meaning that whenever I start spiraling into stress, he pulls me onto his lap or distracts me with something very distracting. It's a great system, honestly.

But there's one thing left to do, and I know Alex isn't thrilled about it. Ethan will be at the ceremony tonight. This means I'll finally tell him my plan—I've set up the center, and it's time to pass the reins to someone else. I'll promise him I'll stay until I know it's in good hands, but after that? I'm done. My future isn't here. It's with Alex. And judging by how he's watching me from across the room, arms folded, jaw tight, like he's bracing for battle, I have a feeling tonight will be… eventful.

I stand in front of the mirror, adjusting the lapels of my white sequined blazer dress, letting the light catch the tiny embellishments. Sami helped me pick this out before she left for Italy; I have to say, she was right on the money. I feel like a boss woman. It's sexy and powerful, feminine and untouchable. The kind of outfit that says *I can handle business and look good while doing it*. And tonight, I need all the confidence I can get. I smooth my hands over the fabric, roll my shoulders back, and exhale deeply. Alex walks up behind me and slides his strong arms around my waist, pulling me flush against him. "You look so fucking sexy tonight, angel," he murmurs, his voice husky. "I'm having trouble keeping my mind from doing very nasty things to you."

A smirk tugs at my lips. "Oh?" I tease, pressing my back into his chest. "Like what?"

He kisses the soft spot beneath my ear, dragging his lips down to the nook of my neck. "Mmm, you don't want to know." I definitely do. I turn into his hold and pull him into a slow, sensual kiss, one that says *thank you for always making me feel like the sexiest woman alive* without using a single word. When we finally break apart, I can feel the way his body is tensed, like he's barely holding himself together. Then, out of nowhere, he pulls something from his suit pocket—a sizeable rectangular velvet box.

I blink at it. "What's this?" I ask, my heartbeat suddenly doing things.

He smirks. "Just a little something that reminds me of the most beautiful woman in the world." I glance at him, then at the box, and slowly open it. I gasp. Inside sits the green diamond necklace from the gala. The same one I saw weeks ago, the one I could barely tear my eyes away from, the one that, if I'm being honest, reminded me of my own damn soul.

"Alex…" My voice fails me. I just stare at it, overwhelmed, because this is not just a necklace. This is so thoughtful. This is him seeing me in ways no one ever has.

"It belongs on you," he says softly, lifting it from the box and fastening it around my neck. I swallow thickly as its weight settles against my collarbone. It's cool, delicate, and breathtaking, and I don't know what to say. "These days, the thrill I chase isn't in deals or numbers. It's in you. Your smiles—the ones that light up your whole face and make my chest ache in the best way. And when I saw this necklace, I was reminded of the exact color of your eyes. Stunning, captivating, unforgettable. Just like you," he declares sincerely, with a heaviness in his voice.

 "I don't even…" I blink up at him, my vision slightly blurry from the sudden sting of tears. "Alex, this is the best gift anyone's ever given me."

His eyes widen, and mild panic sets in. "Hey, hey," he soothes, cupping my face. "Let's not mess up your makeup. This is just the first of many gifts I plan on spoiling you with. My girl gets everything she wants." I let out a small, teary laugh before pulling him into another deep, slow kiss, pouring everything I feel into it. Alex groans into my mouth, his hands gripping my waist like he's one second away from snapping. And honestly? I wouldn't stop him. But before things spiral out of control, he forces himself to pull back, his breathing ragged. "Fuck," he mutters, running a hand through his hair. "If we don't leave right now, I'm going to lose control."

A laugh bubbles out of me. "That sounds like a win-win situation."

He grits his teeth, his eyes dark. "Yasmine."

I sigh dramatically. "Fine, fine, let's go." With one last lingering look, one that definitely promises we'll be picking this back up later, we head outside, where Raul is already waiting with the car. It's time to open my retreat center and close this chapter of my life.

—

The grand opening is breathtaking. The entire grounds is draped in soft florals, candles flickering along the paths, and a soft breeze carrying the scent of lavender and sage through the air. The crowd is a glittering sea of Portugal's elite—artists, politicians, business moguls, and international celebrities, some of whom I've only seen in magazines. Somehow, they're here, mingling in this space. I take a slow, grounding breath and smile as I glance around. This isn't just a celebration; it's a symbol of everything I've worked for.

"Yasmine!" I turn as two familiar figures weave through the crowd—Alaina and Sophia, their faces glowing as they rush toward me. "You did it!" Alaina exclaims, throwing her arms around me. "This place is incredible."

"Breathtaking," Sophia adds, pulling me in for a hug after Alaina. "Every detail is perfect. You've outdone yourself."

Their words warm me, and I smile, brushing my hair behind my ear. "Thank you. I'm so grateful you girls made it out here to celebrate with us."

Alaina waves her hand. "Please. Anything for an excuse to post exotic overseas content!"

Before I can respond, another familiar voice cuts through the soft hum of the crowd. "There she is, the woman destined for greatness." I turn and see Pablo, his serene smile immediately settling the nerves within me.

"Pablo," I greet him, my smile widening as we hug.

He steps back and studies me, his gaze warm with intent. "This retreat center is extraordinary, Yasmine. But it's no surprise. You've always had a rare gift, the power to heal in ways others can't even begin to understand." I'm still blushing, about to thank Pablo, when a dark presence creeps behind me. Immediately, I feel it—that slight shift in the air, the tension curling around me like a snake before I even hear his voice.

"I knew I picked out the right woman for this." Ethan says. I stiffen before turning around, already feeling a sense of unease in the pit of my stomach. His tone is… off. A little too familiar. A little too entitled. And then he does something that makes my entire body go rigid. His hand presses against my lower back. *Oh, no. Nope. Bad idea. Abort mission.* I silently pray that Alex is nowhere in sight. He barely tolerates another man so much as glancing at me. If he sees Ethan touching me, well… let's just say it won't end peacefully.

I exhale slowly, forcing a polite smile. "Ethan, just the man I was looking for. I wanted to talk to you privately about something."

His expression brightens, oblivious to the fact that I am very much lying. "Anything for you, beautiful," he purrs, gesturing toward the terrace. I suppress the instinct to roll my eyes and follow him outside. The night air is cool, crisp, and peaceful—the opposite of the energy radiating from Ethan. The stars twinkle above us, indifferent to the fact that I am about to have a very uncomfortable conversation.

I take a deep breath and dive right in. "Ethan, I wanted to tell you in person that I've decided to step away from this retreat center. My life is heading in a new direction, and I think it's time to pass leadership to someone else." I keep my voice calm, firm, and professional. Ethan's expression darkens instantly.

He doesn't take it well. At all. I see it happen in real-time—the flicker of something ugly behind his eyes, the way his jaw tightens, the subtle way his body tenses. And then? The switch flips. His hand clamps around my wrist, his grip too tight, his fingers digging in just enough to make my stomach drop.

"Ethan," I say carefully, "you're hurting me."

He doesn't let go. Instead, he pulls me closer, his breath hot with alcohol, his expression something I don't like. "I made you, Yasmine," he sneers, his fingers tightening. "You wouldn't have this center without me."

A sick feeling curls in my stomach. "No," I say, yanking my arm, but his grip doesn't budge. "I built this. I made it what it is. You funded it, sure, but you haven't lifted a finger since I got here. And I don't owe you anything."

His lips curl into something that's definitely not a smile. "Oh, you don't owe me? After everything I've done for you? You're mine, Yasmine." I freeze. Then, in one swift motion, his hand grabs my jaw, forcing me to look at him. His grip is rough and possessive. "You're mine," he whispers, low and dangerous. "Don't you forget it."

Panic flares in my chest. My breath catches. And then—

SLAM.

The terrace door flies open so hard it nearly comes off the hinges. "Get your fucking hands off my girlfriend." Alex's voice cuts through the night like a sharp and deadly blade. Ethan doesn't let go of me right away. Instead, he turns his head slowly, his grip still tight on my jaw, his mouth curling into something smug. And then he says the absolute worst thing he could possibly say.

"Ah," he chuckles, his voice dripping with venom. He looks back at me, "Now I see. You're a gold-digging slut, aren't you? Just bouncing from one sugar daddy to the next." I suck in a breath.

Oh no. Oh no no no no no.

Alex moves so fast that I barely have time to register what's happening before he's on Ethan. His hand grips Ethan's neck, yanking him back with so much force that Ethan actually stumbles.

"What the fuck, man?" Ethan yells, his hands coming up to push him off. But Alex doesn't answer. He just punches him. Hard. Right in the jaw. I scream, reaching for Alex, but it's chaos. Ethan stumbles back, his hand cupping his face, his eyes wild with rage. Alex looks like he's about to end him, and I know, deep in my soul, if I don't stop this now, someone's leaving in an ambulance.

"Alex, stop!" I cry, pulling at his arm. People rush over, gasps echoing through the quickly forming crowd. Security pushes through the stampede, separating them before Ethan can swing back.

And then Ethan does what I thought couldn't make this any worse. He spit words at me that burn like acid. "You fucking whore. You used me to climb the ladder."

Something inside me breaks. Tears sting my eyes, my voice shaking as I whisper, "Ethan… stop."

I'm still trying to be the bigger person, trying to de-escalate, but Alex pulls me hard against his chest, his voice low and final. "No, Yasmine." His arms wrap around me, protective and possessive as hell. "Sometimes, you don't need to be the bigger person. He doesn't deserve any more than you've already given him." He glances down at me, his voice gentler. "Let's go." And I let him lead me out. Because he's right. Ethan doesn't deserve anything from me. Not my energy. Not my forgiveness. Not even my anger. I walk away, wrapped in Alex's arms, letting the crowd watch. Their eyes are filled with shock, curiosity, and, most of all, sympathy. But I don't need their sympathy. I'm more sure than ever I've made the right decision to close this chapter of my life. I already have everything I need.

CHAPTER 69

ALEX

Everything in me snapped the second I saw Ethan's hands on Yasmine. Rage flooded my vision so fast that I didn't even think, just acted. And honestly? That punch was long overdue. But more than anything, I'm pissed that he ruined her night. This night was supposed to be a celebration of everything she built, of the retreat center that has her soul etched into every inch of it. Instead of standing in the middle of a room full of people admiring her work, she ended up in some bullshit confrontation with a man who never deserved to be part of her success in the first place. I knew Ethan wasn't in this for the center. He used it as an excuse to stay close to her, and I had to grit my teeth and let it slide because I didn't want to take away from her passion. But now? I regret every second I stayed quiet.

Yasmine is tucked against my chest as we walk back to her apartment, her arms wrapped around my waist like she's trying to anchor herself. She's quiet, withdrawn, not herself, and it fucking kills me. If I had my way, I'd ruin Ethan. I'd make sure he'll never so much as whisper her name again. But Yasmine? She's too good. Too kind. A literal angel in a world full of men like Ethan. And even though she'd never ask me to, I know she'd rather let karma handle him than have me go nuclear. So, instead, I do the only thing I can. I take care of her. I make her favorite tea, draw her a bath, and do everything in my power to wash this night off her, to make her feel safe, loved, and whole again. And when she looks at me, with those deep green eyes full of trust, I know one thing with absolute certainty; I will never let her go again. Even if we ever have to be apart, even if life pulls us in different directions, she has me. She'll always have me.

She exhales softly, pressing a hand to my chest. "Alex…" Her voice is quiet but steady. "I want to leave Portugal as soon as possible."

I pull back slightly, searching her face. "Are you sure?" I ask, brushing my fingers over her cheek.

"Yes." Her eyes hold mine, confident and full of something more profound than words. "The only place I want to be is with you. Wherever you go, if you want me." My chest tightens. She has no idea what she just did to me.

I grip her chin gently, forcing her gaze to stay locked on mine. "You just made me the happiest fucking man on Earth saying that, Yasmine." A slow, relieved smile tugs at her lips, and fuck, I love her. Right now, while she's curled up in my lap, drinking her tea and looking like the most beautiful person I've ever seen, I grab my phone and text Eduardo.

Get the jet ready first thing in the morning. We're going home.

CHAPTER 70

2 weeks later.

It's been two weeks since I left Portugal, and honestly? The situation could've ended better. I wanted to help Ethan transition the retreat center properly, even find the perfect replacement for me, but after how things ended between us…yeah, that wasn't happening. Alex was right—I don't owe Ethan anything. I just pray that the retreat stays what it was meant to be—a space of healing and growth, not an overpriced, influencer-filled money grab. But knowing Ethan, I wouldn't be surprised if there's already a VIP package that includes gold-infused green juices and yoga mats with his initials on them.

After Portugal, Alex and I spent two blissful weeks at his home in Los Angeles—or, as he keeps insisting, *our* home. No matter how many times he says it, the word still makes my stomach flip. It's all happening so fast, but simultaneously, it feels like we've been together for lifetimes. Like our souls have been orbiting each other, just waiting for the right moment to collide. And being with him? It's a level of healing I never realized I needed. I've spent so much of my life guiding others toward their own peace and clarity—who knew mine would come in the form of a stubborn, brilliant, emotionally unavailable-turned-devoted boyfriend?

Now we're back in Tulum, standing in the heart of the place that built me. The *Hana Elise Yoga Center* is thriving and I can't help but feel my mother's presence here. I know she's watching over it, over me. I like to think she had something to do with its success, maybe nudging the universe a little, making sure the right people walk through these doors.

With the money I've saved, I can finally take the next step to launch my dream nonprofit healing center—first locally in Los Angeles, then nationally, and one day, if the universe is feeling generous, worldwide. We came back to Tulum to hand things over entirely to Alyssa. She has been a godsend. Alyssa's been running things effortlessly while I was in Portugal, proving time and time again that she's not just capable—she's *the* person for this. I'll always own the center, but she'll be on the ground, ensuring everything flows, from sunrise meditations to moonlit breathwork sessions. And honestly? Knowing her, she'll probably do it better than I did. So here we are. One chapter ends, and another begins. And somewhere in between lies the terrifying yet exhilarating realization that I might have everything I ever wanted.

I walk through my open-air yoga studio, my fingers trailing along the smooth wood of the windowsill as I take it all in. Alyssa stands at the front desk, focused and efficient, double-checking a schedule on her tablet. She's glowing with excitement, and it makes me smile.

My stomach churns unexpectedly, and I press a hand to it, brushing it off as nerves. I've been feeling off lately—lightheaded here and there, unusually tired, and now this queasy wave. I tell myself it's the emotion of it all, but a small voice in the back of my mind wonders if there's something else. Soft footsteps approach behind me, and then Alex's familiar warmth presses against my back as he wraps his strong arms around my waist. "You okay?" he murmurs.

I lean into him, grateful for his steady presence. "Just… sentimental," I admit. "This place was everything to me. It still is."

He tightens his hold on me, resting his chin on my shoulder. "It always will be," he says softly. "But you're stepping into something even bigger. And Alyssa's got this." I watch Alyssa as she greets a group of students arriving for the afternoon class. She waves at me, and I wave back, feeling a strange mix of pride and loss.

"I know," I whisper. "But it still feels like saying goodbye to a part of myself."

Alex gently turns to me, his eyes searching mine. "You're not saying goodbye. You're evolving. And I'm so proud of you." His words hit me right where I need them most and I blink away the tears threatening to spill over. I've dreamed of this moment—of building something meaningful and then moving forward to create even more. And the fact that Alex is here, standing beside me through all of it, makes it feel like a dream come true. He's been working from his laptop and phone, balancing meetings with moments where he looks up just to smile at me, reminding me that he's here for every step, every decision.

I rest my hands on his chest and smile softly. "Thank you for being here. For everything."

He presses a kiss to my forehead and whispers, "Where else would I be?" I close my eyes, savoring the quiet peace between us. Soon, we'll head back to Los Angeles for our new chapter, our next adventure. My heart swells at the thought of what's ahead—the healing center, the lives we'll change, and the life we're building together. But right now, at this moment, I'm standing at the bridge between the past and the future. My stomach churns again, this time softer, but I dismiss it, focusing instead on the incredible future unfolding before me.

Whatever comes next, I know I'm ready.

—

The sun is just beginning to set, turning the Riviera Maya sky into a masterpiece of soft gold, pink, and lavender. I walk barefoot besides Alex, our fingers laced. Something about him feels… different. His grip is tighter, almost like he's steadying himself. His eyes keep flicking toward the horizon, and when I glance up at him, his jaw is tense, like he's bracing for something monumental. My heart skips a beat. "Alex, are you okay?" I ask, my voice soft, almost lost in the sounds of the ocean.

He stops, turning to face me. The wind ruffles his hair, and for a moment, his eyes fill with so much emotion that I feel it in my soul. "I've never been more okay in my life," he says quietly. He takes both of my hands in his, his thumbs brushing gently over my knuckles. His touch is warm and grounding. "Yasmine…I've spent so much of my life running. From feelings. From people. From the things that scared me. But then you walked in, and suddenly…I didn't want to run anymore."

I blink, tears already welling up in my eyes as everything else fades into the background. "You are my beginning, my end, and everything in between." He continues, his voice steady and soft. "You showed me that love isn't something to be afraid of, and I don't want to build a life unless it's with you." My breath catches as Alex lowers himself to one knee in the sand, the breeze tugging at his shirt as the world seems to hold its breath. He pulls a small velvet box from his pocket and opens it. Inside is the most beautiful ring I've ever seen. A stunning solitaire diamond that gleams in the sun, set in a delicate rose gold band. It's timeless and perfect. My hand flies to my mouth as tears spill over. Alex's eyes never leave mine. "Yasmine…will you marry me?"

For a heartbeat, I can't move. I'm overwhelmed by everything, but then I nod, the answer spilling out of me in a breathless rush. "Yes," I whisper, my voice breaking. Then louder, clearer, as I drop to my knees in front of him, wrapping my arms around his neck. "Yes, Alex. A million times, yes." A soft, relieved laugh escapes him as he lifts me off the ground. Our lips collide in a kiss that feels like *everything*. His arms tighten around me as though he can't bear to let me go, and I melt into him, feeling his love in every part of me.

A sound of cheers breaks through the moment, and I pull back, laughing as I turn to see the entire yoga class gathered at the edge of the deck, clapping and whooping with joy. Some have their hands over their hearts and I realize they must've seen the whole thing.

Alex chuckles, pressing his forehead to mine. "I didn't plan on an audience."

I laugh, wiping my tears away. "It's perfect," I whisper, kissing him again. Everything I've ever dreamed of is standing right here, holding me like I'm his entire world. And I know now, without a doubt, that I've found home.

EPILOGUE

3 years later

ALEX

The house is finally quiet—the kind of quiet that feels earned after the chaos of the day. Yasmine and I stand side by side in our hallway, the soft hum of the white noise machine drifting through the door we've just closed. Hana, our tiny, perfect newborn, is asleep. And by some miracle, our toddler Noah is out, too.

Yasmine lets out a long, tired yawn and stretches her arms above her head, her long hair bundled up in a beautifully messy bun. I can't help but watch her, mesmerized by how effortlessly gorgeous she is, even when we're both running on fumes. She holds up her hand with a grin, and I meet it with mine, giving her a quiet, victorious high-five. "We did it," she whispers with mock disbelief, as if putting both kids down peacefully is some rare cosmic event.

"We deserve a medal," I reply, still holding her hand for a second longer before letting it drop. We both laugh softly, leaning back against the wall, exhausted. Her eyes are heavy, but they sparkle when she looks at me. And despite the fatigue in every bone of my body, I can't stop staring at her—the woman who changed everything. The mother of my children, the love of my life. Even now, I feel that same magnetic pull. But somehow, it's even deeper and stronger.

Without thinking, I step closer and pin her gently to the wall, my hands bracing her waist. Her breath catches and I can see the excitement in her eyes just before I kiss her. I start slow and purposeful, but then our kiss deepens into something fast and hungry, like always. Her fingers slide into my hair, tugging just enough to send a shiver down my spine. I press my body against hers, feeling her warmth through the soft fabric of her silk robe. Yasmine lets out a quiet moan against my lips and her hands slide down my chest, teasing, until her fingers reach my waistband. I groan as she tugs lightly at my sweatpants, and everything in me burns with the need to touch her, to feel her. But I pull back just enough to catch my breath, pressing my forehead to hers as I try to remember common sense. "Angel," I murmur, my voice rough. "Doctor's orders—you're supposed to rest. At least six weeks."

Her lips curl into a slow, wicked smile as she brushes a kiss along my jaw. "That doesn't mean *you* can't enjoy yourself," she whispers. Before I can argue, she slides down to her knees in front of me, her fingers trailing down my sides. I look down at her, my heart pounding in my chest as she tugs my sweatpants down, and I feel a rush of heat course through me.

"Yasmine," I rasp, already breathless.

She looks up at me through her long lashes, her green eyes gleaming with so much love. "Let me take care of you." The second her lips touch me, my head falls back against the wall, and a groan tears from my throat. Her mouth is soft and warm, and every slow movement is deliberate like she's savoring this as much as I am. My hands thread through her hair, tightening reflexively as she takes me deeper, her rhythm steady but devastating. The pleasure builds fast, almost too much, and I'm losing control with every second. She's so perfect, absolutely perfect. And all I can wonder, even as I feel myself unraveling, is how the hell I got this lucky. "You're…incredible."

She hums softly, sending another shock of pleasure through me, and that's it—I come undone, completely, every nerve lit up, my entire body shaking from the force of it. My heartbeat thunders in my ears as she swallows me down, every last drop.

When she finally pulls back, she rises gracefully, a satisfied smirk on her lips as she brushes her loosened tendrils back. I pull her into my arms and kiss her softly, this time with reverence. "You're going to kill me," I whisper, still breathless.

She laughs against my lips. "You'd die happy."

I chuckle, pulling her close and pressing my face into the crook of her neck. We may be exhausted, running on little sleep and surviving on love and caffeine, but this—her, us, our family, is everything I never knew I wanted. And I wouldn't trade it for the world.

YASMINE

The city feels calm in this early hour as we pull up to the airport arrivals lane. In the backseat, Noah and Hana are both peacefully napping. Noah's head is tilted to one side, his little mouth slightly open, and Hana is bundled up in her car seat, her tiny chest rising and falling in perfect rhythm. I glance at them through the rearview mirror, my heart swelling.

"The second the car starts moving, they're out like lights; it's magic," Alex says, shaking his head with a grin before glancing at me, his eyes warm with adoration.

"We really lucked out with these two, huh?" I smile back, my heart swelling at seeing him like this. I can still feel last night's exhaustion in my bones, but today? Today is *everything*.

When I spot my dad, sister, and Chan stepping out of the airport, I don't even think. As soon as Alex pulls up to the curb, I jump out.

"*Yaz*!" Sami's voice rings out as she waves enthusiastically. She's wearing oversized sunglasses and a bright yellow sundress that makes her look like a burst of sunshine. I practically run toward them, arms wide. My dad is the first one I reach, and he pulls me into a tight hug.

"How I've missed you, *Azizam*," he says softly, kissing the top of my head.

I pull back just enough to see his face. His dark eyes crinkle at the corners when he smiles. "Hi, Baba."

Sami and Chan swarm me next, wrapping me in a chaotic group hug. We're all laughing as we sway in the middle of the curb like we've forgotten where we are. As we pull apart, Alex steps around our car, his usual cool confidence softening slightly. "Welcome back," he says, shaking my dad's hand firmly before giving Sami a quick hug.

"You again?" He teases, nudging her playfully.

Sami smirks. "Told you, you can't get rid of me that easily!"

Then Alex turns to Chan and nods. "Chan, it's good to see you, man."

Chan grins. "Likewise. Hope you're ready for the chaos."

Alex chuckles. "I think I've been training for it."

With that, we move quickly as Alex loads their suitcases into the trunk. Once the last bag is tucked in, I glance at my dad. Ready for this?" I ask.

He smiles at me, full of pride. "Yasmine, we've been ready for this since the day you started dreaming it." The words hit me right in the heart and I take a breath to steady myself as I slide back into the passenger seat. Sami and Chan squeeze into the back behind the kids, cooing over them while they sleep.

Alex pulls away from the curb, merging into traffic, while my focus is on what's ahead—the official opening of *The Healing Collective*. A cooperative of local healers, freely offering their gifts to support those seeking spiritual healing and renewal. Three years of hard work, setbacks, triumphs, and relentless dedication have led to this moment. It's the kind of project I always dreamed about—a place where people from every walk of life can come to heal, to breathe, to feel whole again. And it's not just one center; this is the beginning of a movement.

We drive toward downtown Los Angeles, where *The Healing Collective's* headquarters stands—a building full of light and life. The world's biggest stars will be there today, along with community leaders, healers, and everyday people who believe in what we're trying to do. But none of that matters as much as the people in this car—my family. My heart.

Sami's chipper voice breaks me out of my thoughts. "Do you think you're ready to have the world finally see what you've built?"

I turn back to catch her gaze and smile. "It's not just me," I say. "It's all of us."

Chan raises his fists triumphantly and lets out a dramatic cheer from the backseat. "To changing the world!"

Alex and I laugh as my dad shakes his head fondly. The

anticipation thrums in my veins, but beneath it all is a quiet sense of calm. Whatever happens today, I know this is just the beginning. The work we're doing and the love we're spreading will ripple out farther than I can even imagine.

And as we head toward the future, surrounded by love and purpose, I know one thing for sure.

We're just getting started.

Acknowledgement

To my best friend since childhood, Yasmine—this story wouldn't exist without you. You, with the greenest eyes touched by ocean light, inspired the heart and soul of this book's main character. Your unwavering spirit, quiet strength, and fierce softness were the blueprint. Thank you for being my muse, my mirror, and my forever girl.

To Pablo Gomez, my spiritual healer and guide—you cracked me open in the gentlest way and led me back to myself. This book was born from the transformation you helped me begin. Thank you for holding space for the version of me that didn't yet believe in her own voice.

To my brilliant literary sister Stacey McEntire—you believed in Chasing the Calm before it had a title, before I had the nerve to say out loud that I was writing it. Your encouragement lit the path when I doubted it even existed. I am endlessly grateful for your honesty, your kindness, and your cheerleading heart.

And to all my early readers—thank you for your thoughtful, generous feedback. Your words helped me shape this book into something deeper than I could have imagined alone. Thank you for seeing its heart and helping me bring it to light.

With gratitude and love,
Jacqueline Sand

About the Author

Jacqueline Sand is a contemporary romance author based in Portugal, where she lives with her husband and two children. Her debut novel, Chasing the Calm, blends emotional depth with slow-burn romance, offering readers a feel-good escape into love, healing, and second chances.

When she's not writing, Jacqueline can be found reading on the beach with a matcha in hand or filling her growing collection of notebooks with ideas. She's a firm believer that storytelling—like love—is one of the most powerful tools for transformation.

Books in This Series

Unraveled Hearts Romance

They built empires, broke hearts, and buried their pain beneath success. But love doesn't care how guarded you are—or how far you run.

The Unraveled Hearts series follows the four Pierce brothers as they each face the one thing money and power can't shield them from: love.

Set against luxury retreats, high-rise cities, and wild desert festivals, every book in the series delivers explosive chemistry, unforgettable journeys, and the kind of healing that only comes when you lose—and find—yourself in someone else.

Each book follows a different Pierce brother's story.
Each novel can be read as a standalone.
Together, they unravel what it truly means to fall.

Want updates on the next release?

Sign up for my newsletter to get first access to Lucas and Zara's story — releasing 2025.

Chasing the Calm is the first release in the *Unraveled Hearts series*.

There will be a total of 4 books in this series.

Stay Connected

Loved *Chasing the Calm*? If the story moved you, made you laugh, or kept you up past your bedtime (sorry, not sorry), please consider leaving a review on **Amazon** or **Goodreads** — it means the world to indie authors like me. 🤍

I'd love to stay in touch with you.

Follow me for behind-the-scenes content, exclusive sneak peeks, and updates on the Unraveled Hearts Series:

📷 Instagram: @jacquelinesandbooks
🎵 TikTok: @jacquelinesandbooks
📘 Facebook: Jacqueline Sand – Author
🐦 X (formerly Twitter): @JSandAuthor
📺 YouTube: @JacquelineSand
🌐 Website: www.jacquelinesand.com

📧 Join My Newsletter Tribe:
Get first dibs on new releases, bonus content, and calm, chaotic author vibes: https://jsand.myflodesk.com/newsletter

📫 Say hi or share your thoughts:
Email me anytime at contact@jacquelinesand.com – I'd love to hear from you.